Baker

By
Reid Matthias

ISBN paperback: 978-0-6450472-2-6
          ebook: 978-0-6450472-3-3

This edition first published by A 13 in July 2021

Typesetting by Ben Morton

Publication assistance from Immortalise

Back cover Photo by Natalie Kuhl on Unsplash
Front cover Photo by Sneha Cecil on Unsplash

For my grandparents, salt and pepper of the earth people, who brought about so many opportunities to rejoice in sharing life across generations: Elmer and Delores Matthias, Victor and Leota Nacke – such delightful old-fashioned names with beautiful hearts who never got old…

Acknowledgements

Baker, like its predecessor, *Butcher*, is a work of fiction. Some of the place names are real, but Amicable is not. Although its geography and layout may seem to be familiar, at least to many who live in small Iowa towns, Amicable is a figment of my memory. It is situated nowhere near the Boondocks and not even close to Gravity. All characters are composites and exaggerations of my imagination, but any bearing more than a passing resemblance to real life people is unintentional, albeit welcomed. I have borrowed surnames and Christian names from people I have encountered throughout my travels - good and lovely people - and I hope that you who read these pages can connect with them as I have.

A special thanks to my incredible wife Christine who continues to amaze me with the generosity of her joy at reading these books. As she has read and reread the Amicable Circle, her editing skills and eye for details have been extraordinary. To Elsa, Josephine and Greta, my daughters and constant source of love and amusement, thank you for pushing these Amicableans onto the page. To Anji Neil, as always, a woman with an amazing editing eye, thank you.

And to Cees Wesselingh, the original butcher, who helped me find stories in the unlikeliest places.

Prologue

My Dearest Reader,

Hopefully you are perched in your favorite reading chair, reading glasses (or not) clinging to the end of your nose as you prepare to thumb through another episode of my dear hometown of Amicable. I also hope that there is a bottomless pot of coffee brewing on your countertop, bubbling and hissing an endless scent of caffeinated imaginations, allowing you to read, pause, sip, pause, and read again.

The last time we crossed paths was six years ago. Much has happened in this time, not just in my own life — married with children, invested in the life of working with my husband John Thomas and his role in the church and community — but also throughout Amicable.

You would remember our good friend Leo Jensen, Butcher, his wife, Rhonda (and now their children). His arrival signaled a new perspective for us Amicableans (pronounced Ami-CAH-blee-an, if you please; the accent on the third syllable - don't be offended that I've told you how to pronounce the word because that's what Amicableans do). In these last six years, Butcher and Amicable have changed. Not seismically, mind you, just tectonic plates shifting ever so gradually as time moves by.

During this, our second time together, as you meander through Amicable, you may find yourself connecting with specific characters and ways of thinking. This is entirely natural and wholly expected. Don't fear it. Embrace these similarities, if you can. All of us, every race, creed and stereotype have many things in common, not the least of which is that we all desire certain things: love, trust, acceptance, and a desire for moments of peace.

As such, we begin with an explosion.

You might be thinking to yourself, 'Okay, I see what she's doing here - she wants to start the story off with a bang, and we are left wondering whether this particular literary technique might be metaphorical or symbolic and I, the reader, must dig deeply into the metaphors and symbols...' Let me pull the handbrakes on that train of thought right there and then and bring them to a screeching, spark-producing halt.

1

The explosion was real, a gigantic blast which scorched the heavens and shook the earth around Amicable.

Take a sip of your coffee. You might need it. It's going to be a long day (or night) of reading.

Sincerely,

Leslie Deakins

Chapter 1.

If Enrique Fernandez could have lived just ten seconds longer, odds are he would have rued his decision to take up smoking. As it was, Enrique did not survive the blast. Perhaps it was for the best, though, because Enrique was under investigation by the Department of Immigration. Through turbulent seas and vomit-inducing swells, Enrique made his way from Cuba. On the sea voyage, some emigrants lost their lives where they were mourned in the deep orange sunlight of the ancient Caribbean Sea. Their loved ones looked out over bodies floating into the depths and held out an agonizing hope that if at least some of them – maybe only one - survived the journey, it would be worth it in the end.

Making his way into Miami, Little Cuba to be exact, where Enrique felt entirely at home, he was unfortunately, ferreted out by local drug lords to become a drug mule. Through a cleverness well beyond his sixteen years, he escaped their clutches and hitchhiked with other Hispanic vagabonds across the endless stretches of vibrant green hills and escarpments, which covered the Appalachian Mountains like a coniferous bristly beard. On his way northward, Enrique marveled at the expanse, and the variety, of the magnificent country of his dreams.

After being deposited in Evansville, Indiana, Enrique worked for a local building company, which was not particularly concerned where Enrique's visa and passport were located. Their concern was that he work for just under the minimum wage - six dollars and ninety-five cents per hour. For Enrique, this was a fortune. In Cuba, he toiled for six dollars and ninety-five cents *per day*.

Oh, what a country! He blessed God for this fortuitous opportunity. Eventually, he would send for his mother where they could live in this most blessed of all American cities - Evansville.

Unfortunately, the building contractor for whom he worked was as negligent with making sure his worksites were safe as he was with checking immigration documents. One afternoon, Enrique and another co-worker, a Mexican man named Juan, were walking across the rooftop of a new building. Neither Enrique nor Juan noticed that someone had

3

cut through the joist. Enrique was lucky. Though he fell over twelve feet to the floor below, he suffered only minor cuts and bruises. Juan, though, broke both legs. When he was taken to the hospital, the authorities found his immigration status suspect. Even as the bones in his legs were knitting back together, Juan was sent back to Mexico with a sharp reprimand and a 'Don't y'all come back now, y'hear.'

As Juan was taken away, Enrique wisely made sure that he was nowhere near Juan when the Feds came. Instead, Enrique thumbed a ride northwards on Highway 41, away from the South. Always farther away from Cuba.

Traveling north then west, Enrique met wonderful and fascinating people. Because of his rudimentary English, he depended on those he walked with. This, though, led to various problems. Once, he was pickpocketed the forty-seven dollars he'd accumulated on the journey. This caused Enrique ceaseless frustration, but again he came out lucky. His co-adventurer/pickpocket was stabbed by another kleptomaniacal malcontent, who had stooped to robbing illegal aliens.

With neither money nor connections, Enrique accepted a helping hand from a farmer on the outskirts of the Midwest, a generous corn grower in western Illinois. Alas, after the season finished, the farmer could no longer keep Enrique in his employ. In spite of a tremendous non-verbal relationship, Enrique was sent on his way, always north and west. Always away from Cuba. This time, though, the farmer's wife, a blessedly small woman with thin hips and a penchant to wear flower print blouses and blue jeans, loaded up a backpack full of sundries and food. Fussing over him like parents sending a child off to kindergarten, they pulled up his jacket collar, ruffled his hair and waved to him as the bus drove away.

The wheels of the bus purred underneath the passengers all the way into Iowa's capital city. Enrique, entranced by the rural landscape so incredibly different from his homeland, smiled broadly as he disembarked. There was something devastatingly beautiful about the shift from fall and to winter, from autumn leaves to crystalline, glittering snow.

Eventually, the bus dropped off Enrique and his small backpack in Des Moines. Even though he had tried to conserve his meager supplies, his backpack was now less than half-full. As he took his first steps into the icy bus terminal of Des Moines, he found that he had a choice to make. In retrospect, he should have refused the cigarette from the homeless man at the bus stop. The homeless man cupped a lighter in his hands around the cigarette. The flick of the lighter made a scratching sound and, after handing the lit cigarette to the young Cuban, Enrique drew in a breath of smoke that made him cough.

The homeless man laughed. "They'll be the death of you," he croaked.

On the day that Enrique died, he was unaware that a wedding was taking place at St. Clements Church. On that fateful Saturday afternoon, Enrique needed a break. Feeling the urge for a nicotine fix, Enrique took a pack of smokes from his chest pocket, a pocket embroidered with his name holding two pens, and tapped a cigarette from the opening.

On that fateful day, Enrique forgot the rules.

He had survived the treacherous journey across the turbulent Caribbean Sea; he had lived through the desperation of the Miami drug scene; he had escaped with just scratches after falling through a ceiling. After all of this, Enrique thought himself a particularly fortunate person. Ironically, though, on the day that Enrique died, simple flint and fluid ended all of Enrique's good fortune.

A grain elevator was an incredibly *bad* location to have an open flame.

More often than not, what finally gets you is not what you see, but what you can't. As the corn and soybeans were dumped into the grate and weighed, dust particles flew up and out. In and of themselves, these dust particles were not particularly flammable, but strangely, when placed into a compressed space, they are highly combustible. Thus, the NO OPEN FLAMES signs on every possible door and window.

Unfortunately, Enrique happened to be in the wrong place at the wrong time doing exactly the wrong thing. The striking of Enrique's lighter caused the dust in the elevator to ignite and the ensuing explosion could be felt for miles around, not just at the wedding (four blocks away, mind you). The blast leveled multiple silos of the Amicable elevator, killing the young Cuban-American survivor who pretty much assumed he was the luckiest man in the world.

Lucky, that is, until he wasn't.

Similarly, every community has combustible dust particles floating imperceptibly between neighbors and nutcases. These bits of gossip, harmless as day-to-day monotonies transpired, were highly combustible during the hectic times, planting and reaping, when the pressure ratcheted up. After planting and reaping lulls, deep winter, and summer haze, these times were ideal for other things like the wedding between Nash Peterson and Shania Zellner. Those in attendance were brim-full of goodwill for the couple.

St. Clements was bright and airy, warm and packed with Amicableans expecting a beautiful wedding and raucous reception. The aisle between the church pews was adorned with white ribbons and sprigs of green. Candles were lit and organ music floated in the background. Various citizens, dressed in their Sunday finest, waited with anticipation for the bride to be escorted down the aisle. A diminutive flower girl, dressed in pastel pink with accompanying bow, had strewn white rose petals along the purple carpet. As Shania walked gracefully, hand tucked delicately inside her father's elbow, tears filled both sets of eyes. Tears were the sacrifice of the joyful.

At the front of the church, the groomsmen and their female counterparts, stood watching the procession. It was cute to watch both pageboy and flower girl, but it was breathtaking to watch the bride make her way to the front. Nash Peterson watched lovingly as his fiancée was ushered by his soon-to-be-father-in-law, but Nash couldn't look at him — only her.

As Nash gazed at Shania, he couldn't focus on any other part of the wedding service, including the carefully crafted homily delivered by the Reverend John Thomas Deakins, who stood regally in his black, ill-fitting suit and blue tie. Nash would have missed the vows if not for the timely nudge by his identical twin brother, Derek, and his whisper, "Hey, Buttfuzz, you need to promise a few things now…"

Chapter 1.

Butcher stood next to Derek sagely supervising the scene. He smiled at the two young men standing next to each other. As identical twins, their appearances were almost perfect reflections, but their personalities were not. Even in the earliest moments of Butcher's arrival in Amicable, Butcher had noticed the small differences between the boys. Butcher, imbued with an inscrutable and insufferable gift of reading people, was able to interpret the tiniest verbal and non-verbal signals, tell signs, as it were, and within seconds be able to know who they were, who they had been and, with a reasonable degree of certainty, who they would become. When he first encountered Nash and Derek, Nash, the older brother by less than half an hour, seemed more assertive and controlled. Derek, on the other hand, was wildly unpredictable. Using his gift, Butcher had assisted the Peterson twins in their own navigation through life. Because the twins' parents were often out of town, Butcher, though only fifteen-odd years older, had become a surrogate father to them.

"Do you, Shania Zellner, take Nash Peterson to be your lawfully wedded husband, for better for worse, for richer for poorer, in sickness and in health as long as you both shall live?" Shania nodded to the pastor, who smiled at her and then she turned to her betrothed. "I do."

"And do you, Nash Peterson, take Shania Zellner to be your lawfully wedded wife, for better for worse, for richer for poorer, in sickness and in health as long as you both shall live?" Nash took a deep breath, but before he could respond with all the love and excitement he had…

Boom.

The explosion sounded ominously like a detonation. Eight-year-old Ethan Thompson, who had been fidgeting miserably during the wedding ceremony pretending to be anywhere but in the middle of church on a Saturday afternoon, looked up at his mother. His frightened eyes were wide and his head ducked unconsciously. "Have terrorists come to attack us, Mom?"

Shaking her head but looking around concernedly nonetheless, Denise Thompson reassured her son by pulling him close. "No, Sweetie, terrorists would have no reason to bomb Amicable. Clancy, maybe, but not Amicable."

The entire assembly looked around the church as the aftershock of the Elevator explosion rattled the stained-glass windows. Dust bunnies, perpetually perched in the rafters, excitedly hopped down through the diffused light, causing both wedding party and wedding guests to look skyward to see if Chicken Little's prognostication would come to fruition.

A large chunk of cement crashed to the earth just outside the front doors of the church, startling both the ushers and the church cleaner, who had been picking his nails waiting for the service to finish. The piece of concrete, roughly four feet long and two feet thick, weighing almost two hundred pounds, cratered the sidewalk.

"Holy crap!" the janitor exclaimed. "What was that?"

Tina, one of the ushers, hurried to the front glass double doors where, peering through the Methodist Church logo, noticed other bits and pieces of debris falling from the sky. "I think a plane blew up in midair over us!"

Pete the janitor hustled to her side and shook his head. "Unless they've started making airplanes out of concrete, I think you might be wrong there."

"Well, what do you think it is?"

Pete stuck his head out the door and inhaled sharply. "This is way worse than a plane crash." He covered his mouth and pointed to the southern 'skyline' of Amicable where a large black cloud billowed from the top of what used to be the Amicable grain elevator.

Inside the sanctuary, fifteen phones began to vibrate simultaneously including those belonging to all three groomsmen, groom and preacher. Intuitively, Butcher knew what had happened. Somewhere deep down in his soul he knew that the heart of Amicable, the elevator, with its ages of wear and tear, had suffered a coronary.

As the members of the volunteer fire brigade and emergency medical services stood in unison, Nash leaned across to his panic-stricken bride. "I do," he said loudly enough for all who were still listening. "I'll see you in a few minutes." He kissed her deeply and moved off with the other volunteers as they hurried out the door.

Chapter 1.

The time between Nash's departure and the reunion with his bride was at twelve hours. So much for the wedding reception.

Worship services were cancelled at St. Clements Methodist Church the next day. Normally, the only time worship was written off was when there was a cold snap in January or February. If the furnace couldn't keep up, the Amicableans were allowed a reprieve from their weekly, and dutiful, worship to God. Instead, Leslie Deakins sent a message to the congregation members informing them that there would be a meeting at the bowling alley that night for communal commiseration, mutual encouragement and prayer. The bowling alley, with its enclosed bar, the Greedy Pecker (which would have been the site of Shania and Nash's reception) served as the secular wing of community gatherings. John and Leslie both knew that the bowling alley would be packed, so in the communique, they asked that attendees bring a potluck dish to share. More often than not, there were many more than twelve baskets of food left over.

John, after returning home from his firefighting duties, ruefully glanced down at his ruined suit pants. Because of the emergency, none of the volunteer workers had time to change their clothes in order to fight fires, treat the injured and begin clearing dangerous objects. Anyone who happened upon the scene would have seen firefighters shedding three-piece suits, ambulance workers in ties and dress pants and the lone police officer, Louise Nelson, in a beautifully flowered dress. But that was the life of small town Midwest - everyone did their part. Volunteering was a way of life, and in that life, sometimes there were interruptions. Rarely were they large. A few traffic accidents and the random cardiac, but nothing like this.

After taking a shower, Deakins fell into bed next to Leslie, who hadn't slept a wink. It was almost five o'clock in the morning and the sun was peeking through the curtains already.

"How bad was it?" she whispered.

Deakins rolled onto his back and threw a forearm across his eyes. "Horrific. Three dead, four seriously wounded and countless damage to the shops and houses on the south side of town."

Leslie attempted to stifle her gasp, but failed. "Who…?"

"Carl Adams. Poor man, he was sitting in his tractor waiting to dump his load of beans. Might have been asleep, but the fire…" John's voice caught. "Deanne Bauer. She must have been driving on highway 10 when the explosion occurred. The nearest we could guess was that she was on her phone attempting to record the aftermath. She must have stopped too close to the intersection of Highway 10 and Gifford Street. A semi driver didn't see the car and took her out. Then, Enrique…" By speaking the Cuban's name, John's voice and body began to shake.

Leslie rolled into her husband. "Oh, John, I'm so sorry."

They slept fitfully. At seven o'clock, the girls, unaware of the turmoil happening around them in the world, peeked precociously through the door to see if their parents were awake. Still blissfully unconscious, John and Leslie were startled awake by the two-five-year-olds pounding on the side of the bed demanding breakfast and entertainment. Groaning, John felt every last one of his overexerted muscles. His body complained miserably and reminded him that if he was going to take this volunteer firefighting role more seriously, he'd better learn to be a little more active than simply marching briskly across the parking lot to the church from the parsonage.

Leslie, showing concern for her husband, tapped him on the chest. "I'll take care of it."

Without opening his eyes, he felt for her hand. "Coffee. Black. Gallon."

She smiled, pulled herself from the bed and made her way to the kitchen, holding her daughters' hands in her own.

When John eventually appeared at the breakfast table, he arrived haggard; a beard, dark and shadowy, arising from nowhere, made him look ten years older. Eyes, circled by dark rings, reminded them of the darkness, which had occurred and the uncertainty of what was to come.

"Daddy, what was that big noise yesterday?" Gabrielle asked as she stuffed a piece of fluffy pancake into her mouth.

"Use your fork, Sweetie," John said. Gabrielle nodded gravely and did as she was told while Michelle, noticing that she, too, was eating with syrupy fingers, followed her father's advice. "There was an explosion at the elevator."

"What's a espluxion?"

John smiled ruefully. "An explosion. It means that something blows up and goes boom."

"Boom," Michelle repeated.

"What went boom?" Gabi asked.

"You know, the big building, the one with all the big round bins."

"Oh," Gabi responded slowly as if understanding, but her mind had already moved on to the shape that was forming on her breakfast plate.

"So, what do we have to do today?" Leslie asked John as she placed a pancake and coffee in front of him.

"The Emergency Team is going to meet again at lunch time. The crews from Clancy and surrounding towns arrived, so we cycled through the night. Some of the guys have now been working for six to eight hours straight. I'm glad that I wasn't on the crew that helped with Enrique."

John sipped and continued. "My guess is that we'll need time to clear the debris, then take inventory of where Amicable goes from here. My job will get a little more difficult considering the three funerals coming up..." his voice trailed off.

Leslie put her arms around his shoulders from behind. "We'll do this together."

At five o'clock that night, the bowling alley opened its doors and townspeople shuffled quietly inside. Some of them numb to the core, wondering how things could get any worse, stumbled directly to the bar where they were offered a drink by the newest married woman in Amicable, Shania Peterson. Although the wedding ceremony had not officially been completed by Reverend Deakins, both Shania and Nash had verbalized their vows, leaving only the formality of Deakins' pronouncement of marriage unspoken.

Nash and Derek sat at a bar table staring morosely up at a football game on television. Fans with heads covered by triangles of foam cheese cheered loudly. Nash felt a twinge of resentment for the happy faces, blissfully unconscious to the pain in Amicable.

"Shania, can you turn the music on and the TV off?" Nash asked quietly. She nodded and pointed the remote at the television. It blinked off, leaving a momentary vision of dust settling into black.

More and more people straggled in to the bowling alley. As they did, potluck dishes were deposited on plastic tables. Carefully wrapped salads and Jell-O molds were separated from casseroles and meat dishes and placed opposite the brownies and cakes. A few townspeople brought extra food for the emergency medical personnel who had worked fastidiously through the night. No one was bowling and the pinball machines had been turned off.

As they sifted through the details, they also worked through their shock and grief. An hour into the night, the first burst of laughter erupted. Guiltily, James Thompson glanced around the room hoping that he hadn't been disrespectful, but the others smiled at him, willing to forgive, recognizing that laughter, as well as tears, could be cathartic.

At seven o'clock, Janice Stensrud, mayor of Amicable and former runner-up in the county competition for Corn Queen, stood and took the microphone from the front desk attendant. "Hello everyone. Thank you for coming." She paused, waiting for silence so they all could hear her. "Thank you to Ray and Theresa who have allowed us to gather here tonight." Ray, the owner of the bowling alley, nodded from behind the front desk.

"There are a few things that need to be organized. The first is to make sure that those who need support, find that support. Counseling is available; three counselors from Clancy have come to volunteer and of course, Butcher's door is open."

"Secondly," Janice continued, "we'll need to have volunteer clean-up crews clearing debris and rubble. Most of you would know that the explosion sent concrete, steel and even grain all the way to the other side of Amicable, even as far as the Dermot's house." The crowd murmured in disbelief. The Dermot's house was almost half a mile away from the elevator. "I've asked Principal Moganan if school classes can be cancelled tomorrow so that we can mobilize the high school youth to help clear the streets, shops and homes." The youth in attendance nodded proudly.

"Once the debris has been cleared, the town council will meet with other community leaders to discuss possible options for the future."

A hand raised in the back. "Any thoughts yet?"

"No, not yet."

Gravely, the mayor scanned the anxious crowd who had voted for her, or at least sixty-four percent of them. It was time to earn her keep. "I've invited some of the other town leaders to answer any questions also, but Elvin has volunteered to give us an update." Janice nodded to Elvin Meier, the manager of the elevator. Elvin, a sixty-three-year-old lifelong Amicablean, walked slowly to the microphone. His haggard face plainly exhibited his utter exhaustion. As he took the microphone in his hand, it shook.

"Good evening," his voice, caked with phlegm from the dust, trembled. He cleared it and with as much strength as he could muster, launched into the update. "Thank you for all coming tonight and showing your support. The elevator can be replaced, but lives cannot." Janice placed a hand on his shoulder, giving him strength. "Three lives have tragically ended. To respect those who are grieving, I will not mention their names aloud, but you've probably heard who they are already. Four people are currently in the hospital, one in serious condition, but we hope they make a full recovery."

"Thank God for that," someone in the crowd said.

"Yes," Elvin responded, "we do thank God for that." He rubbed his upper lip with a forefinger before continuing. "Here is what we know at this point: the explosion occurred at 3:23 yesterday afternoon. As far as we can tell, a spark ignited the dust in the silos. It could have come from anything, really. We may never know the cause, but we do know the effect: five of Amicable's eight silos have exploded. The last three, by some mysterious chance, did not ignite, or at least not yet."

"Are you saying," another townsperson asked, "that they may still blow up? That we're still not safe?"

Elvin's jaw clenched. "That is a possibility. A remote one, but still a possibility. Although the flames have been extinguished thanks to our brave fire departments, there is still a chance that something could set off one or all of the others." More fearful mumbling and he held up his hands. "Because of this, we may need to tear the whole thing down and start over."

Groans.

Elvin asked for silence. "On behalf of the elevator, I wanted to express my deep sorrow for the loss of life and to all of you…" he held out his hands towards the people but he could not continue and pressed them back over his eyes where he began to sob into them. "I'm so sorry. I'm so sorry."

Reverend Deakins stood and took Elvin Meier's place. "This town," he said with a fierce but loving determination, "will not be destroyed." All eyes looked up at the pastor who had taken his place to stand for them all. "Amicable is stronger than any of us possibly could imagine, because we, Amicableans, are stronger than any storm, any explosion, any accident. During the next months, we will rebuild. Amicable will be resurrected stronger than it has ever been before."

"Be patient," Deakins continued. "Even as we grieve, we will look forward."

Deakins caught the eye of his best friend, Butcher, who smiled sadly at him. It was at that point that Deakins wondered if he had just lied to the entire community. He could read in Butcher's eyes that the devastation could indeed slay the community, but they would do everything they could to stop it.

Oh, Lord, Deakins thought. *We're in for some trouble.*

Chapter 2.

It was mid-morning by the time Stedman Boswell finished flicking through last night's news. As he idly scanned the stories, tragic events, new strains of disease, various fights over correctness and cancellation, he only set his coffee mug down when he read about an explosion in a small town called Amicable. Scanning the details, he frowned and sat back in his chair. *Wasn't Amicable one of theirs?* he mused. *This might be an engaging distraction.*

Boswell was a lead investigator for a large insurance company in Kansas City. Known for its quick response (but slow payment), Baker Insurance was a major player in the Midwest. As one of the top insurance adjusters on the payroll (even at the tender age of thirty-three), Stedman Boswell wondered if this incident was going to be placed in his hands. Jotting down a few notes, Boswell picked up his phone and dialed his immediate superior, Theocrates Baker, the son of the founding owner of the insurance company. After two rings, Theo's voice came to life.

"This better be good, Stedman. We're at the cabin." Baker had purchased a large house in the Colorado Rockies overlooking a scenic, alpine valley replete with pine trees and granite boulders.

"There's been an explosion."

Baker sat up abruptly. "What do you mean?"

"There's this little town in Iowa, Amicable, that had its elevator blow to smithereens last night."

Silence. "I assume that you've called me because we're the underwriters of that policy."

"Excellent guess."

"What is the damage?"

"Catastrophic. Almost complete destruction of the facility, if the reports are correct."

"How much are we insuring it for?"

Boswell looked at his notes. "Fifty, give or take"

Baker swallowed. "Fifty million... whoowee," he whistled. "That's a chunk of change."

Boswell didn't add the fact that three people died in the explosion. It wouldn't make any difference to Theocrates Baker.

"Any idea if it was intentional?"

"No idea, sir. It happened just last night."

Baker rubbed his chin as he gazed out over the picturesque vista. This was the last thing he wanted to deal with on his yearly seven-week 'vacation.' "All right, well, go slow. We'll need to gather the facts and buy us some time. We might have to raise premiums elsewhere..." Baker mused. "When are you going there?"

Boswell smiled and leaned back in his chair. "I can leave tomorrow. It will take about four or five hours to drive there, but I can probably make it by mid-afternoon."

"Good, Stedman. I need you to deliver on this one. If there is some way we can cause a reasonable amount of confusion in the process, we might be able to save some money." A squirrel hopped from one branch to another and Baker almost laughed at its antics.

"Of course, Boss. I'll do my best."

Theo Baker smiled into his phone. "I know you will, Stedman. I know you will. There will be a large bonus for you if we can get this under ten million."

"I think you ought to know, sir..." Boswell was about to bring up the fact that three people died in the explosion, but Baker had already disconnected the phone.

What a putz, Stedman thought and put his phone down.

Three women sat near the front window of Human Beans coffee shop, situated on a sunlit corner opposite Carley's X-Er-Size studio. Now that the Traveler's Choice, Amicable's highway restaurant, had gone bankrupt, Human Beans did a rousing business. As a token of good will to its patrons, Human Beans offered a twenty-cent discount to Amicablean residents. The savings made Amicableans quite happy.

The three ladies, well-known for their close encounters of the gossipy kind, met early on the Monday morning after the elevator exploded. Leona, Linda and Jeannie felt guiltily excited about having something different and drastically difficult to talk about that morning.

16

It wasn't as if Linda, Leona or Jeannie were particularly unkind, they were simply biased in the way that they reported the information. Much of what they discussed with each other (and on a wider scale) was *technically* true, but it was painted like a color-by-numbers, without actually using the right colors. The picture was correct, but the hue was distorted - just like their gossip.

"Well," Linda said slowly and theatrically casually flipping her wrist, her gold ring and large diamond sparkling in the morning sun, "I heard from one of the cashiers at the grocery store, that there was so much damage that we may not be able to clean it all up – maybe even for a year." Linda fanned herself, which the other two copied without thinking.

"Oh my goodness," Jeannie exclaimed.

"I heard talk at the shoe store that most of the farmers are wondering if they need to take their grain to Clancy." She pronounced the neighboring name of the town with a sour face.

"And I heard," said Jeannie, still rubbing her lips, "that... oh, goodness, I forgot what I was going to say."

"It doesn't matter, Jeannie. I'm sure you'll remember sooner or later." Linda's eyes had already strayed outside the window where the first teams of young people began to arrive for cleanup. Each was given a pair of gloves, a high visibility vest and an Amicable baseball cap embroidered with the town's slogan: *We're Nicer in Amicable.*

As the women watched, a group of high school students armed with brooms and dustpans began to methodically scoop and dump. A young girl with long brown hair (each of the women recognized the face, but her name was just past recollection) stopped to adjust her hair. Apparent to both the middle-aged women in the coffee shop and the two young men who were scooping and dumping, the girl was intent on both helping *and* looking good. After readjusting her hair band, she produced her cellphone to check her appearance. Then, calling out to her cleaning comrades, she invited them for a selfie.

"Will you look at that?" Leona pointed to the team outside the window. "Where is the work ethic in our children today? They can't do anything without taking a break, or pausing for a picture. Good heavens," she sighed. "What is our world coming to?"

"It's sad that America can't raise good, wholesome, nice kids who are hard-working and respectful to their elders. I mean, look at that girl out there…" Linda shook her head with derision.

Jeannie snickered.

Leona shook her head. "And those kids with their phones and their gadgets."

Linda tsk-tsked. "No resilience. Like a bunch of snowflakes. They melt under the first little bit of heat."

Jeannie took another sip and burned her lips again. "Dang it," she spoke to her cup of coffee and set it down. "I just don't know where this world is headed."

The youth continued to collect the debris and moved southwards. While they continued working, Leslie Deakins walked along the opposite side of the street with her twin daughters. The girls were carrying shopping baskets in their hands.

"Isn't that cute?" Jeannie smiled. "I'm just so, so happy for Leslie and Reverend Deakins. They're such a cute couple?"

"Yes, cute, but it still seems… unnatural," Leona said softly.

"What do you mean?" Jeannie asked.

"Well, I just can't get used to the idea that my pastor is out there having…." She blushed. "…relations with one of our friends."

Jeannie fanned herself and laughed. "Oh, Leona, you bad girl."

Linda changed the subject. "Back to matters at hand…" The women refocused. "I also heard how much it would cost to rebuild the elevator." They leaned their heads in together. "According to my next door neighbors who have a son named Dylan, some kind of a whiz kid on the computer, he looked it up and rebuilding it might cost… Ninety million dollars." She nodded as if this extra emphasis would make it truer. The original figure was somewhat less (a lot less, actually) but Linda thought that adding a few extra million dollars would be better than costing too little. *Add a little fat to the budget*, her husband would say, *just for emergency's sake.*

"Oh heavens!" Jeannie and Leona exclaimed simultaneously. Because they were the only patrons in Human Beans, they didn't need to worry about privacy or being overheard. Everyone else was out working on the cleanup.

Chapter 2.

"Most of that will be covered by insurance, I'm sure," Leona stated wisely.

"I hope so," Linda said, "or Amicable is going to be Amicrapable."

Jeannie giggled again.

At four o'clock in the afternoon, Rhonda returned home after a ten-hour shift on an Amicable cleanup crew. Butcher was still at the office. After parking the car in the garage, she stiffly pulled herself from the car and slammed the door shut behind her. Looking around the interior of the garage, she noticed the accumulation of junk from the last six years since Butcher had entered her life. The most recently forgotten display pieces were plastic toys shifted from inside the house. *Because*, Rhonda was honest with herself, *the house was just too small for the five of them.*

Connie, Rhonda's mother, still lived with them. Although she had recovered from the trauma of her past, there were still moments when Connie was unable to cope with the present. Butcher was not resentful, thankfully. Rhonda smiled at the thought of her husband who was, in his very being, the kindest (and most exasperating) man she had ever met.

Rhonda stretched her arms above her head, groaning at the effort it took to realign her back and neck. As she exhaled, her eyes took in various unfinished projects: a rocking chair needing new armrests, cans of wood stain and sealant, a visual reminder that the deck was in the latter stages of rotting away if they didn't cover it soon. There was a metal canister, two-stroke motor oil for the unused boat motor. The boat hadn't been taken out for a drive in eighteen months. There were reasons for this neglect, most of them familial; the children and work now took up all their time. John Thomas was a sprightly bundle of four-and-a half-almost-five-year-old energy and his little sister, Georgie, precocious and painfully cute, eighteen months younger.

Georgie.

As her daughter's name echoed in her mind, she thought guiltily of the man for whom her daughter was named. George Hendriks.

Before Butcher, George had been Rhonda's best friend and confidant. Through every trial and tribulation, George, a kind and cantankerous centenarian and next-door neighbor, had been her rock and shield. Now one hundred and three years of age, George had lost much of his liveliness, even refraining from visiting the bowling alley where he had regularly interacted with the high school youth.

Now, George, a shell of himself, (if truth be known, he should have moved into the nursing home a few years ago) struggled to take care of his every day needs. He was slow and getting slower. As his last days were playing out, Rhonda knew, with a deep sense of trepidation, that one day she would walk into his house and find him in his bed, his heart still.

Driven by guilt because she had not visited him all weekend, Rhonda walked over to George's house. After climbing the stairs of the porch, she trundled across the boards and opened the front door without knocking. Even if she had knocked, George wouldn't have heard her. The last time she knocked, he chided her for making him get out of his chair when 60 Minutes was showing an expose on the Clinton regime. George, like most Amicableans, was a die-hard Republican, and it made his eyes water with joy when the Democrats took it up the backside.

Opening the door and walking into the dimness, Rhonda let her eyes adjust. Out of the corner of her eye, she caught movement from the living room armchair. George strained his neck to see who had walked through his door.

"Sorry, I didn't knock," she said as she moved around in front of him so that he wouldn't have to crane.

"You should have," he gurgled as the phlegm in his throat made a wet noise. He cleared it with a loud cough. "I could have been in here naked and dancing."

"You wish," she said.

He grunted. "Sixty years ago, I would have given Butcher a run for his money."

"I'm sure Mabel would have been very pleased about that."

"Yes, my Mabel. One of a kind." The room was silent, save the constant ticking from the grandfather clock: doleful, pendulum swings, the incessant movement of time.

"How are you feeling today, George?"

"Like a spring chicken." He adjusted himself in his chair and winced. "Say, have you ever wondered what that saying means? What's the difference between a spring chicken and a fall chicken?"

Rhonda shrugged. "A fall chicken is usually headless."

George laughed. "Well, I must be a winter chicken then, because I lost my head a long time ago."

"You have more marbles still rolling around in your head than any centenarian I've ever known."

"How many do you know?"

Rhonda sat down across from him. She flipped on the ancient table lamp next to her arm. The shade had dangling faux pearls, but it filtered the light beautifully. "I only know you, George."

"Your one and only, Rhodie."

They settled into a comfortable silence - George, poised on the brink of sleep and Rhonda, still exhausted from the day. "Is the town going to recover?"

Rhonda looked at the backs of her long fingers. Wrinkles had appeared from nowhere. "Didn't life used to be easier? You know, when we didn't have responsibilities as parents, no worries about finances..." She glanced at George who had cracked open his eyes and stared bemusedly, a hint of a smile on his lips.

She continued. "I don't think there's ever been a point in human history where there has been this kind of global chaos." She looked across the room at the photos of George's family, his wife and children, all three gone many years ago. "I mean, there's terrorism and global warming and race relations and diseases and our... our... children are disengaged with their families and communities; they have no work and no urge to contribute and...."

Like a concertmaster summoning silence and stillness from the choir, George interrupted her with his hand. The smooth, transparent skin seemed unbelievably thin as if the thick outer layers had eroded and he was left with one last membrane made of plastic wrap. "In 1939, I was seventeen years old. I remember my father entering my room late one night in September." Again, he adjusted his aching bones in the plush cushion of his chair. "His silhouette filled the doorframe; the light behind seemed to shimmer and as he walked into my room, I could tell something was wrong."

"What was it?"

"He sat on my bed, slouching, his hands worrying in his lap, which was frightening because he was not a worrier." George looked at a photo on the stand near the television, an old black and white, faded in spots by years of exposure to sunlight. There was a much taller version of a man who looked like George and a beautiful woman, thin and pert, wearing a floral print dress.

"'George,' he said, 'the world is about to enter the valley of the shadow of death… again.' Then, he did something I'd never seen him do before – he started crying. My dad fought in Europe during World War I. When he enlisted, he believed he was joining a noble cause, a heroic opportunity to be part of keeping world order. What he entered, though, was the worst representation of humanity's sickness: the trenches, the massacres, the mustard gas, the loss of…" George couldn't finish the sentence.

"But then he said, 'George, that was all child's play compared to the storm that's coming.' The Nazis had just invaded Poland. The rumors about Hitler were coming true before our eyes. The silence in my room was stifling. Even the crickets stopped chirping."

"'So, son,' he said, 'You'll have a decision to make. In the next years, you'll be asked to take part in another war, far worse and tragic and horrific than the 'Great War.' It will change history. If you choose to serve, you will see unforgettable things: acts of terror that will spill over into your dreams even when you are a hundred years old.' I never thought I'd make it, but he was right." George smiled wryly at the memory. "I still wake up in a cold sweat from some of the things that I saw in Germany in 1945."

"It must have been horrible, George," Rhonda said.

Holding her gaze with his rheumy eyes, George's jaw tightened before he spoke. "Every generation believes that they live in the most difficult of times; my great grandparents slogged through the mess of the American Civil War; the change from sails to engines, horses to cars, outhouses to indoor plumbing - every change has a price to pay." He raised an index finger. "But every change has something to be gained, also."

"But George, the elevator exploding…"

He shook his head. "If I've learned anything from one hundred and three years, it's the wisdom of perspective." Rhonda cocked her head to the side. "You don't believe me? How about a story from the Bible? An arrogant young man named Joseph lived through an attempted murder at the hands of his brothers, was sold into slavery, falsely accused of rape and spent years in prison. Later, after God pulled him up by his toga strap and his brothers came back, do you remember what he said?" She shook her head. "'What you meant for harm, God meant for good.'"

Rhonda put her head down. "There's nothing good that can come out of this. Three people are dead; the town is reeling; children are…"

"Children are what?" George's voice was stern, yet kind. "I've heard that they've been asked to help. If I know anything about those kids, they feel honored and valued at the thought of being useful. The dead? We all die, but how do we live together? Amicable?" George's voice was gaining a strength. "This town will be very much like Joseph. Mark my words, it will feel as if Amicable is on the dark ledge of being assaulted and sold. People will be falsely accused of all sorts of things and finally, when the darkest night settles over the town, Amicable will be caged." George transformed into an ancient prophet. "What was meant for harm will turn into our greatest triumph - a paraphrase of Churchill. Rather appropriate, don't you think?"

Rhonda looked up at George to see tears streaming down his cheeks, but it didn't affect his voice. "As we get older, we think that life is getting more difficult, but in actuality, nothing has changed. The older we get, the less flexible we become. Change just seems more painful. Do you understand?"

"Kind of." She waggled her hand.

"The key," George's voice lowered, "is to recognize perspective - all of life is change, and once you stop changing, you start dying."

Rhonda pulled herself up and then knelt beside George, putting her head on his leg and holding his left hand in both of hers. As George stroked her head with his right hand, he wept. "You're a good girl, Rhonda, the best."

Those were the last words George Hendriks ever spoke to Rhonda Jensen.

Chapter 3.

Stedman Boswell yawned loudly into his closed fist as he paused at the intersection of County Road B37 and Highway 10. After what seemed an interminable amount of time driving through endless acres of ripening corn, the young insurance adjuster grew impatient to arrive in Amicable.

Even though he had lived in the Midwest, Boswell had never experienced small town life at any length. With his parents, Mike and Evelyn Boswell, Stedman had vacationed to exotic destinations like Denver and San Francisco, Lake Tahoe and Phoenix, or eastward to Chicago, Nashville or New York. If at all possible, they stuck to the interstates avoiding small towns. The tiny farming villages, dotting the endless asphalt roads, were not sources of wonder, but sources of boredom: *Who in their right mind would want to live in a dusty pothole in the middle of nowhere?* And then, and THEN! The winters…

Mike, Stedman's father, a prominent businessman, who sold airplanes to farmers and thrill seekers alike, needed to mix and mingle with other highbrow Kansas Citians just as he mixed and mingled his drinks. Although not an alcoholic, he was what some might call a whiskey walker. Every night when he returned home from work, he mixed himself a scotch and water and walked around his house (a mansion by Midwestern standards) pontificating on his importance to the world.

Evelyn had been a notch in Mike's belt. A buxom blonde beauty, a Trophy Wife as his co-workers whispered, Evelyn was seventeen years younger than Mike. As a young woman, Evelyn had performed well in beauty pageants with high marks in the swimsuit and talent competition (tap dancing), while 'earning' lesser marks in the interview section. The Boswell family performed their civic charade nicely, posing as a happy, rich couple still in love and admired by the elites.

The truth was, they weren't happy at all, and they really didn't have any friends. For the most part, Mike and Evelyn tolerated each other's presence but preferred to be alone. Evelyn dreaded Mike's return from work at night. Although she put on a smile for him, nodding politely at his descriptions of the way he handled his associates, always making himself the hero, she silently loathed him, and his voice and his 'oldness.' Now that she was fifty-two, she figured that they'd put up with each other for so long that they should probably just stay married. For the most part, though, both Mike and Evelyn were extraordinarily lonely. As was their son, Stedman.

Evelyn was nineteen years old when Stedman made his unplanned entry into the world. Most of the good ol' boys clapped Mike on the back and congratulated him on his virility. After popping a cigar in his mouth (Cuban-illegal, the best), they took him out for beers and barbeque. Meanwhile, Evelyn rested uncomfortably recovering from the birth by herself. Not returning until the next day, as teenage mother and child rested somewhat uncomfortably in the room, Mike patted her arm patronizingly and said 'I'm so proud of you,' then promptly succumbed to his hangover. When he began to snore, the sound woke the infant who began to wail. Mike pushed back the cowboy hat on his head, looked dazedly at his wife, and after standing up, blew her a kiss.

"I've got to get some sleep," he said. "I've got work tomorrow."

As he left the room, Evelyn flipped him the bird.

Stedman grew up in a sterile household filled with every imaginable *thing* except love and attention. When he was two, Mike bought him a remote control car; when he was five, Evelyn bought him a pony; when he was eleven, his father bought him season tickets to the Chiefs home games. When he was sixteen, Evelyn bought him a Porsche. Through it all, as he attempted to play with his remote control car, to manipulate his pony, as he walked the sidelines with some of the Chiefs footballers, Stedman always felt an unconscious, overwhelming sense of rejection. His psychiatrist said that it was a passing phase and he should just be thankful that his parents loved him enough to give him a 'happy' home. What he really wanted was validation for his existence.

Mike and Evelyn breathed a sigh of relief when he graduated from high school and decided to attend Colorado State University. For two years, he partied and pretended to study. After finally dropping out of college for good, his parents sighed deeply when their adult son moved back home.

Stedman's return to his childhood room lasted three weeks until Evelyn grew frustrated about her lack of personal space in the nine thousand square foot house on the rolling eastern edge of Kansas City.

"Stedman," she called up the marble staircase. Lining the stairs were photographs of Evelyn in her glory days wearing a bikini and tap shoes. "Stedman!"

"What!" He yelled down the hallway from the sixth bedroom on the left.

"We need to talk!"

"Later. I'm busy!"

"No, Stedman. Now."

No answer. Evelyn's patience waned until finally she gripped the handrail and clomped up the stairs in her platform sandals, short skirt and silk top. Walking down the hallway, she felt her blood beginning to boil. Without knocking, she opened his door and found her son sitting in his underwear drinking beer and playing video games. He didn't even look up at her.

"Stedman." No response. "Stedman, I'm serious. Turn that silly computer off. I've got a surprise for you." At the thought of a gift, Stedman was both intrigued and resentful at the same time. He didn't stop playing the game, though.

"What is it?"

"Your daddy and I, we feel that at your age, like, you shouldn't, be living at home with us. You need to spread your wings. Fly. You know, test the winds, fulfill your dreams, that sort of thing."

"You just want to get rid of me."

"Stedman," she said sternly, not quite betraying the guilt that gripped her when he had guessed the truth. "We love you and we want the best for you."

Stedman rolled his eyes.

"Your father and I are renting you an apartment in the city so you can be near other young people your age. You know, so you can work and have fun."

"I don't have a job."

"Well, your father fixed that too."

"Really…" Stedman seethed, imagining the humiliation of showing up for work at a job he had neither applied for nor wanted.

"Daddy's friend Theo, you know, Theo Baker, the tall gentleman with the white hair? He owns an insurance company and they were hiring."

"You want me to sell insurance?"

Evelyn took one step into the room and then one step back out. There was a strange odor rising from the floor, a mixture of sweat, beer and something else - moldy cheese? - and she didn't want to gag. "Look, honey, I don't know what you'll be asked to do, but having a job will be good for you and you'll meet some new people, maybe find a… a… um…"

"What, Mom? A girlfriend?" Stedman ground his teeth.

"Well, yes, a girlfriend would be nice. But really, just get out there and meet some people."

Stedman Boswell did indeed move out the next day into the apartment in the city. He began his job writing insurance contracts. He proved to be surprisingly good at it. Enjoying life in the city, he went out on the weekends, sometimes driving his Porsche, sometimes riding the bus. Stedman never brought anyone back to his apartment, and though his mother's hope for a girlfriend did not eventuate, he did enjoy his work. Now that Stedman had been working in the insurance assessment business for thirteen years, Baker had given him autonomy and trust - two things that Stedman had been longing for all these years.

As Stedman's Porsche idled at the crossroads of B37 and Highway 10, he wasn't sure if he had made the right decision in covering the low-profile disaster in the flyspeck town of Amicable. No matter which direction he turned, all he could see were tall rows of corn or shorter rows of soybeans. Utility poles seemed to be the only connections to civilization. Glancing down at his phone, he saw the connectivity icon spin ceaselessly, an endless merry-go-round sucking the battery power from his device.

"Dammit," he said, quietly knowing, in some general sense, which direction he was supposed to go, but unsure of how many miles or cornfields were left to pass. Boswell rolled down his window and the intense August heat blasted his face.

Stedman flicked his blinker and turned east. Revving the engine of his Porsche (a newer version of his high school model), he sped down the humming asphalt in an assumed direction of where Amicable would be. As he travelled towards the ever-distant heat mirages covering the pavement, Boswell was not shocked (though somewhat revolted) by the roadkill lining the side of the road. As the odometer cranked over, so did the number of different kinds of vermin that had met their untimely end on Highway 10. Dead rabbits, gophers, skunks, deer, dogs, cats - he lost track of the species.

Boswell turned his attention to the business-at-hand. In cases like this, delaying payment was always in the best interests of the company. As insurer and insured tousled over amounts and timetables, the insured would settle. Big business always wins. Only a few times in his career had Stedman Boswell allowed guilt to nibble his financial soul: once in the case of a family home burning to the ground and another when a young woman drowned. Unfortunately, the family had been late with their payments by three days. Unfortunate, yes, but companies have to have rules. They can't just pay for pity's sake or there would be no money for the shareholders.

Stedman saw the approaching green sign proclaiming distances - Amicable was sixteen miles to the east. Just ahead was a turnoff to a town called Clancy, apparently one of the larger villages in the area, but frankly, he didn't really care about the names. To him, all policies were nameless; they were all the same – squawking chicks, noisy complainers. *We paid for the insurance. Now give it back.* Unfortunately, for policyholders, there were so many loopholes and so much small print that rarely did the insurance companies pay the full amount. These were the thoughts of the frustrated insurance man as he closed the distance to Amicable.

"When is the insurance investigator coming?" James' worried expression was illuminated by the laptop in front of him. He was trying to work through the family finances as well as have a conversation with his wife, Naida.

Naida was cooking and holding their toddler on her hip.

"According to the mayor, she seemed to think he would be here sometime today."

"What insurance company is it again?" James turned toward Naida and made a face at Nate who giggled and buried his face in his mother's shoulder.

"Baker Insurance," Naida responded and set Nate on the floor. He immediately whined and threw his hands back up into the air to be picked up. "James, can you come get him?"

James pulled himself from his chair and got down on his hands and knees to approach the boy. Nate saw his father coming out of the corner of his eye and hid between his mother's legs. Giggling with glee as James grabbed him, Nate laughed when his father lifted up his t-shirt and blew a raspberry on his belly.

"Baker," he said in a Yoda voice, "How long it will take to reach a settlement, I wonder?"

Naida glanced at him sideways. She'd heard rumors about the potential cost and razing, leaving a World-Trade-Center-sized hole in the heart of Amicable. If James couldn't get work in Amicable, they might have to move.

Teams still roamed through town picking up parts of elevator carcass lying around Amicable. At one point, some youth were walking through Winslow Park when they found a dusty shoe. One high school student was convinced that it was a corpse's shoe and freaked out. Her friends attempted to calm her while averting their eyes from the 'crime scene.' Another bystander called Louise, the town police officer. Five minutes later, the police cruiser arrived. Walking purposefully to the teenage trio, Louise bent down to retrieve the shoe.

"Don't you need to cordon off the area and take some pictures?" the boy asked.

Louise, exhausted, shook her head. "No, Corey. The other half of the pair is over there," she pointed to a tree where a couple were standing barefoot. The man was calling to a dog, which had run away with the matching twin of the shoe.

Chapter 3.

Once the girl saw that the shoe did not belong to a corpse, he pulled her from the ground. Embarrassed, they walked away.

On the other side of town, Nash and Derek began to put the last of the cuts of meat into the cooler, wipe down the stainless steel tables, and prep the shop for the next morning. Peterson Butchery belonged to their father, a swarthy man in his late fifties with a sizeable beer gut and a happily receding hairline. Robert Peterson was rarely in the shop. He trusted his sons to run the business while he and his wife gallivanted across the country exploring all the places they'd wanted to go, but couldn't when the boys were young. After the wedding, Bob and Vanessa had plans to drive to Branson, Missouri, the holy land of Midwestern Baby Boomers, but the explosion kept the elder Petersons in Amicable to help clean up.

The door to Peterson's Butchery opened.

"Tracey," Derek said as he wiped his hands on his apron. "You okay?"

Tracey Thomas, a twenty-three-year-old college graduate and alumnus of Amicable High School, with lustrous sandy blonde hair and sparkling green eyes, panted as she caught her breath. "Yes, yes." She held up a finger. "Give me a second."

"What's going on?"

"What part of 'give me a second' is hard to understand?" Nash and Derek exchanged a glance.

Tracey was Amicablean famous for multiple things, but one of Derek's favorites was Tracey's ability to create a furor by affixing various offensive bumper stickers to her car. One of his personal favorites (even though greatly ironic) was:

BEEF: IT'S WHAT'S ROTTING IN YOUR COLON

Tracey's father, aghast at his daughter's brazen anti-agriculturalism, was appalled and wanted to ground her then, and there. Unfortunately, Dan Thomas found it difficult to ground a college student no matter how many times he said, 'My house, my rules.' She graduated from college with a degree in (much to her father's chagrin) Women's Studies. As far as her father could understand, the number of jobs available to a Women's Studies major were about the same number as books in the Bible claiming that Satan was just misunderstood. When Tracey arrived at her parent's house with the bumper sticker attached, her father, instead of throwing a fit, decided on bumper sticker warfare.

AN ATHEIST, A VEGAN AND A BODY TRAINER WALK INTO A BAR. I ONLY KNOW THIS BECAUSE THEY TOLD EVERYONE IN THE FIRST TWELVE SECONDS

Which, of course, escalated and encouraged Tracey's insolence, pushing her towards the next gem, which almost got her disowned:

IF IGNORANCE IS BLISS, REPUBLICANS MUST BE ORGASMIC

To be honest, most of the town whispered more about the word 'orgasm', but secretly, many thought the bumper sticker was funny, just not as humorous as the father's response:

MY DOG IS A DEMOCRAT. HE JUST LIES AROUND ALL DAY EXPECTING TO BE FED

"Okay," Tracey said after recovering from her breathlessness. "Okay. I'm okay. Guess what? He's here."

Derek raised an eyebrow. "Who's here?"

"The guy. You know, the insurance guy. The assayer."

"I think you mean the 'adjuster,'" Derek corrected.

"Whatever, Captain Grammar. The 'adjuster,'" she put the word in quotations marks, "is here to decide how much money the town is going to get."

"How do you know?" Nash put his hands on the counter in front of him.

"The mayor called Steve Evans, you know, the town Treasurer, who called my dad about coming in for a quick meeting. I overheard them."

Chapter 3.

"What did your dad say?"

"He said, 'Don't say anything to anyone, Tracey,'" she copied his voice.

"And yet here you are…" Derek copied his brother's posture.

"Like, duh. I thought you guys would like to know."

"You got that right. C'mon. Let's go get a look at this peckerwood."

"How do you know he's going to be bad?" Tracey asked.

"Anybody who works for an insurance company is a peckerwood."

"And you know this because…?"

Putting his hands on her shoulders, he smiled. "Remember last year when Dandy Randy crashed his car into the Choke and he made an insurance claim? The insurance company had convinced him to have a five thousand dollar deductible so that he could have a low premium. Well, his car was only worth four thousand dollars, and you know that Dandy Randy is not the sharpest hook in the tackle box."

"Didn't he throw a fit?"

"What could he do about it? It's not like they coerced him to sign on the dotted line, but insurance companies don't give a flying Fig Newton about anyone but the shareholders. Mark my words, Tracey Thomas. This guy is going to be a Grade A premium buttmunch."

Tracey smiled and grabbed Derek's hand. "Come on, let's go. Nash, are you coming?"

Nash shook his head. "No, I'll close up. I've got to get home to the missus."

Derek pretended to vomit. "I'll see you later."

Nash waved to the two and turned to finish the closing routine. It was only later that he realized his brother and Tracey had not let go of each other's hands.

Stedman Boswell and Janice Stensrud faced each other like prizefighters weighing in for the bout. Boswell had four or five inches of height on his opponent, but Stensrud enjoyed twenty to thirty pounds of extra weight. The mayor of Amicable was the epitome of a Midwestern woman: proud, hardworking and strong. Janice easily held her own with male counterparts on the town council.

As she studied the young man facing her, noticing his aquiline nose, high forehead, blue eyes and brown hair, she found him a good-looking young man. But his eyes radiated something else: arrogance - a big city boy. She had seen them before, big city types waltzing into Amicable, expecting everyone to roll over and fawn over their big city ways and their big city clothes and their big city ideas.

Similarly, Stedman Boswell pondered the woman in front of him recognizing that she was a not woman to be trifled with. At the same time, he believed his cosmopolitan charm would melt her iciness. Putty in his hands; butter to be melted. Ice cream on a summ…

"Hello," Janice said simply and without inflection. "Welcome to Amicable. I'm Mayor Stensrud."

"Thank you for the welcome," Stedman responded, his tenor voice echoing in the mayor's office, a 1950's cemented brick room in 'downtown' Amicable with polished floors beneath fluorescent lights above. "I noticed the sign when I drove in - Amicable, 'The nicest town in the Midwest.'"

"Well, we like to think so."

"My name is Boswell, Stedman Boswell. I hope that someone from Baker communicated to you in advance that I'd be coming."

"Yes."

"I don't know how long I'll be able to stay in your nice little town, but I'm looking forward to meeting some of the people and seeing how I can help."

Janice's frown deepened at the word 'little.' Many big city folk thought that 'little' meant 'stupid.' "That would be nice, Mr. Boswell."

"Please, Stedman."

"How can we assist you in your assessment?"

Stedman placed his brown leather briefcase on the table and extracted a manila envelope. From it he withdrew a sheaf of documents and handed them to the mayor. "Over the next weeks, I'll investigate the accident site, interview some of the locals, and write up a report on my findings. I would appreciate some open doors for that."

"I'll do what I can. A few more of the town councilors will be arriving soon. They'll be able to show you around and help you with some of the things that you'll need to see."

"Thank you." Stedman's eyes were distracted by two figures standing outside the tinted window of the mayor's office. Their heads were pressed between the stenciled letters on the window. He raised a hand and waved at them, and thought he saw the young man turn to the girl and mouth the word, *pecker.*
"Who are they?"

Janice turned her head and noticed Derek and Tracey. "Two of our town's great young people."

"What are they doing?"

Janice sighed. "They're being Amicableans."

"Ami... what?"

"Amicableans. What it means to be part of our town. When you say you are Amicablean, it means a pride in many things, but it also seems to give each person the right to be nosy. You'll notice that during your stay. Your business might be a little more public than you expect."

"I'm sure I'll be fine."

Don't bet on it, Janice thought.

Outside the window, Derek and Tracey turned away to face Main Street. On the other side of the street, they recognized the parked pickup trucks of Amicableans, most of them at least partially full of debris. "Did you see what he's wearing?"

"Yeah," Tracey said. "He looks like he's going golfing."

"Or, or, he might be going to his yacht." Derek thrust out his jaw and pretended to put on an English accent, which he was not very good at it. Midwesterners were not good at accents.

They stood in silence watching the traffic pass. Everyone waved to them as they drove by. It was the nice thing to do. Even if you didn't know their name, it seemed appropriate to acknowledge people's presence. When a pickup would pass them, Derek would tilt his head backwards in recognition of their Amicableness, while Tracey smiled politely next to him.

Without turning her head, Tracey asked the question that was on every Amicablean mind. "Do you think Amicable will recover?"

35

Derek frowned and shrugged. "I don't know." They both glanced at the shell of the elevator. Like jagged teeth jutting up from the ground, the cores of the concrete silos looked like cavities.

"I like Amicable," she said simply. "When I was at college, I thought I was done with it. I thought I'd moved on from my parent's rules and restrictions and for a while I did." She leaned into him slightly, not quite touching, but their closeness was palpable. "But after a while I missed having something solid to hold onto. It was like going on a cruise; at first it was fun and exciting and you saw different things and people, but after a while, you just wanted something unmoving beneath you and some people who remember you and your name. You know what I mean?" Another pickup drove by and they waved. "During my second year, I wasn't really homesick, but kind of home-achy. I don't know if that makes sense. I missed Main Street; I missed the bowling alley and our free bowling nights."

"I do know what you mean," Derek said.

"How so?"

"I mean - I don't know what you mean."

Tracey laughed loudly which made him smile.

"My parents left Amicable for vacations and trips and fun stuff, but they never really took us. Nash and I have been locked away in the shop all these years. It's not that we really mind, but someday I want to travel too. Now that Nash is married…"

Tracey picked up on his consternation. "How's that going for you?"

Derek shook his head. He didn't want to talk about it. "Maybe we should get going. We'll see the peckerwood some other time."

Disappointed, and slightly worried that she'd upset him, she nodded and the two began walking down Main Street to her house.

Stedman watched them leave. "I was wondering, Mayor, do you know of a place I could rent while I'm here in Amicable? Do I need to get a place in Clancy?"

"No, no, please accept our hospitality. I know that Liam Wilson, one of our town mechanics, has a place that you can rent."

"Thank you very much. If you could make that happen, I would appreciate it. Tonight, though, I think I'll drive to Clancy and stay in the hotel there."

Janice smiled. The only hotel/motel in Clancy was a dive on the south side of town. A Motel 7 with insect issues. "You do that, Mr. Boswell.... Sorry, Stedman."

Boswell and Stensrud shook hands firmly.

It was very much like an Old West showdown.

Chapter 4.

Stedman Boswell stood with his hands on his khaki encrusted hips staring disdainfully at what had been advertised as a motel but looked more like a cockroach sanctuary. The dark brown siding was peppered with winter salt stains thrown up by the snow blowers, and the front bushes seemed to be wind sieves collecting fast food burger wrappers. The sky above was scrubbed clean of clouds and dirt though.

Pushing a button on his key fob, Stedman opened the trunk of his Porsche. In Clancy, the sports car stood out like a sore thumb. Grabbing his rolling suitcase from the opened trunk, he slammed it shut. Walking to the front door of the Motel 7, Stedman noticed cigarette butts and broken beer bottle glass lying all over the parking lot and sidewalk. Shaking his head, he opened the door with the key, which was connected to a plastic oval with a nearly invisible number 13 scratched from it. He took a deep breath and entered.

Outside the Motel 7, a dark purple Plymouth minivan pulled into the parking lot opposite the rooms.

"Move over, Jeannie," Leona said as she pushed the smaller woman towards the opposite side.

Linda Harmsen, of course, had taken up the coveted middle section of the back seat. As she hooked her elbows over the cushion, she cautioned her friends to silence. "Girls," she said forcefully, "we'll all have a chance to see. Just be patient."

"What if he doesn't come out again?" Jeannie asked.

"He will," Linda assured them. "He will."

"How can you be sure?"

Linda turned to Jeannie, whose face was, in the confined space, less than a foot from hers. "Because it's the Motel 7. He'll be gasping for breath in less than ten minutes. Mark my words," Linda said as she turned back to gaze out the rear window, "we'll see him very soon."

Inside the room, Stedman held his breath as long as possible and then blew it out slowly through pursed lips. Ever so carefully he began to inhale, but immediately recognized his mistake. Unfortunately, the small breath had seared his sinuses.

If Stedman were a connoisseur of odors, he would have been able to pick up cigarette smoke, animal urine, new carpet spray with touches of lemon and a hint of spoiled breast milk. To finish off the bouquet, a flourish of vomit hung in the air. Briefly, Stedman thought that he was about to die. Never in his life had Boswell stayed in anything less than five stars, where the lobby was filled with fresh flowers, the concierge immaculately dressed, and the porters ready and willing to take your leather suitcases to your room for a small tip of twenty dollars. Once, Stedman had stayed at a bed and breakfast where the bathroom was down a hallway. He imagined that hell was indubitably like that. But this Motel 7, made that bed and breakfast seem like Nirvana.

With the back of his hand perched under his nose, Boswell went to ask for a different room. The front desk attendant apologized, telling him that there were no vacancies but mentioned with waggling eyebrows that there was another motel on the other side of Clancy that 'may or may not rent by the hour wink, wink, nudge nudge.' He trudged back to number 13.

Stedman's eyes rolled wildly as he noticed the fraying comforter lying slightly askew on his bed. It looked as if someone had entered Room 13 for a quick fifteen-minute romance, rolled on the sheets and then, like busted teenagers, attempted to throw the cover back into place. For a moment, Stedman's brain imagined the front desk attendant doing that very thing, and bile rose quickly into his throat. Covering his mouth, he threw open the door, raced into the parking lot and vomited his lunch onto the parking lot asphalt.

In the Plymouth Voyager minivan, all three women averted their eyes at the sight of the man emptying his guts. Sagely, Linda scrunched up her face and nodded. "See, I told you so."

"That's disgusting," Jeannie responded. "I mean, it's been a few years since my children have done that, but wow that's a lot of puke."

"Adult vomit is always worse than child's vomit," Leona intoned as if she were the world's foremost authority on the subject. "Different mix of chemicals."

"Look," Jeannie said, "He's got some on his shoes." The man was looking disdainfully down at his brown leather Hush Puppies. Shaking his foot, he attempted to rid himself of the last bit.

"Poor thing," Leona said.

"He's not bad looking," Jeannie said, leaning a little closer to the back window. "Well, as far as a puking man goes."

Linda leaned slightly forward and her arms slipped over the back seat, causing her almost to tumble into the small little trunk space where the spare tire, an umbrella, and three or four fast food wrappers were scattered. As she caught herself, Leona fell into the side window while Jeannie began to helplessly giggle. The movement, though, and perhaps the muffled sound, caught the attention of the insurance man who peered towards the van.

"Shhh!" Linda shushed loudly. "Don't move."

"What is he, a rhinoceros?" Jeannie's hand covered her mouth to keep from laughing aloud. "If we don't move," she uttered slowly through her fingers, "he won't be able to see us."

Stedman squinted his eyes but couldn't quite see through the tinting.

Jeannie mooed like a cow, lowing into Linda's ear. Leona burst out laughing which caused the car to shake. Now, Stedman could see the minivan shaking and he stepped over his pile of vomit to get a better look.

"Go! Go! Abort mission!" Linda shouted, and all three scrabbled towards the front at the same time. Leona, holder of the car keys, pulled Jeannie back, tossing her unceremoniously aside while Linda became wedged between the captain's chairs. The Voyager, rocking back and forth, roared into life as Leona started the engine. Throwing the car into reverse, almost running into Stedman Boswell, the car spun away. Spitting in the dust, Stedman Boswell picked himself up off the ground.

It was only then that he noticed he had fallen into his own vomit.

After pulling himself from the remains of his lunch, Stedman forced himself back inside the small motel room, stripped his clothes off and jumped into the shower. He was not in the least surprised that the showerhead started to howl like a coyote. Boswell reached for the bar of soap, noticing a disgusting curly black hair left embedded in it. Again fighting his gag reflex, he dropped the soap into the bottom of the tub. Grabbing the shampoo, he tipped it upside down squeezing it up into a ball in an attempt to extricate any of the soapy liquid. Obviously, this, too, was not a new bottle. Eventually, he coaxed a small drop of shampoo into his hand and rubbed it into his hair. Grabbing his hair in frustration, he screamed into the shower, which, having enough of his bellyaching, ceased to offer warm water and turned into a brisk mountain cascade. Shouting, Stedman sucked in his stomach and pulled into the rear of the shower where his back came into contact with the plastic curtain which was of the same temperature as the mountain water. Startled, he jumped away and back into the water. He was the ball in a frigid game of shower ping-pong.

Fighting against the stinging water, he turned the spigots off only to realize that he hadn't washed the shampoo from his hair.

After drying off, he repeated his mantra for the night. *Just survive. Just survive the night.*

Stedman Boswell held his cellphone against his ear, the dam of his anger held in check only by the necessity.

Theo Baker answered after seven rings. "What is it, Boswell? I thought we established that I'm on vacation and you're working."

"Yes, sir, I'm sorry," he spoke through gritted teeth. "I just wanted to update you on the events of arriving in Amicable."

"What? Where?"

"Amicable. You know the town where the grain elevator blew up?"

"Oh, yes." Stedman knew that Theo Baker had no idea what he was talking about.

"Mr. Baker," Stedman shouted into the phone to stop his superior from disconnecting the line, "I want you to know that we're dealing with some very, how shall I put this, salt-of-the-earth type people."

"What the hell does that mean?"

"My first impressions are that they are wary of outsiders, and certainly distrustful of insurance companies."

"Not that rare, is it Boswell?" Theo Baker sounded like he was walking. His voice was breathy. "Hurry up and tell me what you need, Boswell, I'm spending time with my family."

Stedman was pretty sure that Theo Baker's family was nowhere near the man. "I'm going back tomorrow to speak with the town leaders regarding the explosion. I'll look around at the damage and pretend that I'm heartbroken. Then, I'll report back to you at the end of the week with an estimate of the damage and a reasonable guess at whether the explosion was due to negligence."

"You will, Boswell, do your best to…" Baker did not want to say any more over the phone.

"Yes, sir, I'll do my job and protect the interests of Baker and its shareholders at all costs."

"Good man. Now, I see my wife. She's signaling me."

"Thank you, sir. I just want you to know that my accommodation is by far and away the most disgusting place I've ever been in my life. Hopefully I…" Stedman heard his cellphone beep, a sign that his boss had hung up.

I hope you have to come here someday, Baker. We'll see how you like it.

Somewhere in the middle of that Tuesday night (it was Wednesday morning, actually), George Hendriks opened his eyes and glanced at the alarm clock beside his bed. After his talk with Rhonda, he was feeling particularly good about himself. He hadn't felt like this for a very long time. His heart felt strong; his lungs were clear, and his skin felt alive. Taking a deep breath, George threw back the covers and noticed the glowing numbers had ticked over to 2:25.

After going to the bathroom, George knew that he wouldn't get back to sleep, so he went to the kitchen table to write a letter. Because Rhonda was the last visitor in the house, he thought he'd express what he'd been thinking after her departure. There was one more thing that he wanted to tell her. For the first time in his life, he had truly felt like a prophet. The narrative of Joseph and his not-so-technicolor dream coat had arisen from nowhere. A few more words had come to him as she had left his house, but he didn't have the strength or the temerity to turn her around. Instead, he had swallowed the words; now at 2:29 in the morning, they were coming back up.

After turning on the light, George situated himself at the old oak table which was scratched and grooved like George's own face. Each mark and line were memories of some better time in life; the kids were little and had gouged the table with a fork, there a mark from a careless push of the green vase, which had held flowers from Mabel's funeral. George ran a finger across some of the scratches, feeling the indentation of time, smoothed as life moved on.

The thought of dying no longer frightened George. Because the three people he loved most in the world had passed before him, he was ready to wander the long corridor between breath and belief to see them again. George pulled a pencil from the mug in the middle of the table and began to jot down his thoughts to Rhonda.

Dearest neighbors,

It's late, or should I say early - 2:29 a.m. to be very exact, and I can't sleep. Rhodie, you and I had a discussion not too long ago about the fate of this remarkable small town. I believe I Butcherized the future and pretended to know something about it that may or may not happen, but either way, it's a future that won't have me in it. I can simply fade into the past and be taken to a worry-less place. Don't think that I won't think about you even as I go; it's just that the end of life has a way of taking the edges off what I used to think was important.

Enough of the fatalism.

A voice spoke to me after you left - don't worry, I'm not going that senile, but I am open minded enough to think that there are angels poking around in places that nobody expects. This particular angel seemed to be urging me to add one last sentence to my prophetic vision from earlier in the day.

When all is said and done, and it seems as if Amicable is about to breathe its last:

One voice, and one voice alone can save this town.
You will recognize the voice when you hear it.

I'm realistic to know that I will not be around to hear the voice. But you must, Rhodie. You must. If you don't, Amicable will be no more.

43

No pressure.
Whatever you do, Rhodie, enjoy your family. Every moment is a blessing from God. Live as if you won't be around tomorrow.
So, I think that I will g

As George was about to write the last words of his missive, the switch flipped. George, still surprised at one hundred and three years of age, felt his heart stop. It was a quick, brief pain, like a pinprick. The pencil fell from George's hand and his head dropped unceremoniously onto the table. His last vision fell upon the wall of the dining room where a black and white photo of four people was positioned. They were standing in front of a shiny new car glinting in the sun.

They were all smiling.

Chapter 5.

Butcher woke with a start. A voice, or a whisper maybe, had raised goosebumps across his soul. It was not a pleasant experience whatsoever. As Butcher's eyes searched the darkness for anything solid, he heard Rhonda's deep breaths next to him. Although he couldn't see her, he reached out to touch her bare arm. The soft skin of her forearm covering sinewy, firm muscles was warm.

Rhonda had been a revelation of wonder. Because of his uncanny ability to read other people, Butcher struggled with trust. In order for him to actually love anyone - Rhonda, in this case - he had to set aside his preconceptions (or precognitions) and trust first. It was incredibly difficult to move from a place of constant distrust to one of vulnerability and openness, but they had made it. Needless to say, Rhonda was compassionate, patient and honest. Now that they had been married six years, Butcher reckoned he had turned the corner regarding trust issues.

Butcher's mind whirred rapidly after his startled awakening. The explosion had certainly traumatized the town, but somewhat arrogantly Butcher had assumed he would be immune to the psychological battering - especially this soon. *Unfortunately*, he thought, *this was something else.*

Something worse.

Butcher threw his long legs over the edge of the bed, unraveled his body and stood up. Rhonda moved, grunted and adjusted herself in the bed, taking up his vacated space. Butcher smiled and moved towards the bathroom. As he quietly crossed the darkness, he made sure that he didn't wake the kids. They were notoriously light sleepers and any movement could conceivably bring one (or both) bounding into their parents' bedroom hoping that it was daytime already.

Halfway to the bathroom, Butcher received another jolt. It almost caused him to lose his footing. He almost called out. Is this what a heart attack feels like? The feeling ended quickly, but a disturbing image arose in his mind.

Oh no.

George.

Quickly finishing his trip to the bathroom, he glanced at his phone on his dresser. *3:12 a.m.* Butcher hoped that he was overreacting. George would berate him for being a nag, but it was better to be safe than ashamed. Even so, Butcher pulled on a pair of shorts and a t-shirt and padded quietly to the front door.

Walking out onto the front porch, he looked towards George's house and noticed that a light was on. *Good or bad sign,* he wondered. Walking down the front step, he accidentally kicked one of the plastic building toys and cursed Playskool.

Butcher felt the unevenness of the sidewalk and the small bits of gravel on the sensitive soles of his feet. Walking on his tiptoes to avoid the brief needles of pain, he found his way to George's deck and approached the door. Opening it, Butcher heard the squeak, and stepped inside.

"George?"

Butcher let the door shut behind him and moved through the small entry where the sight caused his heart to sink. George's head lay on the table. His thin, wispy white hair stuck up at all ends like a floating cloud around his scalp. George's head craned at an awkward angle and his arms hung loosely at his sides. Butcher moved closer to his friend noticing that George's eyes were open. At first, Butcher's hopes rose, but then he noticed George's pupils were dilated.

Pulling out a chair, Butcher moved closer to George's still figure. Reaching out a hand, Butcher smoothed George's hair tenderly, touching the man who had been a significant force in the reconstruction of Amicable's life.

"Ah, George, my friend…" A tear rolled down Butcher's face.

Just as Butcher was about to stand and call the ambulance, he noticed the piece of paper on the table by George's head. Butcher leaned over to see the addressees, *Dearest neighbors,* and wondered what George had been working on. As he scanned the document, his eyes widened and moved back and forth between the piece of paper and the deceased. Without thinking, Butcher carefully folded the piece of paper into quarters and tucked it into the pocket of his shorts. After dialing 911, Butcher went to get Rhonda.

Rhonda's hair, pulled quickly behind her in a ponytail, stuck out at different angles. There was a slackness in her jaw, and her eyes seemed full of fear and shock. She threw herself into Butcher's arms and sobbed. Not long later, with neither lights nor alarm, the ambulance arrived and pulled to a stop outside George's residence. Two emergency medical personnel, wearing blue green coveralls and carrying orange medical boxes, walked purposefully up the stairs.

"Did you attempt to do CPR?" the young man asked Butcher.

Butcher shook his head. "No, he was already... gone... when I entered the house."

"Okay, we'll take it from here."

The EMTs entered the house and began their work. Unable to revive George, they closed his shirt and stood up. "Did you want to pay your last respects before we take him?"

Butcher pushed Rhonda back from himself to look into her face. Her cheeks, wet with tears, glistened in the moon and street light. "Do you want to?"

She took a deep breath. "I think we should."

They walked slowly, hand in hand, to where George had been placed on the floor. George's mouth hung open and Rhonda was mortified at the sight of George without his teeth. Bravely, though, she knelt to the ground beside him and balanced on her knees. Reaching out to touch his face, she found it still slightly warm.

"How long has he been...gone?" She asked the ambulance man who was watching from the doorway, arms crossed.

He shrugged. "Probably not that long - an hour or so, maybe ninety minutes."

Just a few hours after I saw him, she thought.

"Goodbye, George," she leaned in and whispered. "Thank you for living." She picked up his lifeless hand in her own caressing the paper-thin skin. Rhonda's mourning had begun.

Chapter 6.

Demetrius Chandler always felt out of place. No matter where he was, no matter what he was doing, Demetrius simply could not fit in, not in the Midwest, anyway. It's not that he didn't try; he was certainly more than capable of driving a tractor, lifting bushels of hay, hanging out in the parking lot with his classmates, even administering the Midwestern nasal accent with aplomb, but there was one thing that always kept Demetrius on the outside:

Demetrius was the only black person in the town of Amicable.

That he was grateful for his upbringing was constant; Demetrius thanked God Almighty for being adopted into the Chandler family, small farmers (roughly seven hundred acres scattered across two counties) who lived six miles to the northeast of Amicable. His parents, Dennis and Angela, were kind and fun loving (if not somewhat stoic) Amicableans who had lived on the farmstead for generations. Dennis and Angela had not been able to have children of their own, but when the opportunity came to adopt, Demetrius was placed in their hands and hearts. When he appeared, wrapped in swaddling blankets, like a modern-day Jesus, born in April rather than December, both Dennis and Angela wept openly at the beauty of their small child.

Demetrius had always been big. Physically imposing, Demetrius found himself staring into the mirror every morning wondering when he was going to stop growing. At seventeen, six feet six inches and rippling with dark, dense muscles, he was a pride and joy of Amicable.

When outsiders encountered Demetrius Chandler, there was an instantaneous flinch and an immediate sense of fear. But Demetrius' charm, brilliant smile, along with his quick and agile mind, set most people at rest. Most.

According to most students at Amicable High School, Demetrius was a shoe-in to be the Homecoming King.

Now that the explosion had occurred, Demetrius was not so sure that Homecoming would even take place. Although the town and school were taking steps to clean up, there was no certain future for Amicable. Citizens could clear the rubble, but if there was nothing to replace it, Amicable would simply become an even smaller smudge on the map, a flyspeck which cross-country travelers would attempt to brush from their GPS screens.

As Demetrius unshouldered his backpack and slung it into his open locker, he felt a clap on his back. He turned to see Aaron Carlson, a short and bespectacled fellow classmate, staring up at him through smudged lenses.

"Hey, DC," Aaron said as he scrunched his nose to reposition his glasses.

Demetrius greeted him with his deep mellifluous bass, which was in direct contrast with Aaron's tenor. Although they were polar opposites in every physical way, they were actually 'brothers from different mothers' as they often proclaimed. Demetrius and Aaron did most things together; both were on sports teams and in musical groups. Unbelievably to many people, Aaron was actually the better athlete. Demetrius tried out for sports, football and basketball, because he was bigger than any other student in Amicable High School. But when opponents discovered his docile nature, they took advantage of it. Demetrius excelled in the artistic realm. His real talent was in sculpting. Regardless of the medium, whether stone, wood or even wax, Demetrius brought life from the lifeless.

"Are you going to the funeral?" Aaron pushed past his friend like a boat darting past an iceberg.

"What are you talking about?"

"You know, George."

Patiently, Demetrius waited beyond the door of his locker for his smaller friend to finish unpacking before completing his own daily routine. "Yeah, I heard about that."

"Too bad. I really liked him. The dude always seemed like he was doing stuff for kids." Aaron finished putting his books in, closed the locker and stepped back. Demetrius held up his hands as if saying, *Duh, I need to get in there* and rolled his eyes. "Sorry," Aaron apologized.

"When is the funeral?"

Aaron sniffed. "I think it's next week - Friday, maybe."

"That's game day."

"Yeah, I know. But I think it's a morning thing."

"Do you think they'd let us out of school?"

"Dunno."

"Well, if we can get a note, I wouldn't mind skipping Calculus that morning." Demetrius frowned. "Are you even listening to me?"

"What? Of course I am. I'll go with you. We'll just need a note from our parents."

"No problem," Demetrius said as he grabbed the gear he'd need for Chemistry and shut the locker with a resounding slam.

Minutes later, Demetrius approached a stool behind a black, marble-topped workbench next to Carrie Cromwell, his Chemistry partner.

They exchanged meaningless pleasantries waiting for the rest of the class and Mr. Smith to arrive. When the diminutive teacher did appear, flushed with lateness and hurry, he fluffed about at the front desk and pulled out his computer to prepare for marking the class roll. As he called out the names, each child respectfully registered his or her attendance. When the roll was finished, Mr. Smith closed the computer and faced the class.

"We're doing something different today."

Attention drawn, the class leaned forward slightly.

"Less chemistry today and more physics." Groans. Mr. Smith held up his hands. "I know, I know, but I promise that this will be enlightening." He turned to the white board, pulled out a marker and began drawing a series of cylinders and rectangles.

"Does anyone know what this is?"

Puzzled looks. Finally, Demetrius raised his hand. "Yes, Mr. Chandler?"

"It looks like the elevator."

Mr. Smith clapped his hands twice. "Bravo, Mr. Chandler. Bravo. Although I am neither Da Vinci nor Michelangelo, I certainly could give Picasso a run for his money." Demetrius laughed, recognizing the joke, while the rest of the class turned to stare at the large black young man.

"What? Haven't any of you heard of those guys?"

Deidre Jacobsen rolled her eyes. "Like, duh. Da Vinci - isn't that like the guy that, like, Tom Hanks, played in a movie."

Demetrius snorted into his hand.

"And, and, like, I know this, but, Michael Angelo, didn't he, like, um, yeah, wasn't he like, um…"

"Thank you, Ms. Jacobsen," Mr. Smith interrupted. "Mr. Chandler - who were these three people of whom I spoke?"

Demetrius looked down at his hands and the pencil he was playing with. "Da Vinci, Michelangelo and Picasso."

"Thank you, Mr. Chandler."

"Don't mention it, Mr. Smith."

"Now," the teacher continued, pointing back at his drawing, "many of you will now be wondering what Physics and the elevator have in common. I thought we could discuss what happened last week during the explosion." He checked the room for anxiety knowing that the wound was still very raw. "If, during the discussion, any of you feel anxious or overwhelmed, you are welcome to leave the room and go to Mrs. Applebottom's office."

"Okay," Mr. Smith said after a pause. "I thought that most of you would like to know what happened."

Silence ensued except for the ticking of the electric clock above the door. At ten minutes to nine, all knew that this lesson would pass by very quickly.

Mr. Smith cleared his throat and laser pointed at the base of the rectangular part of the elevator. "Most of you would know, I think, or at least I hope you know, that this area of the grain elevator is where the different types of grain are dumped, weighed and tested for moisture." Nods from the farming kids in the room. Many of them had been driving machinery to the elevator for a long time. "When grain is dumped, dust is stirred up into the air." He waved a hand into the air as if simulating the currents. "The dust settles to the bottom of the elevator and into the bins where it is only disturbed occasionally when the grain is then loaded onto trains."

All eyes followed the laser pointer. "Unfortunately, if circumstances are primed - yes, primed, like a gun - and the dust is in sufficient quantities in the air, there is a danger that the dust, if exposed to a spark, or an open flame, will deflagrate."

Frowns across the board. No one knew the term. "Deflagrate. That means a subsonic explosion. In essence…" he was about to continue when Deidre interrupted him.

"That's when the explosion never reaches the speed of sound, or roughly stays under one hundred meters per second." Deidre's entire demeanor had changed.

Mr. Smith looked pleasantly shocked. "That's right, Deirdre. I'm impressed."

"So, the explosion happened because of dust floating in the air?" Another student asked.

"Yes," Mr. Smith responded, and steepled his hands in front of his mouth, "but it's not just having dust in the air - it's the perfect mixture, at the perfect time with a perfect ignitor. In the case of the Amicable elevator, there must have been corn or soybean dust in quantities in the confined space here," he referred back to his drawing, "and then something set it off…"

"What do you think it was?" Gina whispered.

He shrugged sadly. "If I had to guess? A spark from a shovel, or even a cigarette."

"So, it just… what was the word?" She asked. "Conflagrates?"

"Deflagrates," Deidre corrected quietly. "The dust ignites and blows outward and upward."

"Exactly," Mr. Smith said. "The dust in the elevator ignited and burned quickly through the air, the heat expanded and blew out the sides of the silos. But the real damage occurred directly afterwards." The teacher erased the tops of two of the silos leaving them jagged teeth, the jaws of death. "The dust sitting on the bottom of the silos was sucked up into the deflagration and ignited, which caused a secondary explosion, this one much hotter. And, it was this secondary explosion that actually did most of the damage. This was where the true destruction occurred as this explosion may have gone supersonic. With concussive force, pushing air at tremendous speeds across the town, the explosion broke windows and rained down debris upon…" Mr. Smith ceased speaking because of the human life that had been lost. "Well, that's not physics…"

Chapter 6.

Silence ensued as the students digested the information of the elevator's destruction. Half of the class transitioned Mr. Smith's Cubist drawing on the board to the real-life elevator, while the rest of the class stared dolefully at their textbooks in an attempt to ignore the inevitable reality that Amicable might have been dealt a deflagratory death blow.

A question came from the back row, one that was not entirely unexpected, but certainly difficult.

"Mr. Smith," a student asked softly, "what happens when we die?"

All eyes looked up and fastened on the teacher who had had a proverbial can of worms opened.

With that, Mr. Smith came out from behind the teacher's bench, with its swan-necked faucet with safety glasses hanging from it, and pulled up a chair in front of them. Pulling his legs up onto the footrest, he set his hands on his thighs and sighed deeply. "This is a discussion for which I should probably write home and ask your parents' permission, but circumstances don't always allow for parental permission slips."

He ran a hand through his hair. "Okay. This is a discussion, not a lecture, not a sermon and certainly not a diatribe." Mr. Smith could feel a deep sense of relief that someone was actually willing to talk to them about this foundational and metaphysical question. "I'll tell you what I think as a scientist and then I'll tell you what I think as a human."

Deidre was about to raise her hand, but he cut her off. "I know. I know. I've heard and read enough that the two cannot possibly be mutually inclusive – but no physicist is un-human, although some have proven to be inhuman at various times. We all have physical and emotional limitations, and in those limitations are question marks the size of what's left of the Amicable elevator."

Returning her hand back to the bench in front of her, Deidre nodded.

"First, let me respond as a scientist. In studying the effects of time and decay on living things, all humans can recognize that there is a physical and chemical reaction that occurs to carbon based lifeforms. Once birth occurs, the attrition of decay is ceaseless, and the older things get, generally they start to die. It's ugly and painful. Science is trying everything that it can to arrest it. But as scientists, we don't worry about purpose and meaning. We're not looking to understand the philosophy of life. We don't understand *why*, but we know quite a bit about the *how*," he pointed to his head, "we know no breath and no heartbeat causes the cells of our bodies to… cease to function. As our bodies decay, the bacteria that thrive on decaying flesh are fed and transformed into new life. Circle of life stuff which we learned in seventh grade biology and the Lion King." The class laughed uncomfortably.

"But what about our souls…?" The questioner rested her chin in cupped palms on the bench.

"This is where I want you guys to take over for a little bit before I share my own journey." Mr. Smith opened his arms to embrace the ideas of the class.

The entirety of the class fell into a turbulent silence. No one wanted to break the glass of their fear, and yet no one wanted the uncomfortable uncertainty to continue. Although the majority of the town believed in one sort of deity or the other   - some Christian, some mixes of religions, others perfectly comfortable agnostics taking comfort that there could be a God but they couldn't possibly know for sure - when the topic of death arose, all of humanity had one sure and constant hope.

This is not all there is.

Carrie broke the silence barrier. "While I am probably in the minority in this room, I think Mr. Smith has already identified the most possible outcome. We are a result of cosmic happenstance, and although we can enjoy life, this is all there is."

Another student turned to Carrie and forced a smile. "It's popular to believe that the universe was caused by an accident, a detonation of something from nothing, but this brings about many questions. It just doesn't seem like the puzzle pieces fit. Death seems to be like a natural progression of things like…"

"What? What are you going to say?"

"Like the natural progression of a seed, for instance. The plant dies, its seeds are planted in the ground, and something new comes out, something with new life - but substantially the same. But death was the release for it."

Carrie frowned. "That works for plants, but not so much for humans, even if you believe in reincarnation. When people die and you plant them in the ground, nothing comes out of them."

"But how do you know, Carrie?"

"What if," a young man asked, "there was something beyond our senses that we have lost over the evolutionary process? What if we used to have, like, an ability to recognize something beyond sight and sense - ESP, you know? What if we had built within us a God-receptor that could pick up the infinite as well as the finite, and along the way we've lost it, or even forced it out of us. Yet somewhere, not in here," he pointed to his head, "but in here," he pointed to his heart, "there's still this… this… feeling… that we're missing out on something."

Carrie snorted. "That's just religious mumbo-jumbo."

"But is it? Don't you ever wonder if there is something more than birth and eating and procreating and dying? Don't you ever wonder if we just open ourselves up to experiencing something that we can't explain and… don't really want to? What would happen if we did?"

"Come on, Mr. Smith, this is a science class. You've got to put a stop to this." Carrie's expression was scornful.

"Why is that, Carrie? Isn't this how the human mind tries to answer the question of why and how by reconciling the physical and metaphysical world."

Carrie looked unconvinced.

Mr. Smith weighed and counterweighed his next response. "My professional outlook on life wants me to only take notice of that which can be tested, but the human, questioning side of me makes me wonder if there isn't something more, not because I necessarily need a crutch to get through life, but…"

Demetrius leaned forward. "Go on, Mr. Smith. What were you going to say?"

Mr. Smith took a deep breath. "One of the questions that always arises in my mind is this: if I am truly a product of an evolutionary and survival-of-the-fittest model of life, I should never feel one sense of sadness at the death of anyone else on the planet no matter how closely I am related to them. Instead, I should rejoice that another person is no longer soaking up resources from me; I have access to more and more so that I can pass on my predisposed evolutionary advantage to my offspring. Even worse, I should seek the deaths of the people around me so that I can take up my position as king of the hill, cream of the crop, etcetera, etcetera and etcetera. And yet, every time I hear of the untimely, tragic death of people, I am really sad. I can't explain it." The teacher looked out the window of his first story, through multi-paned glass, giving a bird's eye view of the north side of Amicable.

"When I heard of the deaths of those three people, my heart sank and I almost fell to my knees in sorrow. Those people, beautiful and perfectly imperfect Amicableans, had so much to live for. If they were still alive, yes, they would have sponged resources from my own. But they would be investing their breaths in passions and excitements, just like me, and maybe I'd be able to feel that – sense that. Maybe in the fullness of their lives, mine would be made fuller. Maybe other people's lives are not sponges but paint brushes. Isn't that how we started out this discussion? Artistry?"

"For years, I've had these conflicting ideas about the natural order of things and the immensity of life that confounds science and almost destroys it on a human level. Although I believe in the methodology of evolution, I don't believe it erases or even begins to rid us of the question of 'why.'"

For many, the Amicablean disaster had brought about an existential crisis that their minds and hearts could not compute. There was no search engine complex enough to answer the existential question of meaning, so most ignored it. 'Why' was too hard.

Suddenly, the class bell rang. All eyes shifted to the wall clock and then moved back to the teacher who sat quietly in his chair.

"I would like to say 'class dismissed,' but this class will never be dismissed." He smiled wryly at his students. "When you need to talk, we're here for you."

Demetrius Chandler caught the eye of his Chemistry teacher. It seemed as if the universe itself was expanding in his eyes.

As they walked to the café for lunch, Aaron's hands fiddled with his phone. He turned to the right to notice his reflection in the mirror-like pane of glass of Carley's X-Er-Size studio. As was his habit, he studied his appearance closely. The darkness of the glass hid the effects of his teenage acne. He snorted.

Stepping closer to the glass, he stopped and pointed inside as his eyes unfocused from himself to see the interior. "Hey, DC, isn't that your mom?"

Demetrius paused to look through the glass at his mother, Angela, who was waving brightly at him. "Yup," Demetrius responded and waved once back to her. She then began what was intended to be a deep knee bend, but she barely made it past a shallow one.

Inside the studio, past the tinted glass, Donna Humphries huffed out a breath. "He's such a big boy, Angela. What do you feed him?"

Angela turned to face Donna. "The question is not what we feed him, it's what can we keep him from eating. I swear, sometimes I wonder if we'll have enough money to pay the mortgage." She shook her head and laughed. Everyone in the group knew that Demetrius was the apple, orange and nectarine of his mother's eye.

"You must be so proud of him, Angela," Jeannie Dolling chimed in. "Such a beautiful singer. He brings a tear to my eye every time he sings in the choir."

All the women, including Anne Johnson, the oldest member of the women's exercise group at eighty-two years of age, nodded their heads.

"When he sings," Anne responded, "it's like the angels sing with him."

"Either way," Jeannie said as she turned back towards Carley, whose face was a brilliant red and dripping with sweat, "the boy has got some golden pipes."

When Angela looked back towards the window, Demetrius and Aaron had moved on. It was her son's last year of high school. Angela was already dreading the upcoming May when she was sure that Demetrius would move to college to spread his wings and… She shook her head. *No use worrying about that right now. Love him while you got him.*

Carley stood leaning over with her hands on her knees, the universal posture of someone who has had quite enough exercise, thank you very much. "I think we'll take a short break, ladies, grab a drink of water, and gather back in five minutes."

The women broke apart; cliques formed. Three different, and very distinct, conversations took place. Donna and Connie chatted worriedly about the deliberations taking place between Amicable's town leadership and Edmund Bosberg, or whatever his name was. Leslie and Angela spoke openly about George Hendriks' death and funeral arrangements. Anne Johnson merely listened and dabbed her dry skin with a towel; she had not sweated one drop, but she was extraordinarily happy that she was welcomed into the group even at her age.

In a few moments, Carley came back to stand in front of them. Carley had started the exercise class half a dozen years ago in a personal, yet social, attempt to lose weight. Never having been thin, Carley wanted to fit in with people, but even more, fit into clothes. She truly enjoyed the camaraderie and friendship that had formed over the years. As she surveyed her class, she marveled that these women had stuck together the whole time. Even if they weren't dropping dress sizes, they were connecting, which seemed even more important.

Carley stood in front of her class, hands on hips, chubby fingers sinking into her hips.

"Oh, you're all doing so well!"

Donna Humphries blew a hair from her face. "Carley," she interjected, "do you mind if we interrupt our workout..." when Donna said the word 'workout' it was with a generous helping of sarcasm which Carley missed entirely, "to have a discussion?"

Carley frowned, aware that women of Donna's age (Carley was seven years younger than Donna's matronly fifty-two) were prone to blithe conversation rather than hard work to shed serious pounds. "Well, okay, then, but not too much chitty chat chat chat. We've got to keep our heart rates up or we won't burn any fatty fat fat fat."

After clearing her throat, Donna positioned herself like a conductor on the cusp of launching a choir into song; she raised her hand.

"I'm sure that most of you are aware of the conversations occurring in Amicable this week."

"Janice has been working with the town council on the best way to move forward, but has anyone else heard anything about the young man from the insurance agency?"

Linda, Leona and Jeannie smirked.

"The question is," Donna forged ahead, "what shall we do with the young insurance adjuster?" She looked around at the women. "Anyone?"

"Maybe you could make one of your tater tot casseroles, Donna?" Leona said.

Donna frowned.

Carley raised her hand excitedly, the change from teacher to student apparent. "Oooh, oooh, I know. We could invite him to one of our classes to show him what kind of women he's really dealing with." She thrust out a hip, which seemed to be a glacial ridge about to calve. "There are very few men who could resist this." Touching a finger to her tongue, she then placed it on her bottom and made a hissing noise.

"Yes, anyway," Leslie continued, "as true as that may be, this might not be exactly the place to help him change his mind." She spread her hand around the room motioning not only to the exercise machines, but also to the posters on the wall showing slender and fit women clad in 1980's fitness tights including rainbow-colored legwarmers. There were motivational sayings like:

The next time someone asks you how much you weigh, tell them one hundred and sexy.

Or

Of course it hurts, but complaining about it won't make you look good naked.

"... but our task is to help him recognize the immense worth of Amicable. We need to make a stand. We need to band together and let this *adjuster*," spittle flew from her lips when she said the word, "know that we mean business and not," she looked at Carley and added, "that we're open for other kinds of business."

Carley's smile faded slightly. "I didn't mean that I'd be willing to, you know, shed my..." she motioned to her figure, "...morals, but certainly distracting him from his task might be good?"

"I think," Donna said, resting her arms on the chair in front of her, "it would be appropriate to give him some extra motivation to fall on the fair side of Amicable."

"What do you mean?" Jeannie asked.

Donna shrugged. "If he doesn't buy what Carley's offering, maybe we convince him by more… nefarious means?" She waggled her eyebrows. "I mean, if he believes we're pushovers, well, we can push back."

Leslie pushed her hands down in front of her. "Whoa… We don't even know what he's thinking at this point. Maybe we should hear what he has to say first, and then make our plan of attack."

The energy in the room crackled: their quest to save the town assured, but their mission (as of this point) was impossible to determine.

"Good idea," Angela said. "It's best to listen first, act next."

Demetrius and Aaron passed the window again. This time neither the boys nor the women paid any attention to the other.

Aaron carried the remnants of his lunch in a brown plastic bag: half a dozen potato chips and the leftover pickles from his wrap. Demetrius always wondered why Aaron didn't eat the entirety of his meal at Human Beans.

"Are you ready for the game tonight, DC?" Aaron asked as they moved past X-Er-Size.

Demetrius shrugged. "I guess. It's the first game of the season - I don't expect much. I'm surprised we're even going to play."

Aaron shook his head as he swung the brown paper bag at his side. "I hope we play."

"You like losing?"

"I like playing," Aaron said determinedly. "So, if we're going to put in the time to practice, I'd rather play. At least there's some purpose."

"I don't know, man. It's no fun getting our butts kicked week in and week out."

"Maybe if you'd block a little better, we'd be able to win a few games," Aaron said playfully.

Demetrius took a swipe at his friend, who ran across the road. When they reached the school, Aaron reached into the brown plastic bag and finished the rest of his lunch. Scrunching up the bag, he tossed it into the wastebasket and entered the school with his friend.

Stedman was very good at what he did.

And what he was very good at was to make sure that the claimant received as little insurance money as possible. It took a particular talent to dig beneath the claim to find the most insignificant details, which could take ten, twenty or even fifty percent from the final payout. Although he would never speak it, Theo Baker thanked his lucky stars every night for the young and ruthless insurance agent.

Stedman shuffled his papers and frowned. Although the Amicable case seemed to be open and shut, the valuation of the elevator and rebuilding costs in the multi-millions, Baker wanted Boswell to go dredging for something - anything- that might lessen the payout.

For the first time since he had arrived in, or near, the small town of Amicable, Boswell felt a twinge of guilt. As he had spent time mixing and mingling with the locals (he still called them 'yokels' in his mind), he found them collectively to be an intriguing, but stalwart, representation of middle America. The farmers, thick handed and grim faced, shook hands with him and wanted to let him know the importance of rebuilding of the elevator. The shop owners had suffered from a continual lack of sleep since the explosion; already patrons were pinching pennies and zipping wallets (or in some cases, squeezing a rubber coin holder to pull out their change – Stedman thought this decidedly simple) unwilling, or perhaps a better term would be 'unable,' to justify spending the extra dollars on non-essentials.

As he walked around the town, he noticed that the streets seemed well kept and the storefronts tidy. The people, although quiet, were willing to make him feel welcome even though in an awkward, non-verbal kind of way. Two days before, Stedman had rented a house from Liam Wilson, owner of Wilson's Garage. It was a nice house, too, and Wilson had mentioned that the previous residence had burned down which was why the rent was so high. Almost six hundred dollars a *month*! Liam had said this with a slightly embarrassed look thinking that Boswell might question that he was being overcharged, but Stedman suppressed a smirk. He was spending well over six hundred dollars per week for his apartment in Kansas City. At the rental house, Stedman had parked his Porsche in the unattached garage, not because he didn't want to drive, but he didn't want to appear ostentatious in front of these simple folk. They might not take kindly to him showing off his wealth, while trying to negotiate away some of theirs.

Stedman put his phone in his pocket, stuffed the papers into a manila folder, and carefully placed it into his leather briefcase. Running a hand through his hair, he exhaled and blew out a long breath, pushing his cheeks out. Checking his Rolex, now 2:23, he knew that he was supposed to meet the city council at three o'clock.

Walking to the kitchen, he poured himself a glass of water and grimaced. Instead of drinking the water, it seemed like he had to chew it. Another bonus was its sulfurous smell.

Back in the living room, Boswell grabbed his satchel and slung it over his shoulder. As he moved towards the door, he paused to glance out the large bay window at the brilliant, green-leafed maple trees in the front yard with busy squirrels playing in the branches. Grudgingly, he had to admit there was something pleasant about a large front lawn and wide-open blue skies.

After exiting the house, he turned to his right and noticed the hulking shell of the ruined elevator. Fortunately, all the lingering hot spots, had been extinguished. Only the pigeons, like winged parasites, scavenged the cavernous entrails of the dead building.

As Stedman walked to Mayor Stensrud's office, he was acutely aware that every person he passed, stopped what they were doing to stare. *So, this is what it feels like to be a celebrity*, he mused. Pretending not to notice the gawkers, he eventually found his way to the stoop of the mayor's office. With a polite rap on the door's glass, he opened it and entered. The entire town council was sitting around three plastic tables joined in the middle of the room. Stedman gritted his teeth at the thought of sitting in uncomfortable plastic chairs for the next hour, but sacrifices had to be made. All eyes turned toward him as he entered. Putting on his best smile, he led with an outstretched hand to Amicable's female mayor. Stensrud stood and walked around the tables to him shaking his hand firmly, but not warmly. He gave the mayor permission to call him by his first name, but he could see her teeth grind.

"Good afternoon, Mr. Boswell." She pulled him slightly forward to the table where five men and one woman stood to greet him. The five grim, middle-aged men wearing collared, button-down shirts, most of them open one button too many exposing long, curling chest hair, nodded and welcomed him. Various stages of paunches stretched their vertical stripes. Then, Stedman's eyes shifted to the woman: she, a tall woman with lustrous sandy brown hair and beautiful eyes, seemed amused.

Mayor Stensrud introduced each of the council members in turn and then, finally, the beautiful, tall woman.

"Rhonda Jensen."

"Stedman Boswell," he responded.

"Nice to meet you, Mr. Boswell," Rhonda responded coolly.

"Please, as I said with Mayor Stensrud, you can call me Stedman."

"I, also, prefer formality, Mr. Boswell," Rhonda said.

Inwardly, Stedman felt himself recoil from her rejection. "As you wish."

"Now, Mr. Boswell, please, take a seat." Janice motioned towards an empty chair at the table. It was not coincidental that no other chair was placed next to the one she pointed to. "Would you like a cup of coffee? Glass of water?"

Stedman cringed at the thought of a glass of water. "No, thank you."

After they sat, Stedman pulled open his satchel and withdrew the manila envelope and a blue pen with the embossed letters of Baker Insurance standing out in gold. He clicked it open. "Do you want to go first, or shall I?"

Janice opened her hands. "Please, you go first."

"These are the facts." Boswell proceeded to walk them through the insurance policy. "Your insurance cover is for fifty million dollars."

"You have paid the premiums on time and in full every year since the elevator was built in 1964; the policy has been used infrequently, usually accidents, but never for large amounts, thankfully."

Boswell was aware of the effect the word 'thankfully' could have: it could have meant gratefulness that the town had been bereft of accidents throughout the life of the policy, or Baker's thankfulness that they'd been collecting insurance premiums for almost sixty years.

Stedman looked at the woman named Rhonda and lost his train of thought. *Whoever she belongs to, he is a lucky man.*

He cleared his throat and continued. "This morning I spoke with Theo Baker, owner of Baker Insurance Company, and he has assured me that the company is ready to pay out the claim in full." Relieved sighs echoed in the room. Immediately, smiles appeared from nowhere.

Stedman held up a finger. "There are just a few things that I'll need to check off before we all sign on these dotted lines." He pointed to the spots on the bottom of a page.

"And those are...?" Janice asked, suddenly apprehensive

"I'll need to investigate the cause of the explosion. If you read on page seventy-three of the insurance policy, clause 4 in subsection 19, it reads: the claimant will receive funds in full pursuant to an investigation of neglect by Amicable Elevator. If there is doubt as to the ultimate reason for full claim on policy, whether intentional or unintentional, there must be a postponement of disbursement until investigation is finished." The council's faces tightened again. "This means I'll be spending some time in your beautiful town poking around to see if there was any rule bending."

"Excuse me, Mr. Boswell, but are you implying that the elevator was at fault?" Janice asked.

Boswell held up his hands. "I'm not insinuating anything, Mayor Stensrud. I'm not the bad guy. I'm just protecting Baker's interests as well as making sure that Amicable receives the funds legally."

Grumbling.

"Protecting the company's interests," Rhonda said, "is the same thing as saying, 'the shareholders don't want to take a major loss so I'm going to stall as long as possible.'"

"That is certainly not the case, Ms. Jensen. You'd be surprised how many people attempt to manipulate the insurance system. We're here to provide protection for people and companies – especially those, like you who have paid their premiums on time and in full. Protection for those who have been harmed or who have fallen on tough times."

"Which we are," Janice interrupted.

"I hear your pain," Boswell responded, placing his hands directly on the insurance policy. "But this is the brief I've been given. With luck, we'll find that there has been no slippage in judgment and we can get this wrapped up as quickly as possible. What do you think?"

All eight pairs of eyes glared at him.

"So," he continued, "I'll start on Monday. I truly hope the people of Amicable will live up to its name so we can get on with life and get the town its money."

"Yes," Janice said shortly, "let's hope so."

Chapter 7.

Demetrius sat dejectedly on the sidelines, head lowered, his massive hands gripping the facemask of the helmet between his knees. There was a buzz on the field - some excitement, a few players shouting with laughter, voices raised in jubilation. The noise was, of course, from the opposition. Amicable had lost the football game 49-6.

Aaron plopped down on the bench beside him. Aaron's uniform was dirty and grass-stained and it fit loosely over his shoulder pads and frame. Dropping his helmet on the ground, Aaron mirrored Demetrius' posture.

"This sucks."

"Mm hmm."

"Well, we're now seniors in high school and we've won one fricking game in our entire high school career." He ran a hand through his sweaty hair. "One," he repeated morosely.

Coach Clausen walked by Aaron and Demetrius. His large gut, testing both the endurance of his belt and the fabric of his shirt, threatened to expose more than just his furry chest hair sticking out above the V-neck collar. He patted Aaron on the back. "Good game, Eleven." Demetrius snorted slightly. It was one of his pet peeves that Coach Clausen called his players by their numbers not their names.

"Thanks, Coach," Aaron replied. "I'm not sure that 'good' would be an appropriate adjective for this game."

"We'll get 'em next time."

Neither Aaron nor Demetrius responded to the coach's platitude. There was no *getting 'em next time*. This was the last time they would play Orion, with their stupid red and yellow uniforms and their even stupider mascot, a star prancing around the far sideline.

The walk to the locker room was quiet apart from the sound of their cleats on the cement sidewalk. Maple trees in full regalia, brilliant greens muted by the deepening night, stood as sorrowful sentinels embracing the losing team, consoling them (as they always did).

After showering and dressing, Aaron and Demetrius stood in the cool air outside of Amicable High School, gym bags in hand. Aaron's red hair was still wet. It was plastered to his head, and his glasses magnified his eyes in the dim light.

"Do you want to drive uptown and get a soda?"

"Yeah, sounds good."

After stowing their gear in the trunk of Demetrius' white Ford Escort which, by any standards, was far too small for him, the boys squeezed into the front seats. Demetrius started the car, which coughed, rattled and hummed to life.

Looking over his right shoulder, Demetrius pulled the Escort out into the empty street. Even for a Friday night, there would be little traffic. A few fortunate youth with cars and gas money would cruise the streets of Amicable driving slowly and deliberately. After a while, the boys decided to stop at the bowling alley.

Aaron opened the door to the bowling alley and allowed Demetrius to enter before him. As they opened the door, the alley's predictable noises hit them first: bowling balls thudding; the smooth rolling sound made as the ball slid down the oiled lane and finally, with a great crash depending on whether it hit the pins or the gutter, the ball would settle into the abyss.

Aaron and Demetrius had little interest in bowling. After the football game, both sore and bothered by the outcome, they wanted to sit in the Greedy Pecker to drink a cold glass of cola and shoot the breeze with some of the locals.

The Greedy Pecker was a dimly lit, wood paneled room, large enough to house ten square tables and forty metal chairs with fake, black leather seats. If one were to sniff hesitantly, one might pick up the scent of long since smoked cigarettes. There hadn't been any cigarette smoke in the bar for almost twenty years, but people still remembered.

There was one person who was not watching the television though. Between lightshades, Demetrius saw the man was staring at him, which was not altogether surprising. What was surprising was that neither Aaron nor Demetrius recognized him.

"Hello boys," Shania greeted them.

Aaron smiled at her. "Can we have two colas please?"

"Of course." She punched in the amount, took their money and filled their glasses.

While waiting, Demetrius looked back at the man who was still staring. "I'm going to go talk to that guy."

"What? What are you talking about?"

Demetrius pointed. "See that guy? He keeps staring at me."

"Ya think? You're six-foot-six-inches tall and the only black guy in the county. Blind people stare at you because they can feel you moving."

"Very funny."

"Do you need me to protect you?"

Demetrius laughed. "I'll call for help if I need it."

As Demetrius approached, he noticed that the staring white man pushed his chair back to stand up. The man was not old - in his thirties, maybe, but Demetrius could tell there was an innate cockiness about him. It wasn't rare for smaller people to act bigger in an attempt to intimidate Demetrius. It never worked.

"Hello," Demetrius said.

"Shit, you're a big sucker," the man said with a hiccup of derisive laughter.

"We don't say that word around here, mister."

"Oh," the man said, "Sorry about that. I won't say 'shit' again."

"Not that one. 'Sucker.'" Demetrius smirked.

The man extended his hand. "Stedman Boswell."

"My name is Demetrius, Mr. Boswell."

"Nice to meet you." Stedman took a drink of his beer and winced, then wiped his upper lip with the back of his hand.

"Don't like the beer?" Demetrius asked.

Boswell shrugged. "It's not my favorite. I don't normally drink Bud Light, but that seems to be the beer of choice around here." He looked over at the taps on the bar - Schlitz, Old Milwaukee, Grain Belt. "It's not as if it might get any tastier with those."

"I wouldn't know," Demetrius said as Aaron joined them.

"How old are you, Demetrius?"

"Seventeen. How old are you?"

Stedman's drink paused halfway to his lips. "I'm in my thirties."

Aaron arrived at that moment and placed the cola in Demetrius' hand. "Who's this?"

68

Chapter 7.

"Stedman Boswell."

"Sted... what?" Aaron perused the man, noticing first and foremost, his very non-small town clothes: khaki pants and blue striped golf shirt, squared off black shoes and conspicuous gold wristwatch.

"Are you guys in high school together?" Stedman asked

"Yes," Aaron answered.

"What are you doing here in Amicable?" Demetrius asked.

Stedman exhaled. "I'm here to talk to some people about the incident."

"Incident?"

"You know, the elevator explosion. I'm here to... investigate."

"Like a police officer?"

"No. Like an insurance adjuster. Do you know what that is?"

Demetrius kept his face expressionless. "By the context, I think I should be able to figure it out," he said sarcastically. "You'll be investigating the explosion and putting in a report to your insurance company."

Boswell nodded. "Yes, I'll have to look through the damage and assess what happened."

"That won't take long. It's catastrophic."

Stedman nodded. "I noticed. But, if there was neglect or it was done purposefully..."

"That's pretty stupid. Who would want to blow up the Amicable elevator?" Aaron sneered. "It's not like the elevator is the Trump Tower or something."

At that moment, three other people entered the Greedy Pecker.

Symbolically, there should have been a whistle in the background, a whipping sound and some tumbleweed bouncing past. Everyone in the saloon would have known that a showdown was about to take place. One could almost hear the sweat dripping from smooth, cold glasses onto the tables.

Stedman Boswell fidgeted with the drink in his hands. It seemed as if everything was occurring in slow motion.

Sizing up the others, Butcher sensed something strange happening. He knew who Demetrius and Aaron were. Across from them, though, was a slightly built man with brown hair and a large chip on his shoulder. Butcher knew who this was immediately.

Stedman Boswell.

Rhonda had told him about Boswell already - his temperament, the way he spoke to the council and his company-line-toeing. Butcher read him like a book: *He has no chance in Amicable.*

"Hello, Demetrius." Butcher said.

"Hello."

"And who is this?" Butcher spoke to Demetrius, but pointed at Boswell.

Stedman, miffed that the tall man was disrespecting him, stuck his hand out which Butcher took. Momentarily, he felt pity for the outsider, but it passed quickly.

"My name is Stedman Boswell." His voice was reedy thin.

Derek snorted, which made Stedman frown.

"What's so funny?"

"Nothing. Nothing." Derek held up his hands slightly.

Boswell's eyes narrowed as if waiting for the other gunslinger to draw. "What's your name?" He asked the tall man opposite him, his jaw jutting out slightly.

"Most people call me Butcher."

Boswell echoed the snort. "That's a strange name. Is that your last name?"

"No," Butcher said slowly and menacingly, "it's what I do."

Stedman's Adam's apple bobbed furiously, as he tried to control his swallowing.

"What do you do?" Butcher asked, though knowing the answer to his question.

"I'm an insurance adjuster," Stedman responded as he put his beer on the table behind him, unaware that it was occupied by another couple. He crossed his arms in front of himself.

"You're here to investigate the explosion, I take it?" Butcher asked.

"That's right," Stedman said defiantly.

Demetrius and Aaron took a step back from Boswell.

"I assume you're doing everything in your power to quickly resolve the situation," Butcher took a menacing small step closer, "so that Baker will pay out the insurance."

Stedman, not to be intimidated, inched towards Butcher. "We'll see…"

"Okay, okay," Derek inserted himself, "how about we get you both a drink? Maybe we can talk about other things like the weather, or maybe the football team?" He motioned towards Aaron and Demetrius who shook their heads.

"No, thank you," Boswell said. "I think it's better if I get going."

Butcher loomed above him. The air crackled with electricity. "We'll see you later then."

As Stedman pushed past Butcher and the twins, the entire saloon stared at him. After he left, the room reanimated.

"Do you guys want to sit with us for a little while?" Butcher asked Demetrius and Aaron.

They nodded and moved to a table. After Butcher and the Peterson twins purchased their beers, they sat down beside the high schoolers.

"That was interesting," Derek said.

"You can say that again," Nash responded.

"That was…"

"Okay," Butcher said stopping the sentence. "So, boys, did you learn any interesting information from our new insurance adjuster?"

Aaron's mouth flopped open, disconcerted, before he nervously took another sip of his cola. Demetrius smiled. "He seems arrogant."

Derek agreed. "It's unfortunate that we couldn't have had a small-town insurance adjuster, or, or, or… even a woman come. They have a tendency to be a little bit easier to manipulate."

"Is that right?" a voice spoke behind him. Derek froze.

Tracey. "Well… what I mean… is…" his stammering did not help as he turned towards her.

"Women are easier to manipulate? Nice, Derek. Very nice." Tracey turned back to the bar where Shania was waiting. "Do you want to know what your brother-in-law just said?"

"Why did you have to say that, Dipstick?" Nash said with frustration. "Now I'm going to get it too."

"How was I supposed to know she was standing right behind me?"

Aaron stared at Butcher with awe. "Is it true, Butcher, that you can tell the future?"

Butcher laughed and took a sip of his beer. "Not really, Aaron. It's not that I read the future, but I am able to read people."

"How does it work?"

Butcher shrugged. "I don't know how, but it's like... It's like when I look at a person, their stories speak to me. It's in the eyes. The eyes always tell the truth."

"What did you read about that Boswell guy? The insurance man."

"What did you see?" Butcher asked him.

Aaron pushed back from the table slightly, suddenly embarrassed to be put in the spotlight. "Uh, nothing, really. I mean, he's like an old guy with weird clothes. Looked like he'd been shopping online."

The other two laughed. "That's a good start, but when you saw what he was wearing, what did you deduce from his appearance?"

Aaron pushed his glasses farther up on his nose with his index finger. "Is he... rich? I don't know. He just kind of comes across like that."

Butcher nodded. "How about you, Demetrius? What do you think?"

Demetrius' chocolate brown eyes lowered. He fidgeted with his sweating glass. In the background, Shania had turned up the country music to hide the divisive discussion occurring at the bar between the women and the twins. "He seemed like a little man."

"Okay," Butcher said slowly, "but what do you mean by that?"

The young man shifted in his seat. "No ring," Demetrius started, "which means either he never was married, or he is divorced. Either way, his little man personality probably gets in the way of authentic relationships." Butcher's eyes widened in surprise. *The boy shows promise.* Butcher motioned with his hands for Demetrius to continue.

"He gets ahead by pushing others out of the way and he does it with his wealth. Judging by his clothes and the way he walks, I would guess he's probably got a pretty expensive car stashed somewhere in Amicable but he doesn't want us to know about it."

"Why would it be stashed?" asked Aaron.

Demetrius turned to his friend. "Imagine you've been faithfully paying for insurance and you've rarely had to make a claim. Not needing to pay out, the insurer uses premiums to finance his nice car. When you need your insurer to step up to the plate and fulfill his end of the bargain, he shows up in a fancy, $80,000 car, what's your first thought?"

"I'm paying too much money for my insurance?" Aaron's answer was a question.

"Bingo. Easy way to lose customers."

Now Butcher was really impressed. There was much more to Demetrius Chandler than he read first. *This kid had it all together...*

"Is that right, Mr. Butcher?" Demetrius asked.

"You're right on, Demetrius, but let's drop the formality. I'm Leo. I'm a butcher, not the President."

"Okay," Demetrius responded.

"Stedman Boswell is, indeed, a wealthy man, and my guess is that he has either a Mercedes or a Porsche parked at my old house." Butcher's gaze fell on Demetrius, their heads almost touching the lampshades above them while Aaron looked back and forth between the two of them, mesmerized by the exchange. "Anything else?"

"He's not all bad."

Butcher frowned. "How so?"

It was Demetrius' turn to look uncomfortable. "He's a little guy with a chip on his shoulder, but he's accepted a job to come to the middle of nowhere," he made a small gesture with a large hand, "to sort out the 'big man's business.' Nobody wants to do that. It's kind of like 21st century slavery."

Taking in the full extent of the young man's words, Butcher hardened himself. "Don't let him fool you. Wolf in sheep's clothing. Snake in the grass. Whatever analogy you like. We've been dealt a losing hand in Amicable. This guy has no soul for small towns."

"How do you know?" Aaron asked.

"His whole body screams it. He's had a horrible home life; his father is older than his mother and they have been 'absent' for much of Boswell's young life. His mother didn't really care for him, which is why he is invested heavily in his looks. Probably got his job through his dad, also, which must drive him insane." Butcher looked back and forth between the teenagers.

"He's come here with his fancy car assuming that we'll all roll over and want our stomachs scratched." Butcher's face hardened. "He's listening to the big-dog voice in whatever city he's come from and we have no choice but…"

"But what, Mr… Leo?" Aaron whispered.

Butcher leaned in to the two young men. "We have no choice but to help him decide that Amicable is not the place for him."

Aaron's face lit up, but Demetrius remained impassive.

"You disagree, Demetrius?"

Butcher had forgotten his own past in Amicable. Arriving in the town as an outsider, Butcher had experienced the very things he was considering for Stedman Boswell, but he justified them by believing that he, Leopold Jensen, had come to Amicable to improve it, not to tear it down.

"I just think that everyone deserves a chance…" Demetrius responded softly.

"A noble thought, but be careful. Before you invite the snake into your house, remember his fangs."

Demetrius nodded slowly.

The disagreement at the bar had ended amicably. Nash and Shania were staring lovingly into each other's eyes – newlyweds. But what intrigued Butcher was the intense static coming from Derek and Tracey. Now as he watched Tracey, he noticed certain things: she held her hand delicately, but strongly, gesturing with polished confidence. Just once, she tenderly touched her hair, flirting. She wanted Derek's gaze not just drawn to her hair, but the gentle slope of her neck and the cleft at the bottom of her throat, where her pulse was tapping out a romantic Morse code.

It was obvious that Derek was attracted to her, and even more obvious that he had no idea what to do. Although he stammered a few responses, his smitten-ness would have been apparent to anyone with one eye, much less two. Butcher smiled. Even in the midst of tragedy, life seemed to find a way.

"Look, Derek," Tracey said, "I know you're intelligent, but you have to escape this kind of…" she waved her hand in the air, "tiresome patriarchy and its embedded oppression. In one of my Women's Studies classes in college, we read a book about the dangers of adhering to a good ol' boys club mentality as the world moves forward. We need to understand that there is no difference between men and women, old and young, gay and straight, black and white, American and Mexican…" She paused as Derek's mouth was open. "What is it?"

"I'm going to have to take that class." Derek said.

"You don't even go to college," Tracey laughed. Absently, her hand strayed down to her leg; it alit briefly on Derek's leg.

He stiffened and sucked in a breath.

"Sorry about that," she apologized but moved her hand only after she had pressed it slightly.

Butcher could see that Derek's pupils could not possibly dilate any further. The young man probably couldn't hear a word that Tracey was saying.

Butcher turned his attention back to the high schoolers. "Okay, boys, what do you think we should do about our newest visitor to Amicable?"

Aaron smiled. "Let's take him down!" Aaron punctuated his response by tapping the table. Butcher smiled.

Demetrius leaned back in his chair and put his hands behind his head. "I don't know, Leo. Patience might be the best course. Maybe we can turn this guy away from the dark side?"

It was going to get interesting.

Chapter 8.

The white terrycloth robe hung open allowing Theo Baker to feel the tepid summer breeze flow across his waxed chest. Absentmindedly, Baker fidgeted with his phone while the steam from his coffee curled upwards from its resting place on the patio table. Although the beauty of the surroundings were unparalleled, majestic mountains capped by a mane of ancient pine trees, sun shining from the east illuminating eddies of early morning fog rising from the pristine alpine lake below him, Baker was more concerned with the rising stock market than the rising fog.

A voice from the door behind him called out. "Mr. Baker, is there something that you need me for this morning? If not, I'm going out for a walk around the town."

Theo looked up from his device but did not turn around. The voice, dissociated from the body, was irritating, but Baker was begrudgingly grateful for his secretary's organizational skills. On these trips, he usually brought her to organize his daily agendas, pick up groceries and supplies and retrieve coffee for him in the morning. Often, his secretary, Summer, would remind him that her skills ran much deeper than being a go-fer, but Theo only waved his hand and sent her on her way.

When graduating from the University of Kansas, Summer Teichman ranked third in her class in Business Marketing. Finishing internships in medium-sized companies, she sent her resumés to corporations across the country. Summer ended up choosing Baker Insurance because of its opportunities for advancement. When presented with the current opportunity to travel with the owner of the company to Colorado, she had jumped at it, thinking he was wanting to pick her thoughts and ideas regarding the future of the company. *How naïve I have been*, she thought.

"No, Summer, I don't need anything from you," he said crossly. "But Baker opened half a point higher this morning. The shareholders will be happy."

She rolled her eyes. *As if he really cares about the shareholders.*

Theo finally turned to find Summer standing in the doorway. She was wearing her black running tights and tank top. His leering eye made her feel like covering herself, but she didn't. *He wasn't a bad guy, just a...* she tried to think of the word... *a lecher.*

Theo's phone rang.

Thank God, they both thought at the same time.

"I've got to take this call. It's Stedman."

"Okay," she turned her back to him. "I'll be back around lunchtime."

"Take your time," he mumbled and pushed the green button on the phone. "Boswell."

"Good morning, Mr. Baker," Stedman said brusquely. "I'm updating you on the progress of the claim in Iowa."

"Go ahead."

"I've been meeting the locals."

"And what did you find out?"

Baker could hear papers rustling in the background. "My gut instinct is that they're hiding something. Someone knows something about the elevator. At the council meeting the other night, a few of the councilors couldn't maintain eye contact with me. There was one person there, a woman who seemed a little more confident than the others. I would guess she's a key cog in this."

"So you need to spend more time with her, is that what you're saying?" Baker responded with a licentious grin. "Don't be mixing too much pleasure with work."

Like you ought to talk, Stedman thought. "No, sir," he said. "Strictly business."

"What is your plan?" Baker asked.

Boswell spoke softly. "I'm going to church on Sunday."

"Excuse me?"

"From what I understand, almost everyone goes to church on Sunday mornings - some kind of small-town thing. One of the locals, a..." he checked his notes... "Jeannie Simpson invited me. I think it will be well worth the pain."

"You'll definitely need a raise after this case, Stedman." Theo looked at his fingernails.

"You'll definitely need to give me a raise, sir."

"Good work. I'll wait for your call next week. Don't feel like you have to call me unless it's important." Theo disconnected the call without saying goodbye.

Stedman shook his head and set his phone down on the desk.

On Saturdays, Amicableans poke their noses between the lintels of their front doors, sniffing the air and nuzzling the sunshine (or clouds, on some weekends), and nod contentedly as they don their blue jeans, t-shirts, comfortable New Balance white shoes and grab the keys to their pickup trucks. Most Amicableans drive Fords or Chevys, although there are a few smug citizens of questionable descent (usually Germans) who choose Dodges. On those halcyon mornings, Amicableans drive slowly to various meeting places; a few park their trucks at Human Beans Café; some men, farmers and agriculturalists, shuffle slowly to the butcher shop. Peterson's Butchery had installed its own small, portable coffee maker. On Saturdays, some of the men would drink their way through two or three cups (four would be considered gluttonous, but one cup would be downright rude) while pondering the weather, the forecast, and the state of affairs of the high school football team. Many of them had attended Amicable High School and would wax nostalgic, when 'men were men' and 'boys played in the marching band.'

As pickup trucks moved from street to street, Amicableans would wave, or gesture to each other, depending on the level of their relationship. If the pickup wasn't recognized, one index finger would poke up from the steering wheel like a prairie dog checking for danger. Two fingers from the steering wheel indicated an acquaintance; three, a friend; four, a close friend. And for best friends, the middle finger and a guffaw of laughter.

Butcher drove from his house, turning left, where, after seeing two pickups and a tractor rumble by, each given three fingers in salute, he maneuvered down the street and pulled into the parsonage next door to St. Clements Methodist Church. The front lawn had been cleared of debris from the explosion, but divots had yet to be filled.

John and Leslie stood on the front porch; Leslie's hands were on her hips, while John's hands and chin rested on top of a broom. Over the last years John had lost weight. This had been a cause of amusement for many of the parishioners, who were sure that Leslie had whipped him into shape. But the truth of the matter was: John's weight loss was a result of his activity in the community. Previously, he had worried more about dogma and routine, but now John's efforts were largely concentrated on protecting the interests of the town and its people.

Butcher killed the engine and opened the door. Waving to John and Leslie, Butcher pulled himself from the front seat and with great excitement, he retrieved his children from the back of the car. Once outside, Georgie and John Thomas scooted straight up the stairs to where the Deakins' twin girls were waiting inside. J.T. and Georgie loved spending time with the twins.

"Howdy, neighbor," Leslie called out and embraced Butcher after he'd climbed the stairs. John and Butcher shook hands.

"Where's Rhonda?" Leslie asked.

"She has an emergency meeting with the council today."

"Are you up for a glass of iced tea?" Deakins motioned towards the house where the delighted screams of the four children could be heard through the screen door. "I'll bring it out so that we don't have to sit inside the sonic whirlwind."

"Good idea," Butcher responded. As he watched his friend turn back into the house, he read some worrying things about him, exhaustion and grief included.

They sank into Adirondack chairs and waited for John to return with the iced tea.

"How is Rhonda doing?" Leslie curled up a leg underneath her and rested a fist to her temple.

Butcher shrugged. "As good as can be expected, I guess. Each day, I suppose, she moves a little bit past the sight of George's death, but she keeps flashing back. It's like a skipping record. His body hunched over the table…"

"I'm so sorry, Butcher. George was such a good man."

Pushing open the screen door with his foot, John carried a tray laden with a sweating pitcher of iced tea, submerged lemons and a cup of sugar. He set the tray down on the small table and poured glasses for each of them. The pouring was cathartic, like an ancient ritual designed to bring peace from chaos. Hunkering down in a chair next to Butcher, he lifted his glass.

"To the future," he said with a wry smile.

"To the future," they repeated.

"Now," John said, "I'm intrigued by the mention of George's prophecy…"

Butcher set his drink down and pulled a sheet of folded paper from his back pocket. "These are George's last words. His thoughts were interesting to say the least."

Deakins nodded sympathetically. "Go on."

"As I approached the table where he lay, I noticed he had been writing something." He pulled the letter away from his chest. It made a crinkling sound in his shaking hands.

A voice spoke to me after you left - don't worry, I'm not going that senile, but I am open minded enough to think that there are angels poking around in places that nobody expects. This particular angel seemed to be urging me to add one last sentence to my prophetic vision from earlier in the day.

When all is said and done, and it seems as if Amicable is about to breathe its last:

One voice, and one voice alone can save this town.
You will recognize the voice when you hear it.

I'm realistic to know that I will not be around to hear the voice. But you must, Rhodie. You must. If you don't, Amicable will be no more.

No pressure.

Whatever you do, Rhodie, enjoy your family. Every moment is a blessing from God. Live as if you won't be around tomorrow.

So, I think that I will g

Deakins stood, put a hand on Butcher's shoulder and read from behind.

One voice can save the town…

Who is it? What words will that voice say? How will Rhonda recognize this voice? John's thoughts raced.

"Was there anything else?" John asked.

"No," Butcher responded as he looked out over the front lawn, the wind dancing in the midst of the rustling leaves - life in Amicable had not changed visibly, but spiritually. "Nothing written, but while they were talking that night, he said something more, something that we've been pondering over and over and I thought maybe you two could help us put the pieces together."

"What was it?" Leslie asked.

"He said, 'Amicable will be like Joseph, and it will feel as if it's on the dark cusp of being assaulted and then sold. People will be falsely accused of all sorts of things and finally, when the darkest night is settling over the town, Amicable will be caged." He paused. "Do you think Rhonda's crazy? Could she really remember that?"

Deakins nodded. "Sure, people who have witnessed traumatic things can either remember everything, or remember nothing. Sounds like she's got the best of both worlds in some ways."

"What does it mean?" Butcher asked.

Leslie spoke. "Joseph was the second youngest son of twelve brothers born to Jacob. He was given a robe, more beautiful than all his brother's. Joseph was proud – far too proud, and eventually his older brothers had enough of his lip so they decided to kill him." Butcher nodded, following the story. "At the last moment, Reuben, the oldest brother, pleaded to save Joseph's life and instead of killing him, instead of throwing him into a pit to let him die, they decided to sell him instead. A caravan of nomads was passing by, so they sold Joseph into slavery."

"Where does the love of God part come in?" Butcher asked.

Deakins lifted an eyebrow and smiled. "God's love comes when you least expect it. In my opinion, Joseph had to grow up, had to recognize his part to play in the world, and sometimes that part arrives with pain. So, Joseph's whole life was blown up - he has nothing - no money, no family or friends, not even clothes and he was left at the bottom of the hole. Now, if Joseph was a normal person, he probably would have given up and thrown in the towel…"

"Or the technicolor dreamcoat," Leslie laughed.

"But he didn't have that anymore." John smiled. "Instead, he built up trust among people he encountered and somehow found God at the same time - in the depths. But, then everything goes to crap again. He is put into jail. Through strange twists and turns, he leaves jail and becomes a very powerful man."

Leslie nodded. "And everything that had been intended for evil - the attempted murder, the false accusations, the nakedness - turned out for God's good."

"So, are you saying that all this that has happened, the explosion, George dying, that self-satisfied, arrogant punk coming to Amicable, is all being planned for good?" Butcher frowned.

"Well, I don't know if these things turned out in the way that they should have, but the consequences can certainly be seen with perspective. In two years, or five years, maybe fifteen, we might see a different and stronger Amicable, maybe. That doesn't set aside the grief and pain of what happened to people and certainly not for those who lost grievously. All we can do is wait and see how God might use this."

Butcher's frown deepened. "But what are these parts about false accusations, being sold and Amicable being caged? What does that mean?"

Deakins shrugged. "To be honest, I don't know. We don't even really know if George's words are prophetic. For the moment, though, let's assume that they are."

"What do we do next?" Butcher asked.

"I guess we have to see what will take place with the insurance adjuster."

Immediately, Butcher clenched his jaw at the sound of Stedman Boswell's title. "Yes, about him…"

John and Leslie moved further forward to the edge of their seats. Expectantly, they raised their eyebrows and simultaneously breathed out their question. *And?*

"Boswell is no fan of small towns, obviously, but he's also got a real hang-up with authority figures. His dad, according to what I read about him, was absent - probably a big shot businessman with no parenting skills and no desire to find them - and a mother who married for wealth."

"So what do we do?"

Butcher paused. In that moment he had a choice to make. Over the years, his instincts had invariably proved correct, but in this case, there was a worm of indecision burrowing around in his brain.

If Butcher would have paused and reflected on that feeling, that hesitation, Amicable may never have reached the nadir, which occurred in the ensuing weeks. If he would have paused just fifteen seconds more, he would have realized that Stedman Boswell's journey was akin to his own - an outcast, abandoned by his father, his mother lost to him, afraid of a world that spoke a different language than kindness. To accept Stedman Boswell into the community, overwhelm him with hospitality, invite him to understand small-town, Midwest life, and the comfortable and nice people who inhabit those small towns, would have been the better choice.

Unfortunately, Butcher's instinct was to do the opposite.

"Look," he said spreading his large hands in front of him, "Boswell will attempt to discredit the accidental nature of what happened to the elevator. Somehow, he will manipulate the narrative. He's going to ruin us, because that's what he has been asked to do."

"And you read this?" John's voice trembled slightly.

Butcher nodded.

"What we need to do is…"

"Good morning, neighbors!" A woman's voice called from the front lawn.

Linda Harmsen was leading, flanked closely by Jeannie and Leona. Strangely, Jeannie had a pair of binoculars hanging by a strap around her neck.

"Hello, everyone," Leslie called out, but her voice could not entirely hide the evident frustration of being interrupted. "What are you doing?"

"We… um… noticed Butcher's car parked here and… um… we thought we'd see if you could use more company," Linda answered.

Leslie swallowed her irritation. "Why are you wearing binoculars, Jeannie?"

"I thought, well, it's a beautiful morning for bird watching, don't you think?" Jeannie picked up the binoculars and peered through them at a nearby elm tree. "Robin. Nice."

Leona asked, "Do you think we could join you on the porch?"

Leslie sighed. "Of course, ladies. Please, join us. Would you like some iced tea?"

"Oh yes, please," they responded with one voice and each found a spare chair to pull into the circle of trust. Leslie gave John a look who then retreated into the house for three more glasses for tea.

The ladies settled into their chairs, all three crossing their legs primly in unison.

"So anyway," Linda broke the silence, tapping her knee with her hands, "what are we talking about today?"

"We were just discussing the events of the week - George's death, of course, and the continued cleanup after the explosion."

"Mm hmm."

"How about you?" Leslie returned the question. "What have you been discussing today?"

"Well," Leona stretched out the word, broadening it with anticipation, "as we do, we got together at the café today to gather information for the sake of helping others." Leslie couldn't help clearing her throat and shifting in her chair. "And then, we decided to see if anyone else was getting together this morning also."

"And bird watching," Butcher included with a smirk.

"What?" Leona snuck a look at Jeannie who was gently tapping the binoculars. "Oh… yes, of course. Bird watching."

"See anything amazing yet?"

"Not yet. But the day is still young."

John pushed open the screen door and handed a glass of iced tea to each one of the visitors. The women accepted their drinks from the pastor and thanked him. "Now," he said as he pushed himself back into his seat. "What did I miss?"

Linda took a sip while waving her hand in the air signaling that she would like to be the first one to speak. They waited. "Leslie was just beginning to tell us about the topic du jour (she pronounced it 'deh zher') which," she wiggled her eyebrows, "should be a juicy conversation. Right?" Leona and Jeannie nodded supportively.

"Yes, well, I suppose these conversations need to occur so we can find our way forward," John replied.

"What exactly are these 'conversations' we're talking about?" Butcher asked.

"Well," Leona said fingering the drips of sweat on her glass, "what are we going to do with Mr. Stedman Boswell?"

The mere mention of Boswell's name seemed to spark the electricity on the porch. "We've been talking..." Linda said

No kidding, John thought.

"And? Have you come up with any solutions on how the *town* can move forward?" Leslie asked the pointed question, emphasizing the communal nature of their discussion

"We have a few ideas." Linda situated herself back in her seat pretending to choose her words carefully. "The insurance adjuster is... problematic. I've heard from a trustworthy source..." this 'trustworthy source' was usually her own intuition, "that Boswell is going to rip us off."

"That's not really new information, Linda," Leslie said. "That's what they are paid to do."

Linda's face reddened. "I know that," she said testily, "but I wouldn't put it past him to fabricate new facts in order to taint the 'evidence' if you will."

"There's no way you could possibly know that," Leslie said.

Interestingly, Butcher interrupted. "But she's right," he said softly, which caused Linda's eyes to widen with both surprise and happiness.

"Last night, when I was with the Peterson twins at the bowling alley, we ran into Boswell."

"He was at the bowling alley?" Leslie sounded surprised.

Butcher nodded. "He was talking to some high school students after the football game. Our discussion was interesting and I... read in him a few things that worried me." Various murmurings from the women: *oh my goodness, a double tsk tsk*, "and I immediately wanted to..."

"Wanted to what?" Leona pushed forward.

Butcher, for his part, was wise enough to choose his words carefully knowing they would be broadcast quite dramatically through the grapevine. "I wanted to help him understand the error of his ways."

Leona leaned back again in disappointment.

"The man is bad news. If he's not dealt with, he could destroy the town."

"What are you suggesting?" Linda's voice lowered conspiratorially. Leona had spilled some of her tea on her blue jeans, but she didn't seem to notice or care.

Butcher looked at John and Leslie. "Boswell needs to be encouraged to reassign himself to another case so that a more… sympathetic insurance adjuster will look into our claim."

"I like the sound of that," Linda said. "We'll get right on it. Maybe we can have a discussion about what we, the good women of Amicable can do to 'encourage' Boswell." Leona and Jeannie nodded their excitement.

"Wait, wait," John said, "we can't go off all half-cocked. This has to be done quietly. There can be no evidence of tampering."

Linda, Leona and Jeannie were no longer listening. Their heads nodded autonomically.

John continued, "Be careful."

"We'll be gentle." The twinkle in Leona's eye proposed the opposite.

"What will you three do?" Linda asked.

"We don't know yet." Butcher took a deep breath. "Perhaps it's best if we can discuss a few more sensitive things…"

Leslie decided to be blunt. "As in we will need some privacy. No offense."

The three women started, suddenly aware that they were being brushed off. "Oh, I see," Linda spoke with feigned hurt. "Well, okay then, we'll just be off. Thank you for the tea and the company."

Opening the front door of X-Er-Size, Carley flipped on the lights. Flashing and blinking, false starting like a car on the last legs of a battery, the lights eventually caught and began to hum.

Chapter 8.

Whistling through the empty space, across the carpet and weaving between exercise machines, Carley placed the boxes she'd been carrying on top of the counter next to the cash register and dropped her keys into the wicker basket. Removing her purse from her arm, Carley placed it on the seat and began to rummage through it looking for something - she couldn't remember exactly what it was - but something. At that moment, there was a knock at the door. The sound jolted Carley to remember that she was searching for her lipstick.

Carley's eyes fell on the figures at the door: Linda, Jeannie and Leona. *Interesting. They weren't usually here on weekends.*

Carley smiled and raised a finger then mouthed the words, 'Hold your horses,' grabbed her lipstick and began to apply as she walked.

Opening the door, Carley ushered the women into the room with an open arm.

"Thanks for letting us in, Carley," Linda said as she pushed into the studio.

"I was just setting up for the workout this morning," Carley said as she finished putting the lipstick on. Bright pink.

"We need to talk," Linda said breathlessly. "And, we need to call in reinforcements!"

Carley clapped her hands enthusiastically. "Tell me! Tell me! What's going on?"

"We just met with Butcher, Reverend Deakins and Leslie," Leona interjected. "We've got to summon the troops to get down here."

"Just tell me what this is about."

Linda silenced the other two and explained, balancing deliciously on the edge of fact and fiction, what had been discussed on the parsonage porch.

Not long after, the entire X-Er-Size group began to assemble like the Avengers at the door of the studio. In her active wear, which was only used on active days, Donna Humphries strolled quickly and purposefully southwards on Main Street looking over her shoulder (twice) to see if she was being followed (as were the instructions of Linda Harmsen). Pushing the door open quickly, she moved towards the dance floor where stools had been placed. Carley stood behind them at the counter nervously humming and bouncing back and forth between feet, getting physical to Olivia Newton-John's old songs.

"What's going on?" Donna called out excitedly.

"We're waiting for the others to arrive before we share, that way we won't have to repeat everything two or three times. We'll take questions after." Frustrated, Donna sat on a chair, took off her tennis shoes and pulled out a pair of exercise shoes, which to anyone else, looked exactly like her tennis shoes.

As Donna transitioned footwear like Mr. Rogers in his beautiful neighborhood, the door opened and Angela Chandler and Penny Reynolds appeared. Like Donna, they wanted to ask questions, but were stopped in their tracks. As Penny turned to put her bag on a chair, she rolled her eyes. Carley caught the expression, which made her snort.

Connie, arriving soon after, sat next to Angela where they entered into quiet conversation beneath the speakers detailing Madonna's plea for her papa not to preach. Lastly, Anne Johnson's walker pushed through the door and her face, soured to match her personality, scrunched up as she moved into the exercise area.

"What in the Sam Hill am I doing here on a Saturday morning? Did somebody light a fire in your Spandex?" Anne noticed the three women perched in the front on their thrones, smirking smugly at their courtiers. "What are you smiling about?"

"No, Anne. No fire. We've got something very important to talk about. Something that affects the very soul of Amicable." Linda tapped her chest dramatically.

The wheels of Anne's walker squeaked as she finished traversing the dance floor to a chair. All eyes followed her until she plopped down next to Connie, who reached out to pat her arm. Anne frowned and focused her eyes on Linda. "Well, go ahead. I'm waiting."

"Wait," Penny said. "Where's Leslie?"

They had purposely not invited Leslie, not only because they had recently spoken to her, but they didn't want her correcting any factual discrepancies.

In spite of her annoyance with both Penny and Anne, Linda smiled. "You've been summoned today because a terrible scourge is about to sweep through Amicable." She paused for dramatic effect.

"Carley, can you turn down the music, please?" Carley did and then Linda continued. "We're talking about Stedman Boswell."

Anne shook her head. "You mean that insurance fella from Kansas City? We've already had this discussion."

Leona clasped her hands in front of her chest. "New information has arisen about the young man."

"Yes, from a very reliable source, we've learned that Mr. Boswell is about to make some serious inquiries and, perhaps… accusations against members of this community when the elevator exploded."

"Why would he do that?" Connie asked.

"It's always about the money. Supposedly, according to my source…" Leona jabbed Linda with her elbow. "Sorry… our source… this insurance adjuster will be looking to take millions off of the settlement to save the insurance company upwards of…" she pretended to calculate the figure in her head. In reality, Linda attempted to decide what amount would most motivate the women. "Thirty million dollars."

Gasps.

"Wait, wait, wait," Penny said, holding up her hands, "Are you saying that Baker is trying to renege on the policy because of technicalities?"

"Technically they aren't technicalities. If Baker can prove that either someone deliberately destroyed the elevator or, worse yet, the elevator was at fault for its safety procedures, they can pay back whatever they believe is fair."

"That's horrible," Angela whispered.

"But how can we know this information is true?"

"Our source is very trustworthy."

Anne had had enough. "Enough with this 'our source' crap. Who is this omniscient source you are quoting? How do we know this isn't you three coloring the facts like you always do?" Anne's eyes narrowed.

"I resent that," Linda said.

"Resent away," Anne responded as she leaned forward on her walker. "But before I do anything, I want to know that this isn't just a little imaginary situation made up between the three of you to stir up trouble in Amicable."

"We can't reveal our sources. That would be a breach of confidenti…"

"Linda," Penny interrupted, "We know that the three of you mean well, and that you truly do believe that you are doing the town a great service by… sharing information that would best be kept private, but it would certainly help if we could know where you're getting your information from."

All eyes turned back to Linda, who looked back and forth between Leona and Jeannie. She nodded. "All right, we'll reveal their name, but none of this must leave this room."

"Get on with it," Anne responded.

"With apologies to one person in this room, our source is Butcher."

All eyes shifted to Connie Redman, who shrugged.

Pleased by the reaction, which gave credence to their words, Linda pushed forward. "Now that you have the information you asked for, we've called you all together for action."

Leona spoke next. "Each of you has specific gifts and talents that lend to… how shall we say… helping Mr. Boswell choose a different location."

"Are you asking us to help you sabotage the legal obligations of the insurance company?" Angela asked.

"No, no, of course not," Leona said hastily tapping downwards with her hands. "Butcher has simply invited us to participate in an orderly sort of small town, willful civic protection."

"You mean civic disobedience."

"Please, of course not. We would never want anyone to endanger their reputation or risk reprisal, but there are ways to influence people without actively hurting them."

Carley came out from behind the counter. "What do you mean?"

"I don't want to put any ideas into your heads," Leona said, but by the tone of her voice, she meant exactly the opposite. "…but killing him with Amicablean kindness, such as when Butcher first arrived, might be in order…?" She left the sentence to trail off into the infinite realm of possibilities.

Chapter 8.

"Give it to us straight, Linda. What exactly are you asking us to do?"

Linda grinned malevolently. "Your mission, should you choose to accept it…"

"Oh, brother," Donna muttered.

Ignoring the snide remark, Linda continued. "…is that each one of you finds a way to ingratiate yourself with young Mr. Boswell and, well, grate on his nerves. Make him edgy. We don't want him angry, just… well, uncomfortable."

"Do we need to make a coordinated plan?" Angela said.

Jeannie's eyes were drawn to the motion over Anne's shoulder, outside the X-Er-Size window, where a figure had just walked by. Stedman Boswell.

"Yes. Yes we do."

Happily, Stedman Boswell whistled as he wandered down Main Street, hands in pockets enjoying the sunshine on his face. He had slept well the last couple of nights. The only noises were a few barking dogs, a chorus of crickets and the random semi rumbling through town.

Along Main Street, the stores were neat and well maintained. From the grocery store to the hardware store, the bank and shoe shop - all were open for business on a Saturday. Walking down the street, Stedman looked to his left and saw Peterson's Butchery where the young men and the giant worked. When all was said and done, Stedman looked forward to celebrating his victory.

A few people who did not know him wished him a good morning, while all of the passing drivers, whether pickups or cars, waved to him - one index finger. He wondered what that meant, but he nodded his head and kept moving.

Checking his reflection in the shop windows, Stedman recognized that he looked different than the people of Amicable. These hicks and their blue jeans, t-shirts, pickups and close-cropped hair, were throwbacks to a previous generation frozen in time. Although there were pockets of modernism, a few tattoos, some brilliantly dyed hair and a nose ring or two, (wildly frowned upon and universally condemned by the stalwarts as a vulgar, attention-seeking display), much of Amicable seemed perfectly content to ignore that there was a bigger and brighter world out there.

Boswell checked his Rolex and estimated the time until his meeting with the town council that afternoon. The mayor wanted to check in with him to work through a timeline for the upcoming weeks (or months, if Baker had his way) and push through with a plan for when the funds could be distributed. She would not be happy with his proposal.

Stedman glanced at the sign to his left. It was a workout studio with the name X-Er-Size. Briefly, he wondered how many people took advantage of it, but then moved on.

Turning left again, he saw the steeple of St. Clements Methodist Church and the opposing building on the other side of the street - Amicable High School. Both were built from the same kind of brick, the color of clotted blood. Where the school seemed blockish, a Tetris piece settled into the middle of town, the church was angular and pointy.

Stedman stopped at the corner and leaned against the side of the exercise place waiting to see what would happen next.

Steve Evans, the city treasurer, tried to keep his emotions in check as he listened to the mayor, but his hands began to tremble. "This is impossible."

"Listen, Steve. We have to figure out how to keep the town afloat, whether we need to borrow money, or ask for donations, maybe a GoFundMe page...?" Janice's attempt at humor missed Steve's funny bone by a country mile.

"We simply can't do that, Janice. How is it that you can't understand this? Due to the upgrades at the school, Amicable is already deeply in debt. We've raised taxes, but made cuts to the budget. Unfortunately, what we're talking about is a catastrophic fiscal failure. When the elevator blew up, the last bastion of income for our town went with it. Farmers are driving grain to every other town in the county; people have stopped buying groceries in Amicable because they can do one stop shopping in Clancy." Steve paused and then cleared his throat.

Chapter 8.

"Mark my words: if we don't get the insurance money, Amicable will fold." Steve tapped the folder in front of him with each word.

David Thomas shook his head. "There has to be another way."

"If you have any ideas, now would be a great time to put them forward," said Janice.

He leaned back in his chair. His thick dark hair, streaked with grey at the temples, gave him the look of an aristocratic nobleman. "Okay, look, we can choose to undermine Boswell which could cause endless delays. But, let's be honest," David spread his hands, "he thinks he's a big fish in a small town." Nods around the table.

"Why not try the opposite tack? Instead of sabotaging his movements, maybe we should massage his ego, you know, maybe give him every courtesy short of bribery? Make his stay here in Amicable a positive one. If we're lucky, he'll look out for us instead of having it out for us."

Rhonda Jensen glanced at her fellow town councilors. "What are you proposing, Dave? How do you see this working?"

"I don't know. This is all theoretical - it's kind of running real time in my mind."

"Well," Janice said, "We've got four hours to figure it out."

Stedman looked at his watch. At 7:33 p.m., he was both tired and elated. Strangely, the events of the afternoon had confused him more than he ever could have imagined. After showing up five minutes late for the meeting, he found the town council full of smiles and come-on-ins. Mayor Stensrud greeted him with a hearty handshake - she even called him by his first name - and then, as the rest of the table repeated their names for his benefit, they made him feel entirely comfortable.

As Stedman walked to the rental house at 184 Peppertree Lane, he worked through the other events of the meeting. The city treasurer produced the financial statements without being asked. One of the councilors brought the elevator logs and manifests – a starting place. And lastly, the councilor named Rhonda (he couldn't remember her last name) had spoken to him separately from the others and said that 'she would do whatever she could to help make his stay in Amicable a pleasant one.' He wasn't used to women coming onto him like that, or at least sober ones anyway. Obviously, she was attracted to him. As much as he might detest his time in Amicable, certainly a little fun shouldn't be out of the question. He'd have to be careful, though.

Crossing Highway 10, Boswell's stomach rumbled loudly. Looking up to his left, he noticed the shell of the elevator reflecting the deepening light. Although the sun would still be up for an hour or so, this was his favorite time of day. Oddly, the colors seemed brighter here in the country. Consciously, he attempted to suppress any thoughts that might taint his work for Baker Insurance, but after an afternoon like he'd had, it was difficult to suppress positive feelings.

Stedman approached his rental property. On opposite sides of the path leading to the front door were matching maple trees, green leaves fluttering in the wind. Liam Wilson had told him that these smallish trees were replacements after a fire had ravaged the old house. Insurance had covered the contents and building, Liam told him. Stedman was sure that Liam stressed that insurance had covered the entirety of the property even though the reason for the fire had never been found.

The house, a rambling ranch, was quaint in a rustic sort of way. Brown siding, replicating a log cabin finish, gave the house a Northwoods kind of look. Along the side of the house, bushes and flowers stuck up at regular intervals. Liam had taken very good care of it.

Striding up the sidewalk, Stedman's belly voiced its displeasure again. Pulling his keys from his pocket, he opened the front door, placed his briefcase inside the house and grabbed his car keys. Smiling, he touched the Porsche key and strutted to the detached garage where he manually lifted the creaking door. *How can there not be an electric garage door opener?*

After pulling out from the garage and closing the door, he backed the car out onto Peppertree. Peeling out of town heading west, he retracted the convertible roof and stuck his middle finger in the air towards Amicable.

He and Amicable must have been the best of friends.

Chapter 9.

John Deakins looked out over his congregation. In any other year, Labor Day Sunday would have been one of the smallest worship services. Some of his parishioners would make a last mad dash pilgrimage to their 'summer cabin', which, for most of them, was on the shoreline of any number of Midwestern ponds or lakes. On this Labor Day, most, if not all, Amicableans stayed put to help with the cleanup.

This Labor Day Sunday, the church was three-quarters full and filling quickly.

As always, Leslie and the twins sat in the fourth row from the front, on the left side in front of the lectern. John did not use the lectern very often anymore, but when he did, it was a relief to see his family sitting (usually uncomfortably) not far from him. During the service, he was quite sure his daughters would be fidgeting and poking each other, but that was childhood for most kids. Scattered throughout the sanctuary were families, older couples, a few singles and the odd stranger. Although he'd been trying to break them of the habit, he'd not been able to succeed in having them sit closer to one another, or to the front of the church, for that matter. For some reason, there was always a human-sized space between families, friends and strangers, an invisible wall between relationships.

A small clot of people appeared in the back left-hand aisle. John squinted to see who it was and why they were blocking the path into the sanctuary. He was not surprised to see many of the town council members. They seemed to be chatting animatedly about something, and then stopped suddenly, looking backwards into the narthex and down the stairs. At that moment, Jim the Organist (who also doubled as Jim the Mailman) broke into an opening fanfare on the upper rank of the organ sending traditional attendees scrabbling for their service orders and hymnals.

As the opening song began with ironic joyfulness, the clot broke open and a new cell entered the cluster. Reverend Deakins almost stopped singing when he saw who it was.

Stedman Boswell.

What bothered him most, though, was the fact that the town council members seemed to be welcoming Boswell like a prodigal son. After his discussion with Butcher the day before, he knew that they should be cold-shouldering, not warm-welcoming the wastrel. Deakins frowned but continued singing. All eight of the council members (plus Boswell) settled into the fifth row from the back, which caused excitement in the ranks of parishioners. Jim the Organist/Mailman finished the opening hymn with a flourish and turned exultantly from his place in the balcony, expecting to see at least a few of the worshippers staring rapturously up at him, but his smile crumbled when he found the sanctuary was held captive in strained silence.

Reverend Deakins, dressed in dress slacks, shirt and tie, stepped to the center of the transept, adjusted the microphone and addressed the crowd. "Good morning everyone. A blessed Labor Day to you all. Welcome to all who are members and our guests in attendance today. As we begin in worship today, I want all of us to remember as we confess our sins to God, the most heinous of sins - pride." Much of the congregation shifted uneasily in their seats. This was an odd opening from the normally easy-going pastor.

"In order to properly prepare for worship, let us think deeply about the ways that we transgress against the Almighty by placing ourselves before Him." Deakins turned piously toward the altar, aware that every person in the pews that day was wondering what in the world was going on. *What did pride have to do with Labor Day?*

As Mayor Stensrud and Councilor Evans flanked him, Stedman Boswell scanned his surroundings. Boswell hadn't been to church in years. Neither Christmas nor Easter seemed to hold any kind of magical feeling for him. His parents had not been raised in a faith and, frankly, he had no urgency to understand a deeper meaning in life. For goodness sake, Stensrud and Evans should be the first ones to recognize the fact that Amicable's main source of life had just exploded should be a clue that there was no universal cosmic benevolence. Crossing his arms, he pondered the wisdom of keeping his agnostic thoughts to himself. As the community confessed its sins silently (which Boswell also thought was strange - *Were people actually checking off all the errors that they'd made before an equally silent deity?*), Boswell's eyes strayed to Mayor Stensrud's left where Rhonda sat. Surprisingly, she seemed to be taking seriously this part of the service. In his experience, beautiful people had nothing to confess. It was simply something weak people did. Regardless of what she was doing, Boswell enjoyed her profile: her delicate and full lips, high cheekbones, long lashes closed. *Would she look like that when she whispered his name?* He smiled to himself, but then stopped when an old woman gave him a dirty look.

A young woman read a Bible passage, something tedious and read in monotone, about a young boy being sold into captivity by his brothers. When she finished, the young woman mumbled 'This is the word of the Lord,' invoking a similarly mumbled response from the congregation, 'Thanks be to God.'

The crowd was of varied ages, although there were more older folks than younger. In general, they were well dressed and predominantly Caucasian. Dotting the back rows were a few of darker skin tones, probably Mexican or Latino. After his cursory glance around the church, Stedman's thoughts strayed again to Rhonda. *What was it about her that was so... so... intriguing?* Yes, she was beautiful, but there was something mysterious about her. Certainly she had to be married, or at least with someone. Glancing at her left hand, he spotted the wedding ring. He felt disappointed and aroused at the same time.

A challenge.

Meanwhile, on the right side of the church, Leopold Jensen tried his hardest to entertain his children during what was the longest twenty minutes of their week. Even though John Deakins was Butcher's best friend (and best man at his wedding), Butcher still struggled with the weekly monotony of the sermon. It wasn't that John's words weren't applicable, it was just that they weren't particularly helpful to parents who were trying to corral their children. First, Georgie decided that John Thomas was a little too close for sibling comfort, so Butcher situated himself between them. Then, J.T. had had enough coloring and wanted something else to distract him. Butcher produced a small sandwich bag of little green army men. Unfortunately, J.T.'s advanced creativity brought sound effects. As the little green army men began to snipe each other off the tops of the pews with a *peeuw, peeuw,* where they flew dramatically to their deaths ending up in various distracting places such as Doris Olson's immaculately coiffed hair. The old woman turned around, and with a practiced death stare, handed a grenade-launching specialist back to the little boy's father. A father sitting one pew back, put his hand on Butcher's shoulder and whispered, "We've all been there, Man. Hang in there."

What Butcher wanted to do was not to distract his children. He wanted to catch Rhonda's attention. He knew that she was supposed to be sitting with the town council as a sign of unity, but certainly not with Boswell in the middle. What did they think they were doing?

Butcher glanced in Rhonda's direction hopeful that she would be able to sense his gaze, but she stared resolutely forward in stern concentration. Just as he was about to turn away, his gaze fell on Stedman Boswell.

What the...

Boswell was staring at his wife and Butcher could read everything. Because Rhonda was paying attention to John's sermon, she didn't notice the lascivious look. It was subtle, yes, but Butcher had seen enough, and his gift allowed him to know, that he would have to be very careful. Very.

Butcher searched his thoughts. He trusted Rhonda completely - so much so, that he was unable to read her anymore. When you trusted someone implicitly, there was no fear of rejection and life was ablaze with beauty and mystery. *But what if she was tempted by...? No, she would never do that.* Once, though, she had wanted to live in a big city; she fell in love with a big city guy. *No, not anymore. Her life was here with him and Georgie and J.T.. Still...*

After one last look, he turned away. *Stedman Boswell needs to go.*

Near the back of the church, in the glow of a stained glass window portraying a young man being pulled from a dark hole, Linda, Leona and Jeannie furiously scribbled notes to each other passing them back and forth like teenage girls. Leona was most adamant in her ministrations, scribbling furiously on her bulletin and pointing at the object of their disaffection ensconced between the town council members.

Chapter 9.

Linda received the bulletin, read it and replied quickly. Then, noting her thoughts, she handed them back towards Jeannie, who waited impatiently for the private message.

On the other side of the church, Carley chewed her fingernails. Not prone to the habit, but momentarily defenseless against it, she spotted the three women on the other side of the room passing notes. Staring, she saw that Penny Reynolds was pondering her bulletin very closely as if it were the Bible itself. But Carley was certain that Penny's phone was behind the bulletin. Penny was only a few seats away, so as quietly as possible, Carley pushed her way past the other residents of Pew 3 and out into the aisle. Reverend Deakins, caught by the movement, followed her with his eyes but continued his onslaught of sinful pride. Carley actually hoped he'd go another ten minutes (this was a first for her) so that she could connect with Penny.

Looking up from her phone/bulletin, Penny put it aside guiltily and questioned Carley with her eyes about the invasion into Pew 5. *What are you doing?* Penny mouthed the words.

"We need to talk," Carley whispered. A few religious souls turned slightly to see what the commotion was. Strangely, a whisper was just as loud as a shout in church.

Not right now. Penny motioned with her head to the front.

"But…"

Penny frowned deeply. *No. Just wait.* They both looked towards the front in expectation of Reverend Deakins catching them like a school teacher and sending them to detention.

Carley had an idea. She took out her phone and began to text Penny.

What do u think they're talking about? She pushed 'send' and waited for Penny's phone to buzz, or at least show up on the screen.

Unfortunately, Carley Hennesy missed an important digital detail and instead of texting Penny Reynolds alone, she sent the message to the entire exercise/conspirator/saboteur group. Immediately, two phones pinged, one buzzed, three twinkled, one car horn went off and another a recording of Donna Humphries' husband snoring. As the sounds echoed throughout the church, one-hundred-and-forty-two faces turned towards the sources of the sounds. The women simultaneously reached for their phones at the same time. If the scene had been recorded, it would have looked like a jolt of electricity had passed underneath the seats of the entire congregation.

Carley looked at the message that she sent, smacked her head and cringed. Looking over at Linda, Leona and Jeannie, Carley noticed their scowls. Carley embarrassedly shrugged, raised a hand in apology and looked towards Reverend Deakins who, although frowning, hadn't given up the ghost of his homily. Carley pointed to her phone so that they would text her.

Without being too obvious, Linda texted the group to *meet after church at our table - but DON'T be too obvious about it!* Unfortunately, Carley had forgotten to turn her own phone off and Olivia Newton John sang loudly, "Let's get Physical! Physical! I wanna get physical!" It startled her so badly that she dropped the phone under the pew.

"For heaven's sake," Penny whispered. "What are you doing?"

"I'm sorry," Carley said as Olivia finished her urging for some body talk.

Interrupted again, Reverend Deakins finally paused, put both of his hands on the wooden pulpit and put his head down. Everyone knew that they were now on probation. The next one to peep would be expelled from the sanctuary.

Demetrius Chandler looked to his right and downwards at his mother. She was particularly embarrassed. Glancing over his right shoulder to where Aaron and his sister Penelope were sitting, Demetrius found them both smirking. Shrugging, he turned his eyes toward Butcher who was staring at the insurance adjuster.

On the homestretch of the sermon, when Reverend Deakins usually threw in the ubiquitous 'Jesus went to the cross and died, rose again for your salvation,' Butcher casually glanced at his wife whose head sank lower as if a previously un-thought thought had crossed her mind. Butcher's adrenaline pulsed. What was she thinking? *I wish I could read her now!*

"Amen," Reverend Deakins said, as he mercifully pulled the covers up and over his sermon, putting it to bed.

Deakins looked up into the balcony where Jim the Organist/Mailman was perched, hands ready to launch into Luther's hymn, *A Mighty Fortress Is Our God.* As the fanfare began, Deakins walked down the steps into the nave and took his seat beside his wife. Leslie reached out for his hand and gave it an apologetic squeeze.

"What the heck is going on in here today?" Deakins asked her. She shrugged and pointed to the hymnal.

> A mighty fortress is our God.
> A bulwark never failing.
> Our helper he amid the flood,
> Of mortal ills prevailing...

After the worship service, in the basement of St. Clements church, the women joined together circling their usual table like Arthur's knights. Sitting in uncomfortable metal chairs with wooden backs and stenciled letters *SCMC,* the women looked expectantly at each other. Even though cups of coffee sat in front of them, they didn't drink. As the women spoke in low tones, careful not to be overheard, Butcher, Derek and Nash watched from a distance, observing them and the opposing table where the town council and their 'esteemed guest' sat. Butcher noticed that Boswell was not impressed with the percolated coffee.

"Do you have any idea what's happening?" Derek asked Butcher.

"No idea whatsoever," Butcher responded as his eyes fell on the man who had been ogling his wife.

"Why are they sitting with him? I thought we were all in this thing together?" Nash asked.

"It's like they've changed sides," Derek stated mirroring his twin brother.

"There's much more going on here than we expected."

"But why is Rhonda sitting at that table?"

Butcher shrugged. "She hasn't let me in on the secret."

"But can't you..." Nash widened his eyes.

"Nope. I can't do it with Rhonda, and believe me, I tried this morning. It doesn't work on her anymore."

"That's too bad," Nash said. "I'd love to have the ability with Shania. I swear the woman is as complex as a Rubik's Cube."

Both Derek and Butcher looked at Nash and the unfortunate description of Shania's complexity. "Okay…" Derek said slowly.

"It's all about trust, Nash. If you trust the person you're with, you don't need to… read them."

"Are you struggling with trust, Butcher?" Derek asked.

"Of course not." Butcher hesitated, and the twins caught it, but they didn't say anything.

"Do you know what's going to happen?" Derek asked.

Butcher shook his head. "I wish I did. I really wish I did."

Nash turned to Butcher. "Hey Butcher, do you think you'd be able to close the Chop Shop for a week and come help us out in the locker? Mom and Dad are driving to Kansas City to get some building supplies for the town. The store is closed tomorrow but we have to catch up."

Butcher looked over at Rhonda's table across the room where his wife was cupping her chin in her hand and smiling at the insurance adjuster.

"Yeah, I can do that," he said. Maybe he needed a week of butchering to vent his growing irritation.

Chapter 10.

After the worship service, Labor Day passed without note, but the citizens of Amicable could feel deep in the marrow of their bones that something was changing. Although Labor Day was supposed to be a holiday, many Amicableans were working; businesses were repaired; front lawns, cleared, re-sodded and watered. It felt as if the town was beginning to overcome its despondent inertia and scrabble towards hope. Yet the town felt deeply the loss of its heart. Not one member of the community didn't daily look to the hulking shell on the south side of Highway 10 and wonder if the future was as bleak and hollow as it seemed.

In the afternoon, kids played in neighbors' backyards while the adults, after working through the day, set up camp on porches, decks and lawns with beer coolers and barbecues. Brief spurts of laughter cut through playlists of music. Even though the edge of worry seemed to scrape like a strigil over the town's skin, it was a beautiful day for relaxing,

Stedman Boswell knew that he was an outsider - a stranger in a strange land. He was not naive enough to believe that it would only take a short time for him to ingratiate himself, but he thought that with his charisma and charm he'd be able to at least make inroads. Other than the eight-member town council, the rest of the community warily kept their distance.

As Stedman sat on his own small front deck, cold beer in hand, he watched the idyllic town spend its holiday. Strangely, he was caught up in the simplicity of their collective life. The connections that they had created and maintained with each other seemed to give them true contentedness. Stedman couldn't believe how many kids wandered freely through the streets, parading from house to house, backyard to backyard. Of course, city life was preferable with its culture, its pace and the variations of people, but Amicable seemed to have one thing that the city didn't.

Peace.

One member of the community remained resolutely in his consciousness. Briefly, he thought of her green eyes and sandy brown hair, long slender neck, her tanned skin and strong arms. For the rest of the night he imagined his interactions with her.

On the other side of town, Butcher and Rhonda sat on their front porch with their children and Connie, and attempted not to look at George's house. On previous Labor Days, George would have taken up residence in his sturdy, wooden Adirondack chair, beer in hand, glasses perched precariously on the end of his nose. Raising a hand, George would have invited them to sit with him and have a beer.

"You okay, Hon?" Butcher asked as Georgie and J.T. entwined themselves around and in between the deck chairs.

"Hmmm?"

"Are you okay?" Butcher looked into her eyes, desperate to read what she was thinking.

"Yes, I suppose."

"What's on your mind?"

"Just trying to figure out a few things."

"Can I help?"

"No, not really."

"If you want to talk about it, I think…"

"No," Rhonda replied testily.

Connie watched the exchange from the other side of the porch and frowned. It wasn't like Rhonda to speak to Leo like that, but she had learned not to say anything. Suddenly, Connie's phone buzzed. Though she was accustomed to the cell phone, she never grew used to its obtrusive nature. Reaching into the pocket of her pants, Connie withdrew the phone and opened the text app.

Phase I beginning tomorrow. Move into position at 11:05 a.m.

"Who was that?" Rhonda asked.

"Just the exercise group," Connie said noncommittally.

"What do they want?"

Connie shrugged. "They want to get together this week, I think. Some extra exercise before the cold sets in."

The phone buzzed again. This time from Angela. *Seraph and Gabriel will be in place. We have the ammunition. Michael, do u have comms?* The conspirators decided the best way to 'hide' their intentions was to have call names. Deciding early and quickly on the names and kinds of angels (to which Anne Johnson rolled her eyes, not just because she thought the idea was easily 'one of the most stupid things I've ever heard,' but because she was given the name 'Uriel' which she thought was far too close to the word 'urinal'), the group thought this would be an appropriate, yet wholesome, way of keeping their identities secret.

Donna/Michael responded quickly. *I purchased the walkie-talkies in Clancy yesterday. Everybody owes me $4.37.* This set off a flurry of texts. Connie moved from the porch and onto the grass. The conspirators grumbled at the excessive price of the walkie-talkies, but Donna mollified them by explaining their long-range capabilities.

Eventually, Linda/Azrael (the Angel of Death) interrupted the complaining by refocusing their thoughts back on the future of Amicable.

We can work out the price later. Focus. Archangel, do you have the props?

That's a copy, Azrael.

What does that mean? Jeannie/Cherub wrote.

It means, 'yes,' Jeannie. Leona was shaking her head as she typed this.

You're not supposed to write our real names. Carley/Raphael smirked as she sat on her stationary bike and watched the communication take place.

WE'RE TEXTING, EVERYONE! DO WE ALL UNDERSTAND WHAT THAT MEANS? OUR REAL NAMES POP UP ON THE SCREEN!!!!! Penny's/Gabriel's use of capitals and a frustrated emoticon was enough to let everyone know how she felt.

That's exactly why I bought the freaking walkie-talkies! Donna raised her hand exultantly. The walkie-talkies only cost four dollars apiece, but she wanted to spread around the cost of the drive to Clancy to the other ladies.

Connie watched the exchange take place. Her call name, Raguel, one of the archangels - a lesser known one, though - seemed appropriate as she felt her part was such a small one. As the second oldest member of the conspiratorial team (younger than Anne by a considerable distance), she believed her biggest asset would be the wisdom of age. More importantly, though, she didn't want to betray Rhonda.

What time will Satan be walking by? Leona/Archangel asked.

Approximately 11:15. The meeting finishes about 11:00. Raphael and Uriel will be waiting outside X-Er-Size and will escort Satan to ground zero.

Carley did not think it was appropriate to name her studio so 'publicly.' *Do we really need to expose my business to this public forum?*

For heaven's sake, Azrael wrote, but didn't think of the irony, *this is a closed message. Is everyone ready?*

Eight responses, like a roll call, all with answers ranging from *Affirmative* to *Roger* to *For cripes sake, Yes!*

The day after Labor Day was going to be a good one.

As was his routine, Butcher woke early. When his eyes popped open, he saw that light was already filtering into their bedroom. The evening before had been filled with terse conversations; Rhonda had gone to bed early complaining of a headache. Guiltily, Butcher watched her go, and as much as he wanted to kiss her goodnight, a selfish sense of obstinance took hold him. When she had plodded off to the bedroom, he remained resolutely stuck in his armchair.

Rolling back over, he noticed that Rhonda was already up and out of bed which was odd because she was not a particularly vibrant morning personality. Pushing himself up on the edge, he stretched his torso, getting the blood moving, and then yawned deeply into a closed fist. After finishing his morning routine, he moved into the kitchen and saw a note lying in the middle of the table.

Leo, I've gone out for a walk. I'll be back at 7:15. If you need to leave early, just wake Mom. She was going to take care of the kids anyway.

He noticed that there was no signature and worse, no term of endearment at the end. By 7:00, Butcher began to worry. Even though she said she'd be back by 7:15, Butcher's thoughts had flown to distant places they had never been before. Was she meeting with Boswell? Where were they meeting? Was he losing her? Heart racing, Butcher paced from kitchen to window, peering intently towards the street hoping to see her appear.

Moments later, Connie appeared. Butcher thanked her and, after one more worry of where his wife was, set off on a brisk walk towards the butchery. Instead of going into Peterson's first, Butcher went to his office in the Chop Shop. Retrieving the key from his pocket, he opened his office door and made himself a cup of coffee. He left a note for Hossein, his receptionist, to cancel appointments for the next few days and reschedule for the next week. Once finished, Butcher left the office and locked the door behind him. Just as he was taking the step downwards onto the sidewalk, he looked to his right where Derek was approaching with a cardboard carrier containing three coffees.

"Morning, Boss," Butcher smiled as he looked down at Derek.

"Hey, Butcher!" Derek exclaimed as he clapped the tall man on the shoulder, which caused the coffees to precariously list to the side.

"Careful," Butcher cautioned, flinching to help Derek.

"I had it all the way," Derek said, as they moved one door west to Peterson's Butchery. Nash was already prepping the display cases. Wearing his traditional light blue shirt and work pants, covered by a thick plastic apron, Nash waved to them.

Walking up the two steps, Derek grabbed the handle of the door expecting it to be open. When it didn't open, his hand slipped from the handle. As if in slow motion, he began to tumble backwards down the stairs. Fortunately, Butcher could see what was about to happen and he reached out to steady the young man. Unfortunately, one of the cups of coffee tipped and coffee spurted from the opening splotching the front of Derek's shirt. Providentially, the lid did not separate or Derek's entire shirt would have been covered by coffee.

"Dangit, Nash!" Derek shouted through the closed front glass. "Can you just unlock the freaking door!"

Laughing, Nash traipsed to the door and un-snipped the lock allowing his brother and Butcher to enter. "Morning," Nash said. "Boss number two."

"Why do you have to lock the door, Buttfizzle? It's not like people are going to bust in here and steal something." Derek grabbed a paper towel and began to daub the coffee stain from his shirt.

Butcher stood with hands on hips in the front waiting area. *Some things never change.* Peterson's Butchery had been upgraded: there was a new set of table and chairs situated in the front window. The walls had been recently whitewashed and the large glass windows had been replaced. A set of electronic scales sat on the front counter and the display held new cuts of meat of all kinds, whole chickens, pork chops, beef brisket, and even (to the great joy of many little children) a cow's tongue. Nash had already turned on the stereo system. Even though the stereo had been replaced, the music had not changed. Echoing in the carpetless room were the sounds of the '80's.

"Well, I'm not paying you to stand there, Butcher. Put your apron on and get to work." Nash smiled. "Derek and I are going to sit at the front table and drink our coffee while you do all the work for us."

"Whatever you say, Boss." Butcher saluted Nash and made the nostalgic journey lifting the bench top and walking through to the back. He smiled as he pulled the apron over his head.

For the next hour, Butcher sliced, diced and sawed meat. It took him ten minutes to find his rhythm but eventually, muscle memory took over. Derek shook his head as he watched the mound of meat grow higher and higher. Nash laughed as they sipped coffee and prepared for the first patrons to arrive.

Later in the morning, across the street, a silver, late model Porsche arrived. Most of the patronage inside and outside the butchery turned to stare. Seeing a Porsche in Amicable was like seeing a cheetah running free in Antarctica. The door opened slowly; Amicableans everywhere turned towards each other and derisively crossed their arms.

"Hey Derek," Nash said, "Get a load of Stedman." He pronounced his name 'Studman.'

Derek whistled. "I can't say I envy the guy his life, but boy, I wouldn't mind driving his car around."

"What do you think he's doing?"

Derek watched Stedman approach the butchery. "Probably going to pee on our front door."

"What?"

"He's going to come in and buy some meat, Dipstick." Derek grinned malevolently and rubbed his hands together. "This is going to be fun."

Chapter 10.

Stedman Boswell checked his reflection in the rearview mirror, first his hair, eyebrows and teeth. Fully satisfied that he was, in fact, a handsome man, he opened the door of the Porsche and stepped outside. After straightening his shirt and pushing out the creases, he put his sunglasses on and confidently strode across the street to the sidewalk outside the butchery. Four grizzled farmers stood in a semi-circle facing the young man. Conversation stopped, but one of the farmers twirled a toothpick in his mouth.

"Good morning, gentlemen," Stedman approached them and stuck out his hand. One farmer looked at it, paused and glanced at his friends who raised their eyebrows and shrugged. They shook.

"Beautiful day today," Stedman added. The group looked at the sky. As Stedman pushed past them, one remarked under his breath, "Who's that?"

A bell hanging over the doorway tinkled as Stedman entered. Boswell encountered the smirking set of twins he had met a few nights before standing behind the counter.

"Good morning," Stedman said. "I don't know if you remember my name but I'm Stedman Boswell. I'm here…"

His words were cut off by Derek coughing into his hand the word 'jackass'.

"I'm sorry," Boswell said with a frown. "What did you say?"

"What?" Derek raised his eyebrows in mock confusion.

"Did you just call me a jackass?"

"I was coughing," Derek said, as his brother coughed into his hand. "See, it's catching."

"I'm not stupid," Boswell said. "You can't say that. It's offensive."

"Is it true?"

Stedman's eyes widened in surprise and he reddened. "You should be fired."

Derek snorted and leaned forward on the counter. "You shouldn't be offended. You're the one judging us."

"I don't know what you're talking about."

Derek moved towards the fold up door, pulled it upwards and stepped out towards Boswell. Stedman took a step back, but then planted his feet. In the background, the saw had stopped. "The minute you arrived in Amicable, you've judged every last one of us. You've labeled us small town hicks, red necks, ignoramuses, backwards and stupid. You look at us and you see people who are beneath you."

"I've done no such thing." Stedman's eyes darted to the ground and back to Derek. Butcher had taught them a thing or two about recognizing lies.

"You're lying."

"How dare you!"

"You should finish that sentence like you wanted to. 'How dare you, you small-town, closed-minded, bigoted hick.' You couldn't be any more judgmental if you wore a neon sign that said, 'I'm better than you are.'"

Stedman's mouth flopped open. He wanted to protest, but the words weren't coming.

Derek continued his tirade. "You imagine that all people from small towns are morons. I got news for you, Strawman Buttswill, we Amicableans can smell a large pile of crap from a long ways away."

Boswell's voice returned, but he was astounded that the young man opposite him had read his thoughts so clearly. "Stop calling me names, that's off…" he stopped his words knowing that he was self-fulfilling the prophecy of Derek's words. "Either way, you've been judging me for something I never thought."

Derek looked at Nash who smiled. "Wanna bet?"

"There's no possible way that you could prove what's going on inside my head."

"Fifty bucks says I can prove it."

"Okay, prove it."

Derek motioned to Nash who shrugged and opened the till. They had never done this for money before, but the jackass, Boswell, needed to be smacked off his pedestal. Nash retrieved two twenties and a ten and placed them on the counter. He raised his eyebrows at Stedman who confidently reached into his wallet and placed a fifty-dollar bill on top of the other notes.

"Now," Derek said, "if I can prove to you not only your motives, but also how you came to your understanding of culture and life, i.e. your arrogance and snobbish disinterest in Amicable, I get to keep your fifty bucks."

"You're on." Boswell took a step back.

The twins looked at each other one more time and then Derek called over his shoulder, without taking his eyes from Stedman.

"Butcher. You're needed in front."

Like the calm before a storm, an eerie stillness settled over the room. If not for Eurythmics, the only thing that would have been heard was the motors in the coolers.

Without sound, a form filled the doorway. Butcher's head almost reached the upper frame. He entered standing next to the twins.

"What is it, Boss?"

His eyes fell on Stedman Boswell.

"Butcher, Mr. Butthole here needs to have his thoughts read. We've got a fifty dollar bet that 'we' can do it."

Stedman moved towards the trio. "The idiot bet me that he could 'read me,'" he used his fingers as quotation marks. "Tell my motives, my history, and my," more quotation marks, "'Arrogance.'" He motioned towards the twins who were now standing a step behind Butcher; both of them had folded their arms like identical sphinxes.

Butcher moved glacially through the bench. "And you've already put your money down?"

"Yup," Stedman said confidently.

"Okay," Butcher pretended to sigh deeply, but inwardly was reveling at the fact that he was about to destroy the man. Butcher slowly opened the flip top counter. It creaked like a rusty door in a horror movie.

In seconds, Butcher had a complete read of the man.

"Obviously, you are a man of means."

Stedman looked beyond Butcher to the twins who pretended to face off against each other like prizefighters. "Is this the best he can do? You can look at my clothes and tell the difference between me and you." Derek pretended to make a jab towards Nash's face, who dodged it artfully.

"You've got a Porsche," Butcher continued, "or at least I think that's yours. There would only be one reason to drive that in Amicable, and that would be to show your superiority."

"Whatever," Stedman said. "So I've got a Porsche."

Butcher continued. "No one has ever really liked you."

Now, Boswell looked up.

"Your father is an executive; your mother is what his workmates consider a trophy wife. My guess is that your father is at least twenty years older than your mother."

Boswell's eyes widened.

"Neither of your parents think much of you and no matter how hard you try and no matter what kind of car you buy, you can't quite seem to get in their good graces, especially your father. You've taken on a job as an insurance adjuster so you can stick it to father figures everywhere."

"Wait a minute. Who have you...?" Derek and Nash were faking punches with every barb that Butcher was throwing.

"Your most recent relationship with a woman ended when she decided she'd had enough of your..." Butcher waved his hand trying to find the right word. "...possessiveness."

"Obsequiousness," Derek shouted, as he pretended to punch Nash in the face.

"Now, now," Butcher cautioned, "Let's not show off to our big city guest." He winked at Derek then turned back to Stedman. "Your girlfriend grew tired of your snobbishness and arrogance. What was her name was..." He studied Stedman's face, which had grown white, "Tahlia..." He studied Stedman's reaction. "No, it's Tania. Almost.... Ah, Trina!"

Stedman Boswell's legs began to quiver. "Holy sh..."

"You've come to Amicable to overcome your failed attempts at love by giving in to your greater love for your work. You've got an inferiority complex the size of the Empire State Building, so you've come here and expected us small people to fawn over you, a big city insurance adjuster." Butcher moved menacingly towards him and spoke in a low voice. "But you have no interest in helping us at all."

Chapter 10.

"I…I…How…. I mean…" Boswell's stammering sounded like a coughing outboard motor.

With each stammer, Derek punched Nash until he was staggering behind the counter like a boxer on the ropes.

"And now that you've come here, you will do whatever it takes to humiliate the town including…" Butcher's eyes widened, "… seduction?" Butcher frowned. Who was he after? He looked at Derek and Nash and immediately worried about Shania and Tracey. Then, he moved forward. "Be careful, little man."

At this point, Derek moved in for the kill and in slow motion, he pantomimed a gigantic uppercut, which Nash turned into a drama-filled knockout all the way to the floor. The two of them, laughing hysterically, pulled each other into a standing position. When they stood, the front door was swinging loudly shut behind them.

"Wait," Nash said, "where did he go?"

Stedman Boswell was already across the street to his Porsche. Within seconds, he was driving rapidly down Main Street.

"I guess he'd had enough," Derek smirked and grabbed the money. "Ten for you," he counted out and handed to Nash. "Ten for you, Butcher. You did most of the work."

"Why do you get thirty?" Nash asked grabbing at the bills.

"Because," Derek said, "I'm the brains of the operation." Nash laughed and took a quick swipe at his brother who was already moving towards the back room.

Butcher stood stock-still staring out the front window, shocked at what he had just read. *Rhonda?*

Stedman Boswell's hands were shaking. So were his knees, his feet and what seemed to be every other part of him, too. How did he do it? Who had he been talking to? There was no way he could have known about Trina. That was not public knowledge, and his relationship with his parents was so intimate, it was as if the man truly was inside his head. Stedman placed his hands back on the Porsche's steering wheel.

Stedman's watch read, 10:30. He had fifteen minutes until his meeting with the town council.

Chapter 11.

"Azrael! This is Cherub! Satan is moving! Repeat, Satan is moving. He's early!" She paused and then added, "I mean, over!"

Eight other women adjusted the volume of their walkie-talkies as Jeannie's voice rang out. Each one of them, Jeannie included, looked down at their cheat sheets for the call signs of the other women to know exactly who was supposed to be responding to the message.

Donna = Michael
Carley = Raphael
Angela = Seraph
Anne = Uriel
Penny = Gabriel
Connie = Raguel
Linda = Azrael
Leona = Archangel
Jeannie = Cherub

Okay, Linda thought excitedly, *we're on.* "Listen, everyone. Remain calm. We've prepared and planned for this attack; no need to rush things. This is what we trained to do. Over."

Connie rolled her eyes and depressed the button on the walkie-talkie. "Do we have to treat this like we're taking out Saddam Hussein? This seems kind of stupid."

"This is Archangel. You have to use your call sign otherwise we don't know who is talking! Over."

Anne attempted to respond to Leona's demand, but couldn't quite figure out how the walkie-talkie was supposed to work. She had listened during the pep talk, but these newfangled gadgets with all their buttons and pushy things seemed too complicated to remember. Eventually, she turned to Penny and handed her the walkie-talkie. "Can you let all the other ladies know that this is extremely confusing. I can't remember where I put my glasses most of the time and they want me to remember nine silly names. Over."

Penny smiled and pushed the button repeating the message. Anne crossed her arms and smiled.

"Gabriel, this is Azrael, I copy that, but for our anonymity, it's best if we don't use our real names. Roger. I mean, over and out."

"Azrael, this is Michael. You can't say over and out. That means that you are leaving and turning off your walkie-talkie. You say, 'over,' or ask a question like, 'copy?'"

Jeannie had been pushing her button seven times during the interchange. "Everyone, this is Cherub! Just a reminder, Satan is walking the streets of Amicable."

"This is Azrael. Seraph and Raphael, what's your 20?"

Carley and Angela looked down at their piece of paper and realized that Linda was talking to them. Carley jumped. With both hands, she held the walkie-talkie next to her lips. "Oh, that's me! I'm so excited. This is Raphael. I have no idea what you're talking about. What do we need twenty of?" She waved her hands in front of her and then remembered she forgot to finish the transmission. "I mean, over!"

"Raphael, this is Archangel. Hold the walkie-talkie farther away from your face. We can't understand you. Over."

"Oh!" Carley exclaimed and then depressed her button again. "I said, 'I don't know what you're talking about.' Twenty what? Car... I mean, Raphael over." She giggled again.

"Raphael, this is Azrael, it means 'what's your location?' Are you in position?"

Angela put a hand on Carley's arm. "Azrael, this is Seraph, we are not in position. Repeat, we are not in position. Satan has arrived too early. Over."

On the north side of the street hiding in the bushes, Linda swore under her breath. Jeannie was still looking through the binoculars at the approaching insurance man. As Boswell approached the corner of Main Street and 2nd Avenue, Jeannie looked up to the rooftop above the X-Er-Size studio to see movement. Carley was waving towards them.

"Abort! Abort! This is Azrael. We'll have to bide our time until Satan exits his meeting with his minions." *Dangit*, she thought, *we almost had him.*

Penny and Anne breathed a sigh of relief. Penny's eyes wandered to Anne, who was leaning on her walker. "Do you think this is really going to work?"

Anne snorted. "Which part? This idiotic plan or the idea in general?"

"Then why are we doing it?" Penny shook her head.

"Because," Anne said, as she put her chin onto her forearms, "even dying bodies kick a little bit."

"Hey," Demetrius said, as he stuffed his Spanish textbook into his locker, "what did you want to talk about?"

Aaron crossed his arms. "Don't you think things are getting weird here?"

"What, at school? It's always weird at school."

"No, stupid. In Amicable. Haven't you noticed the way the adults are acting?"

Demetrius shrugged. His mother had been edgy, but he assumed that was because of the explosion. It didn't explain her going out for chicken chores with him last night, though. That was his job and it was strange to have her following him but not talking. "I suppose. But what does it matter?"

"I don't know, but it seems like something is about to go down."

"Like what?"

"On my way to school today, I saw a few of the women, you know those gossips and a couple others, walking through the bushes. Even that old lady, Mrs. Johnson, was pushing her walker through the grass and into the shrubbery. I slowed down to watch a little bit, but I had to get to school."

"That is weird."

"Do you want to go see if they're still there?"

Demetrius smiled. "Sure, and after that we can get some lunch up town."

Five minutes later, after signing out of school, they paused at the front desk. Mrs. Bender smiled at them over her glasses, which had been pushed down to the tip of her nose. "Have a good time, boys," she said and went back to her tapping at the computer.

As the boys descended the steps that faced St. Clements, Aaron looked up at Demetrius, who had stopped at the corner. He was staring upwards and across the street.

"What is it?" Aaron asked.

Demetrius shrugged. "No idea, but someone is on that roof."

Aaron followed his pointed finger.

Not one person, but two.

Although the meeting went well, Stedman was still shaken by his encounter with the three butchers. It wasn't hard for Stedman Boswell to dislike people; sometimes it only took one word, or even a look. This Derek Peterson - he was a real piece of work and certainly lived up to every one of Boswell's stereotypes. He was ignorant, racist, bigoted, small-minded and decidedly offensive. His brother was not quite as bad, but the largest problem lay in the fact that they were so similar in appearance, so identical, it was easy to hate them both.

Then, there was the tall one. *Where had he found out those intimate details?*

Boswell looked up from his walking to notice the two young men on the corner across the street. It was the two boys he had met at the bowling alley the other night. They were staring up at the sky.

Strange...

"Seraph, Raphael, stand by. Satan approaching. Deploy decoys."

"This is Raphael, who's speaking please?"

"Oh for Pete's sake, this is Azrael."

"This is Raphael, Azrael, you told us that we need to use the call signs." Carley giggled into her hand again.

"Just be ready, over."

"This is Raphael, copy, ten four, good buddy."

The plan had been Leona's brainchild. One of the first things that they had noticed about Stedman Boswell, of course, was his clothes.

The Angels were convinced they hadn't seen a man so nicely dressed on a weekday since Tom Grismere had attempted to apply for a job at Human Beans Café. But now this cosmopolitan boy entered town like a dandy, with his fancy tan pants and button down shirts (they hadn't seen him wear a t-shirt yet!) looking like a model out of GQ magazine (not that anyone in Amicable read, or even owned, GQ magazine). Perhaps he wouldn't take so kindly to having his threads soiled.

Thus, Phase I.

Angela Chandler had been tasked with securing the ammunition. Journeying out into the chicken yard, Angela had loaded chicken poop into a bucket and added water. When the consistency was just right (somewhere between diarrhea and Jell-O), she ladled it into squeezable icing bags used for decorating cakes. *Poop cannons.*

As Stedman Boswell paused beside Carley's X-Er-Size studio, Carley perched a pair of dead pigeons on top of the building. Both pigeons had been shot by Donna's husband, Henry. Henry was unsure why Donna wanted two dead pigeons, but he had learned early in the marriage that too many questions led to many more questions.

Thus, Carley held onto the dead pigeons while Angela waited for the signal. Although the birds slumped dangerously over the wall, Angela was sure they would fool Stedman Boswell if he looked up.

Jeannie excitedly looked through her binoculars. "Uriel, Gabriel, this is Cherub, move into position."

Anne and Penny moved around the western corner of the wall and began walking slowly towards Stedman Boswell. As they neared him, they cornered him beneath the dangling birds.

"Good afternoon, sir," Anne said, producing her rehearsed lines mechanically. "How are you today?"

"Fine," Stedman said backing closer to the wall and frowning. "And how are you?"

"Michael, Raguel, can you see anything?"

The sound of Linda's voice blurted out the walkie-talkie that Penny was carrying and Penny scrambled for the piece. Embarrassed, she smiled at Boswell. "Sorry about that."

"What's going on?"

Anne thought quickly. "It's a popular thing in Amicable to follow police scanners."

"Aah."

"Azrael, this is Michael, all systems go, over." Connie and Donna were standing on Main Street watching surreptitiously from underneath the awning of the clothing store.

"Azrael, this is Seraph, we don't have a clean shot. We might hit Anne and Penny!"

"Don't use their names, dangit!"

"Sorry, we might hit the other two Angels! Over!"

From her position in the bushes, Linda could see their window of opportunity closing quickly. Anne had used up all of her lines; she was beginning to mumble and their tactical positioning was fading. The time was now to make a decision.

"Stay on target! Stay on target!"

"For goodness sake… Azrael," Angela had to search for her call name, "we can't hit the other two."

"Seraph, this is Azrael. They are acceptable casualties." Linda looked at Leona and Jeannie who were nodding with tension.

"Okay," Angela said. "Dropping missiles. Go one! Go two!"

Angela aimed the icing bag over the edge at Stedman Boswell. As if in slow motion, she watched the large gloop of chicken poop float downwards, with the second following it. Then, like two bombs exploding, one hit Stedman Boswell on the side of his head running down his cheek and onto his shoulder where it trailed down the front of his shirt. The second missile, unfortunately, wandered off target and landed directly onto the seat of Anne's walker.

"What the…" Boswell exclaimed as he bounced away from the wall feeling the excrement running through his hair and sliding down his face. He looked up and saw two pigeons affixed to the top of the wall. One of them was listing badly to the left.

"Bullseye!" Jeannie whispered loudly. "You got him!"

Unfortunately, Carley stopped to celebrate and clapped her hands. Too late. The dead pigeons toppled over the side of the wall, spiraled to the ground and landed with a thud at the feet of the three people previously engaged in strained conversation.

Penny and Anne looked at each other with horror. Stedman was aghast at the two lifeless pigeons.

"What is that? What happened?"

Penny leaned over to pick up the dead pigeons. Thinking quickly, Anne said, "The heck. It looks like they shit themselves to death."

Penny's eyes widened and she snorted.

Seeing the pigeon poo on her walker, Anne said, "Give me one of those."

Penny handed Anne a dead pigeon and she began to wipe the seat of her walker with its dead body.

Stedman Boswell looked on with revulsion as the old woman used the dead bird as a wet wipe. "What is wrong with you?"

With just the right amount of faux sympathy, Penny extended the remaining bird. "Sorry," she said, "did you want one too?"

"Did you see that?" Aaron said. "Those people just… just… I'm not sure how to explain what just happened."

"Yeah," Demetrius said, "I saw it. But I can't believe it."

"Can't believe what?"

Demetrius looked up to the roof, where two figures were standing. "That's my mom."

"Seraph, Raphael, this is Azrael, mission accomplished! Return to base." Linda's voice registered extreme excitement.

"Who is this?" Another female voice asked over the radio.

"I already told you. This is Azrael. Who is this?"

The walkie-talkie came to life. "This is Officer Louise Nelson of the Amicable Police Department. I need to know what you are doing, immediately."

Linda's eyes widened. "Uh, Officer Nelson, how long have you been listening?"

"I've listened to the entire conversation, but I can't seem to figure out what's going on, so, I'm asking you, what did you just do?"

A male voice came over the airwaves. "Officer Nelson and Unidentified Angel, this is Tom Busman, I've been listening, too. You've really got me curious."

"Tom Busman, this is Officer Nelson. Who are you?"

"I'm a trucker hauling from Omaha to Minneapolis. Me and the boys have been tuning in. You helped us stay alert."

The Angels stared with wide eyes at each other. *Oh, crap.* Six more voices echoed over the airwaves, all truckers. All laughing.

Stedman Boswell retraced his steps and made his way southward on Main Street into Norwood's Grocery Store. As he pulled open the glass doors, the air conditioning hit him in the face, which, mixed with the smell of bird shit, caused him to gag. Shoppers paused to stare. Although he had wiped off as much as he could, some was still plastered to his cheek, in his hair, across his shoulder and down his arm.

"Where is your bathroom?" He asked the nearest person, a grocery worker in her mid-twenties. Her nametag read *NAIDA*.

She pointed to the back of the store. Stedman stomped through an entire aisle of cereal and bread, almost careening into an old woman who was comparing the prices of corn flakes. "Get out of my way," Stedman grumbled.

The woman, surprised that someone would speak so gruffly, (especially on a Tuesday), pulled her cart to the side. She watched warily as the young man pushed past her, through the hanging plastic strips into the back of the grocery store where a bathroom was located for the convenience (or inconvenience) of shoppers. Stedman closed the door behind him and yanked the chain on the light and looked into the mirror. His anger turned to rage.

They were laughing at him.

Not only had the day started badly, but this series of events was unacceptable. Stedman moved closer to the mirror to inspect the damage and grimaced at the remains of the pigeons' lunch.

"How can a pigeon eat that much?" He grumbled. As he stared into the mirror he wondered, *What are the odds that a pigeon would crap on me at that moment?* He pushed the thought out of his mind and turned the faucet on. Pulling the last paper towels out of the dispenser, he wet them and wiped his face, cheeks and hair, then he leaned in and found more on his collar. Swearing again, he scrubbed it furiously and checked his reflection. It looked like he'd been hit with a water balloon.

"Well," he said to his reflection. "There's not much else that can go wrong today."

How wrong he was.

Demetrius Chandler found concentrating difficult. The last class of the day, Choir, was taught by Mr. Kocik, an amazing vocal teacher. Adept at both piano and voice, Mr. Kocik could bring out the best in every young person. The mustachioed teacher (one of the few public smokers in Amicable) required that the students not only learn how to sing solos, but also wanted them to learn to be part of a vocal team. This, of course, had ramifications in all areas of life. Many Amicable alumni would give honor to Mr. Kocik for teaching them the value of working with people and not against them.

"Demetrius, where is your brain today?"

Demetrius blinked twice. He had been pondering the sight of his mother on top of a roof dropping something on top of the insurance investigator.

"Sorry, Mr. Kocik."

"No, really, what is it?" The Bohemian's eyes were alight with inquisitiveness.

"I… um… well, I've just been wondering what the point of music is." Demetrius blushed.

"Okay, everyone, take a seat." Mr. Kocik motioned with his hand and then spoke to the choir collectively. "I'm not understanding your question."

"Why do people make music? I guess the question for me is: when all this has happened in Amicable, you know, and the town is dying, and, I mean, why are we in here on a Tuesday afternoon singing?"

"Interesting question, Demetrius. What does everyone else think?" Mr. Kocik closed the music and walked around to sit in front of the piano.

A tenth-grade girl raised her hand. "It expresses emotion."

"Okay," the teacher responded, "but we can express emotions in many different ways. Art does it, I suppose, but certainly we could simply tell people, 'Hey, I'm feeling sad,' or "I think I hate you today." This made the kids laugh.

"Yeah, I guess," another girl said, "but music changes the meaning from thought to feeling. You can tell me you're sad, but when I hear it in a song, something makes me understand. It makes me reflect on it."

"Or," a boy sitting to the left of Demetrius broke in, "music does something to our brains; some kind of drug maybe."

"Good. Good. Music has been shown to release endorphins just like eating good food, being intimate or even listening to stimulating conversation." These kinds of discussions did not always happen in high school, but in Mr. Kocik's class, all topics were allowed simply because music was part of every kind of event under the sun.

"But," Demetrius pushed, "isn't it a bad thing to be singing when there is so much... pain outside these walls?"

Mr. Kocik's eyes narrowed. "You know, Demetrius, you've got a great mind, but when you answer this question for yourself, something deep inside you will fundamentally change. The abyss of your soul will fill with amazement."

"I have no idea what you're talking about, Mr. Kocik," a tenth-grade girl responded, which caused snickers.

Scratching his head, Mr. Kocik leaned back in his chair. "Since the beginning of time, humankind has been singing - in fact, most of creation has its own song - and humans sing most profoundly in their grief. Sometimes, music is the only thing that can bring people from grief back to life. Some of the most powerful songs of all time have been written when the composer was in pain, or terrified, or horrified. The greatest composers, Beethoven, Mozart, The Beatles, Aretha Franklin, Eminem, you name them, were inspired by tragedy to put their pain into sound."

"But why?" Demetrius was insistent.

"I don't know, Demetrius. I only know that it works. I don't know why gravity works, only that if I throw my pen up into the air, it will come down. I know that for me, if I have encountered pain, there will be a song that speaks to it. And when I find it, I'll hold onto it like a drowning man holding an upside down lifeboat, until I'm rescued."

"What are you saying, Mr. Kocik?"

He smiled sadly at Demetrius and his eyes flicked towards the blue sky outside the window. "I'm saying that Amicable needs to keep singing or we'll drown in our sorrow."

Stedman slammed the door. Although it was hot in the car, he sat fuming in the front seat. Pounding on the wheel twice with his hands, he produced the key from the pocket of his pants and started the engine. He revved it furiously then pulled out into traffic. He wanted to give the one finger wave to Peterson Butchery, but he didn't take the time to roll down his window.

Turning left to drive in the opposite direction of his residence (because Main Street was one way) he pulled into the 'flow,' which was all of two pickup trucks putzing down the road. When a yokel stopped in the middle of the street to allow another car to back out from the white strips on the side, Stedman finally lost his cool and pulled around the pickup truck, narrowly missing the car, which was pulling out. With a blurt of his horn, Stedman swore out the window, squealed his tires and peeled down the street. Turning left, he looked up at the top of the brick wall and angrily flipped the bird to where the pigeons had been. As he did so, he heard a squawk and spotted flashing lights behind him.

A police car.

Gritting his teeth and shouting profanities into the windshield, Stedman Boswell pounded his fists again on the steering wheel. *Great! Just great! What is this stupid small-town cop pulling me over for? Boredom? Idiocy?*

Louise Nelson opened the door of her police car and stepped out to approach the Porsche. Nearing the window with curiosity, she tapped on the window of the sports car. When the window finished rolling down, Stedman Boswell's red face appeared.

"Good afternoon, Sir. Can I see your license, please?"

Boswell stared ahead at the window, hands grasping the steering wheel so tightly that his knuckles had turned a sickly pink and white.

"What seems to be the problem, officer?" His teeth were clenched so tightly it was hard for Louise to understand the words.

"You were driving a little dangerously back there, werntcha?"

He shook his head. "I swerved to avoid a pickup truck that had stopped in the middle of the road."

"Be that as it may, you roared past them pretty good. Swore at him, too, sounded like."

"Oh, please. Are you going to write me a ticket for profanity?"

"No, I'm going to write you a ticket for reckless driving." Louise pulled out her ticket book. "License, please."

"Look, officer, I've had a really bad day. I even got shit on by a bird." He pointed to his shirt.

"There still is no need for that kind of language."

"You know what…?" Stedman had had enough. "Shit! Shit! Shit! Damnit! Bullhockey!"

Louise gasped. "All right, sir, I'm going to have to ask you to step out of the car." She backed up and put a hand on her Taser.

"This is ridiculous. I wasn't even doing anything wrong. It's just this little Podunk, fly speck town on a map that is seriously f…"

"Do not finish that statement, sir. You have exactly five seconds to get out of the car or I'm going to have to take you in for resisting arrest."

Stedman laughed maniacally and opened the door. "Where are you going to take me? Your cousin Janie's basement, or the back side of Farmer Pete's hog shed?" He pushed the door open, almost hitting her.

"That's enough, sir."

Stedman, though not a tall man, stood menacingly above the diminutive town police officer. Reaching into his wallet, he produced his driver's license and handed it to Louise, who placed it on her board and began to write him a ticket.

"This is all just a misunderstanding, don't you think?"

"Sir, please move back."

"Look, I just want to get home and out of these clothes." He reached out a hand and placed it on Louise Nelson's shoulder. Not the right thing to do.

Faster than what seemed possible, Officer Nelson brought her knee up into his groin sending exquisite, torturous pain from his balls to his head. Doubling over, Stedman wilted in front of Officer Nelson who pushed him to the ground and put a knee into his back. Grabbing her handcuffs from her utility belt, Louise shackled the young insurance adjuster.

"Why are you arresting me?" he said with panting breath.

"Assaulting a police officer."

"I didn't assault you," he said.

"According to the law, the minute you touched me is the minute you assaulted me. Now, you have the right to remain silent…" Officer Nelson had always wanted to read a 'perp' his rights. Although she had known who this person was after she had seen his license, Louise had no idea the hornet's nest she was stirring.

Stedman Boswell would fume for five more hours before someone came to get him.

Chapter 12.

An affair never begins with the eyes; it begins with the imagination. The Figment, the mind's sliver of discontent, which can imagine both beauty and woe, begins to create that which was not. The Figment sees a back turned at the wrong moment, feels a quiver of distress in the voice, hears a word of discord and assumes, then ultimately believes, that the person to whom their soul has been stitched, is ripping away from them. If conditions are right, the Figment will begin to whisper elsewhere.

So it was with Rhonda Jensen.

Stress and anxiety have a way of negotiating with, or even encouraging, the Figment to give it life. When this happens, the Figment has access to both psychological and spiritual resources, appropriating them for its defense system, to enslave the mind chaining it with false narratives. For Rhonda, Amicable's tragic events were the catalyst for a dialogue with the Figment.

That they loved each other was not in question. But did she trust him? Did he trust her? Her Figment claimed her contentedness simply because they had stopped communication. The ashes of unkindness floated in the air between them. This trajectory, from love to distrust, so sudden and unexpected, gave free rein to Rhonda's Figment, which imagined an entirely new world beginning in the most unlikely of places.

Amicable's jail cell.

Outraged, Janice Stensrud called Rhonda. Louise Nelson had arrested Stedman Boswell for assault and resisting arrest. Both charges seemed odd, considering Louise's mild nature and her genuine inability to write tickets for Amicableans. Sure, sometimes there was the odd noise ordinance violation or an occasional speeding ticket, but a warning almost always did the trick. To arrest someone? It would have taken a lot for Louise to get that riled up. What had Boswell done?

When Leo returned home from the Butchery, she told him what had happened. Butcher, who was washing the dishes, clapped his hands tossing suds into the air, and threw his head back laughing uproariously at the news. Her mother, Connie, who was sitting at their kitchen table holding Georgie in her arms, put her head down.

"Why is that so funny?" Rhonda asked her husband.

"The guy deserved it."

"How so? It seems to me like he's just trying to do his job."

Butcher spoke into the sink as he washed methodically. "His job? Are you joking? He's not trying to do his job. He's trying to do his employer's job. He's a minion of injustice, that's what he is." Butcher shook his hands twice and turned for the towel. When he turned around, he noticed Rhonda standing with arms crossed and eyebrows frowning. "What?"

"I think that there is some injustice about… what happened to *him*. I mean, what could have happened to set him off like that? Janice said that Louise arrested him for assault. Don't you think that's hard to believe?"

Butcher shook his head and walked past Rhonda. "No. He probably tried to manipulate Louise into letting him off because he was an outsider, and when she didn't, he probably did, or said, something stupid."

"But what set him off? Every time I've met with him, he seemed like a nice guy just trying to do his job."

"A nice guy? A nice guy? Be careful, Hon." The hair raised on Butcher's neck and he stopped to turn back to her. Connie was studying her fingernails intently at the table.

"When we met with him today, he was quiet and withdrawn. Eventually, he came around."

Butcher's jaw clenched. "I'll bet."

"What do you mean?"

"He came around because you guys are helping him…" he crossed his arms mirroring his wife. "You're helping him rip the guts out of this town."

"I can't believe you, Leopold Jensen! Six years ago when you showed up in Amicable, everyone thought YOU were trying to rip the guts out of the town. Remember? YOU!"

"Oh, here we go. Always about Leopold Jensen and if he would have just left nice old Amicable to its own, everything would still be nice and friendly."

"All that I'm saying is: give the guy a chance to do his work, get us our money, and leave."

"You don't understand, Rhonda! This guy is bad news! I read it in him. He has no intention, NONE! of helping us rebuild Amicable!" Butcher's voice raised with each word.

"Can we just..." Connie interrupted softly. Georgie tensed in her lap.

"Can't you see, Butcher, that your endless reading of people is actually part of the problem? You're the one who actually makes them self-fulfilling prophecies." Rhonda's anger was getting the best of her.

"Oh, so now this is all my fault? That's rich." Butcher opened the front door. "I'll see you later." Just as he was about to slam it behind him, he stopped and pointed a finger at her. "Be very careful, Rhonda *Jensen*." His stress of her married name brought a frown from both Rhonda and Connie.

Rhonda grabbed the car keys from the bookshelf by the front door. "I have to go to the jail, Mother. Please look after the children until I get home."

Connie squeezed Georgie as her daughter followed Butcher out the door.

Ten minutes later, Rhonda pulled up in front of the one cell police station. The cell, an open-aired cage locked with an old-fashioned skeleton key lock, was situated in the corner of the main room. In the back of the station there was an 'interrogation room,' but for the last few years, its typical purpose was that of a storage closet.

Peering through the police station window, Rhonda spotted Louise at the front desk typing notes into her computer. Without knocking, Rhonda entered and strode through the waiting area lined with uncomfortable looking plastic chairs and a row of snack machines. A happy little coffee pot sat in front of the windowsill. The coffee inside appeared more like crude oil than coffee.

"Hello, Rhonda."

"Louise." Rhonda's gaze was drawn to the cell where Stedman Boswell was sitting, bent over. His eyes met hers when she walked in, but then ashamedly went back to his hands. "Do you have a few minutes to tell me what happened?"

Louise shook her head. "I can't discuss the details of an investigation…"

"Come on, Louise, you know I won't say anything," Rhonda said quietly. "I'm not a frickin' New York Times journalist... Talk to me."

Louise sighed and came out from behind her desk. Almost a foot shorter than Rhonda, Louise stared up into her eyes and recounted the incident.

"Has he said anything else about why he snapped?" she asked quietly.

"He said he had a bad morning and then a bird crapped on him."

"Do you think that he's a danger to himself or the town?"

"No," Louise replied quickly. "He doesn't seem like he would hurt anyone, really." She lowered her voice. "I actually regret having to get physical with him, but he put his hand on me. I didn't want to get hurt." Louise looked guiltily at the cell.

"It's not your fault," Rhonda replied. "How about we let him go home to cool off and then we can talk about it tomorrow?"

"What do you want me to do with the charges?"

Rhonda leaned in. "Would it be appropriate for me to suggest we drop the charges? You could still ticket him for reckless driving, but maybe assault and resisting arrest can go away."

"Yes, you're probably right," Louise said. "Do you want to talk to him?"

Nodding, Rhonda moved towards the cell. His anger had dissipated. He was left with strangely vacant eyes. Unlocking the door, Louise ushered Rhonda inside leaving them to speak quietly. Rhonda moved to the bench beside Boswell. She sat apart from him and leaned back against the wall stretching out her long legs in front of her.

"Been quite a day."

He didn't answer.

"Do you want to talk about it?"

He cleared his throat. "Not really."

"Officer Nelson has agreed to let you go home. She also dropped the assault charges, although there may be a fine for the moving violations. Does that sound all right with you?"

He nodded, saying nothing. He looked ashamed. Then, he turned his eyes up to hers. They were green, ringed with emotion, not from what he had done, but something deeper.

As she looked into his eyes, the Figment stirred inside her hungrily. Unconsciously, she began to feed it.

He was a beautiful, but delicate, man. His brown hair framed his face nicely. Unlike Butcher, Boswell was still young enough not to be going grey. There was a wiry strength about him: thin arms covered by light peach fuzz, broad, but skinny, shoulders; his jaw muscles stood out from years of chewing gum. Although he was not quite as tall as she, he possessed an inner largeness, or at least that what's her Figment whispered. As he stood up, she noticed his clothes, the cut and fit were perfect.

Feed me, her Figment whispered.

"Can I offer you a bite to eat?" Rhonda asked without thinking. Tongues would wag in Amicable if she were caught sharing a meal with him, but at this point, her Figment had convinced her that she was doing the will of the town council. Technically, they wanted her to grease the wheels, make the process go faster.

Stedman couldn't quite control the quizzical expression crossing his face. Certainly, he knew which side she was on. Was she going to feed him sugar and then switch it to salt?

"Why would you do that? It seems like everyone else in this tin-pot town has it out for me. What's in it for you?"

"Nothing," she said simply. "I think you've had a rough day and it would be nice to end it well. I know a great place in Clancy if you want to get out of Amicable."

"That's the understatement of the year."

"Do you want to get changed?"

"Yes." He looked down at his clothes. He could still smell the dung on his collar. "Can I meet you somewhere? What's the name of the restaurant?"

"How about I'll wait for you by the elevator and you can pick me up in your fancy car. I've never ridden in a Porsche before."

Stedman Boswell smiled and nodded. "I'll see you in forty-five minutes."

Rhonda and he exited the cell door together and, after retrieving his phone, his keys and personal items, they walked outside.

I'm hungry.

Demetrius strolled up the front path to his house, one hand in a pocket, exercise bag held by the other. Cats sprawled across the front steps like furry bumps while cicadas hummed slightly in the trees. Still the tail end of summer, the trees had not yet begun to turn color, but there was a scent in the air as if things were about to change again. Demetrius trudged up the steps and moved one of the cats out of the way hissing. Pulling open the noisy screen door, Demetrius held it with his foot as he maneuvered the large exercise bag into the house. Football practice had been predictably long tonight. After their lopsided loss on Friday, the coach thought more practice would un-lop the losses.

Demetrius opened the front door of the house and ducked to enter. His mother was finishing preparations for dinner while his father sat at the table watching the news on TV.

"Hello, Demetrius," said his dad. "How was school?"

"Interesting," Demetrius padded through the kitchen to put his dirty clothes into the laundry. He looked at his mother who was whistling as she stirred the meat and sauce mixture in a pan. Angela smiled at him, then at Dennis, and went back to stirring.

After returning to the kitchen, he pulled out a chair and sank into it. It groaned under his bulk. "Classes were fine, but something weird happened at lunchtime."

Dennis responded without looking away from the screen. "What was it?"

"When Aaron and I walked uptown for lunch, we noticed that new guy in town, Boswell, walking towards us. A couple of ladies - one of them for sure was Mrs. Johnson, I could tell by her walker - were talking to him and all of a sudden…" He looked up at his mother whose eyes had gone wide. "Something dropped on him from the top of the building. I mean, why would anyone drop a water balloon from the top of a building? That would be weird."

"Yes, that's very weird," his dad replied.

"But what was really strange, was that I saw two people on top of the building, and one of them looked just like you Mom."

Momentarily speechless, Angela giggled and laughed too loudly. "That's silly. I've been here all day. Maybe it was some kids having a practical joke. You know how kids are these days."

"That doesn't make sense."

"I don't know," Angela's voice trembled, "but I hope they catch them. Can't have that kind of hooliganism going on in Amicable. Anarchy, I tell you."

Demetrius frowned, but said nothing more.

"Anyway," Angela said, "let's eat. I'm sure you're all hungry."

What was she hiding? Demetrius thought.

As they drove to Clancy for an evening meal, Stedman Boswell retracted the roof of his Porsche allowing the wind to blow freely through Rhonda Jensen's hair. While the ride passed, Stedman glanced at her in the passenger seat. The western sun made her face glow. Her eyes were closed. "What do you think of the car?"

"It's beautiful," she said without opening her eyes.

"I bought it a few years ago after my promotion at work."

"Hmmm."

Stedman was frustrated. *She's so small town…*

"So, have you lived in Amicable your whole life?"

"Yes."

"Do you like it?"

"Of course. Everyone I love lives in this town: my mother, my family, my friends, my work. I don't have to drive a long distance to get anywhere. I enjoy the lifestyle." She sighed. "How about you? Do you like the small town?"

"Not so much."

"Why not?"

He shrugged without releasing the steering wheel. "I guess it's just what you get used to. I grew up in the city; all the people I know are cultured, they have big hopes for the future, they have lots of expensive things."

"You don't think those happen in Amicable?"

He snorted. "No, I don't think those things happen here." She raised an eyebrow. "Okay, it's like this: who has the most expensive house in town?"

"The Cromwells."

"What do Mr. and Mrs. Cromwell do for a living to have such a large mansion?" His voice dripped with sarcasm.

"They sell fertilizer." Stedman's mouth twisted into an ironic smile. "Ah, you think it's not a worthy business?" Her cheeks flushed with anger.

"No, no, it's not that, but they sell shit for a living."

"That's the pot calling the kettle black."

"What do you mean?" He looked to his right at her flashing eyes and clenched jaw.

"Insurance. It's a crock. Insurance companies rip customers off. People pay the insurer to 'protect' them, yet when it comes to paying out, they find inventive ways to circumvent living up to their end of the bargain. Highly excremental, if you ask me."

"Interesting," Stedman said.

"Look, I know you've come to Amicable to assess whether the town will be compensated for its loss. The town has paid its premiums for decades. Now that a tragedy has occurred, you've been sent to work us over. You take our money, invest it in something else, then delay payment as long as possible until the policy holder gives up, isn't that right?"

"That's a bit unfair," Stedman pouted.

"Admit it," Rhonda pushed. "If Baker fails to pay up the fifty million policy, Amicable is finished." She crossed her arms. "And some very good people - almost all of them - will have to watch their town slowly suffer and die before their eyes. How's that for a nice broadside on your conscience?"

Chapter 12.

"What makes you so sure that I'm going to attempt to screw the town?"

Rhonda's eyes flashed again and her husband's face appeared. Briefly, a stab of guilt punctured her conscience. "I have my ways of knowing."

"Women's intuition?"

"Something like that." She paused. "Mr. Boswell, would you please turn the car around? I think I need to go home."

Stedman frowned. "But we haven't eaten yet. I'm hungry. I need to be fed." He manufactured doe eyes and pleaded with her. "Please."

Rhonda sighed. *The council was depending on her.*

"Fine, but I need to be home by ten."

"No problem," Boswell eyed her profile beside him. "I'll certainly have you home before then."

Unsure what to say or how to say it, the last miles to Clancy passed in silence. After arriving at the Creek Restaurant, Stedman parked the car across two parking spaces. He noticed Rhonda's frown, but this type of parking was second nature to him; the Porsche was his everything.

The restaurant, situated on the banks of a beautiful little river, had a watermill burbling on the back side. A few cars dotted the parking lot, but business was obviously slow. A Tuesday night.

Stedman held the door for Rhonda and they entered the reception area. An older man was holding a coat open for his wife who was roundly criticizing his help. In the dining area, two tables were occupied by mute, middle-aged couples who were out for an 'exciting' date. The men were staring morosely at a television on the wall while their partners forked their way through the salad bar offerings.

A young server seated them at a table near the window overlooking the waterwheel. Rhonda thanked her and they sat.

Perusing the menu, Rhonda was suddenly transported back to her first date with Butcher. An eerie, guilty feeling settled over her and she smiled uncomfortably at the man across the table from her.

"What's good to eat here?" Stedman asked.

"The burgers are good. If you like steak, they do that pretty well, too."

135

"What about drinks?"

Rhonda shrugged. "You can have something if you want."

"You don't want anything? I'm buying."

"No, no, you go ahead."

While she pretended to scan the menu, he stared at her. "Is something wrong?"

"Why do you ask?"

"You seem nervous. Jumpy."

Rhonda's eyes shifted to the mill. "Why would I be nervous?"

"Because you're sitting across the table from a handsome man." He laughed, but she blushed.

"I think I'll have the chicken."

"I'm sorry if I've offended you," he said.

"You haven't offended me," she corrected, "my discomfort is that I don't do this."

"Do what?"

"I don't go out to eat, ever, not even with my family."

Stedman's eyes narrowed. "With your husband?"

"And my children."

"How did you and your husband meet?"

At that moment, the server interrupted the conversation and took their orders. Rhonda smiled uncomfortably and pointed to the chicken while Stedman ordered the steak. The server nodded after he asked for a beer and then turned to make her way to the bar.

Leaning back in his chair, Stedman raised his eyebrows. "And...?"

"Mr. Boswell..." Rhonda started, desperately trying to keep her mind from the growing physical attraction. There was something so enticing about him, not just his appearance, but also his confidence.

"Stedman."

She sighed. "Stedman, I would prefer not to talk about him or my family. If you want, we can talk about the elevator."

Rolling his eyes, Stedman leaned forward. "Come on, Rhonda. We'll be talking about that for weeks in Amicable. We're not there now. We're here – apart from everything. Let's talk about something else. Something about you – who you are. What makes you tick?"

"I'm not that interesting," she replied untruthfully.

"Let me be the judge of that."

"What do you want to know?"

The server brought Stedman's beer and placed it on a coaster in front of him. Rhonda thanked her.

"Have you always lived in Amicable?"

There was a hitch in Rhonda's reply, one moment too long before lying to him. "Yes." Her traumatic history flashed, but she squelched it.

"I'm not sure if I believe that."

"Believe it."

"Tell me about Amicable. Why you stay?"

Relaxing, she told the story of Amicable's hold on people. Rhonda spoke of a history of caring people, founded on principles of solid citizenship undergirded by an agrarian lifestyle. Growing up in the small town had not only shaped who she was, but defined who she would be. From a talented athlete and student, to a devoted mother and wife, the people of Amicable had supported her through the journey.

"And now that you're settled, don't you ever want anything more?"

"What do you mean?"

He laughed. "Adventure, excitement, I don't know, life with a few risks." His eyes captured her. Rhonda tried to look away, but she couldn't.

Feeling her throat dry, she took a sip of water. Mercifully, the server came out with their meals and placed the plates in front of them. Stedman was irritated by the second interruption.

As Rhonda began to cut up her chicken, Stedman sipped his beer. "We keep getting interrupted."

Rhonda nodded, swallowing.

"Isn't there anything more to life than eating, sleeping, loving and dying?" His question bore a hole into her heart.

Mouth full, she covered it and swallowed before answering. "Yes, I had designs of a different life at one time, but I'm happy now."

"What did you want to do?"

She wiped her mouth and changed the subject. "Do you have dreams?"

He snorted. "What do you mean, like visions when I fall asleep or goals in life?"

"Either. Both."

"Yeah, of course." He took a bite of his steak. "I want to have the finer things in life. You know, a big house, nice car, maybe a wife…" When she blushed, he cleared his throat. "But sleeping? I don't know. I suppose. How about you?"

Rhonda continued to eat her chicken. She punctuated her sentences with her fork. "When I was a little girl, I used to have dreams about all sorts of things - the typical stuff: bicycles, ponies, friends and such. But I had one recurrent dream."

Stedman followed her movements, the graceful way she moved, the tendrils of hair floating just behind her ears. As she spoke, the waterwheel in the background plodded along steadily, pushed by a never-ending stream.

"It's morning, and I'm leaving my house. My mother has fixed my hair in pigtails. I'm wearing a little jumpsuit, pink, I think. My shoes are white - so white that they look like they're actually shining. As I walk out the door, my mother doesn't say anything to me, but I can somehow tell that she is worried. When I walk down the front steps and onto the road, I'm aware that a solitary bird is singing *Girls Just Wanna Have Fun* in the background."

Stedman laughed.

"As the robin is singing, I bop down the road, but it gets darker and darker and I meet three different people, or objects. They are blurred, and even though I can't see them, I can feel what they are. Does that make sense?"

"Yes. I know what you mean."

"The first is a rapidly rising green balloon. It snags on a tree but doesn't pop. The wind takes it from the branches, farther and farther into the sky until a raven flies by and pops it. The pieces fall back to the earth. When it finally reaches the ground, limp and lifeless, along comes a big, old grizzly bear, which picks it up in its hands and re-inflates it.

138

Chapter 12.

Somehow, it fills. Slowly, almost tentatively, like it's going to pop again. The outside of the balloon looks like it's stitched together."

"Fascinating. Does it burst?"

Rhonda shook her head. "No, but it always seems to be close."

"Then what happens?"

"The grizzly bear carries it for a while, like, I don't know, it's teaching it how to fly again, and then it does, but the balloon doesn't go quite as high. It just kind of hangs around the bear waiting for the ravens again."

"Do they come again?"

"I don't know. I don't think so. I used to wake up at that point. It got too dark."

"Do you ever have that dream anymore?"

Rhonda set her silverware down and stared at Boswell aware that she was revealing something very personal. "A few nights ago." *It had been a very long time…*

"What do you think it means?"

"I have no idea."

Boswell picked up his napkin and wiped his mouth. "Why did you tell me? Did you think I could interpret it for you?"

Rhonda frowned. "No… well… I'm not sure why I told you."

"Do you want me to try to interpret it?"

She laughed and motioned with her hands. "Sure. Go ahead and try."

"You're the balloon."

She shook her head. "No, I'm the one carrying the balloon, remember?"

"Yes, you are the little girl, but you're the balloon, also. The balloon is filled with your hopes and dreams." Rhonda's eyes widened. "As you grew up, you flew high. Your dreams came true until…" He watched her eyes to see if he was on the right track. "You met someone who popped your balloon and you came crashing back to the earth, back to Amicable. Is any of this right?"

"Oh gosh…. That's amazing."

"So the pieces of the balloon were your shattered hopes for a life outside Amicable. This grizzly bear, an untamed animal, a friend -

maybe even your husband, who knows - put you back together and now you float by his side afraid to fly high again."

Rhonda was silent. Frightened. Butcher was the only one who had ever done this for her, *to her*, although in a very different way.

"You're old enough now to look back and realize that you missed out on something, some higher calling. And that grizzly - you know that he can't come with you?"

Rhonda's hands shook. She hadn't realized how much she wanted to do something different in life. Amicable did not scream life-fulfilment. She had always wanted to live in the big city - travel - let her hair down, cut her hair off - she just hadn't thought about it for a while. Rhonda knew contentedness with Butcher, but was this the happily-ever-after she'd always wanted? Or, was it just a settling for second-best-safe-place that kept her from experiencing the fear that comes with pre-meditated failure? When he finished interpreting, Rhonda felt a warmth growing in her stomach, a growling of discontent. Sitting across from her was a way out. A way to fly. And yet...

"I need to go."

"No, but, wait..." Stedman said as he reached his hand out to her. She recoiled. "I'm sorry if I upset you. I'm sure I'm probably way off base..."

"It's not you. I have to get home."

"But it's still early. Let me at least finish my dinner." He pointed at his half-eaten steak.

Sighing, Rhonda nodded her head but pushed her plate away.

Conversation remained shallow as Stedman finished his meal. The other diners had since left; only a few remained at the bar chatting amiably with the bartender who was busily washing dishes while listening to the tales of the lonely with one ear.

While he ate, Rhonda attempted not to watch him, but she was caught by his soft, white hands, his delicate cheekbones and his long eyelashes. Everything about him was the opposite of Butcher and yet she continued to find herself powerfully attracted to him. Stedman didn't speak with his mouth full, but he paused to wipe his lips with the paper napkin before answering. His lips, thin with just a shadow of a moustache bordering them, seemed curiously kissable. Rhonda blushed.

"What's wrong? What are you thinking about?" Stedman asked.

"Nothing. Oh, nothing."

Once again, he wiped his mouth, reset the napkin in his lap (Amicableans normally set the dirty napkins on the table), and smiled bemusedly at her. "You look like the Cheshire Cat."

Rhonda shook her head. "I was just thinking about your life in the city and how different it is to here."

"And that's a good thing?"

"Different. Just different."

Stedman held her eyes and then, with a resolute nod, said, "Let's get out of here."

Rhonda's heart quivered. *How beautiful he is.* "Great."

After paying the bill, Stedman led Rhonda back out to the Porsche and opened the door for her. She thanked him and moved into the seat. The full moon hung suspended above them, a string-less white balloon released into the heavens. The moon's illuminating glow shimmered across Stedman's face as he dropped into the driver's seat. Smiling at her, he started the car and it rumbled to life. Putting the top back down, Stedman drove out of the parking lot and back down the road to Amicable.

"Did you have a good night?"

She nodded, knowing that any words she spoke now could be misconstrued as encouragement.

"I had the worst day," he said, "with the meeting and then the bird crapping on my head and then the arrest, but then you made it turn out good."

A slight, wary smile touched her lips.

"Funny how better than average food and good conversation does that."

She didn't respond.

Lips pursing, Stedman turned toward her again. "Have I done something to offend you?"

She shook her head.

"Is it about our conversation, you know, the dream thing, in the restaurant?"

Shrugging, she looked to her side to see the rapidly passing landscape whiz by. Blurry, the dark stalks of corn, shaded yet shimmering in the moonlight, seemed like watchers; faces accusing her of much more than a misdemeanor. As judge, jury and jailors, they held court over her thoughts. Did she really want to leave Amicable again? Her life? Was she missing out on something?

"No," she finally responded, "you haven't offended me. I'm just reflecting on the way life turns out."

"Is this what you want?" he asked boldly, uncaring of the way it sounded.

"Look, Stedman, you don't understand…"

"No, I don't. Help me to understand."

"My husband, well, let's just say our meal together would not be a particularly positive thing for you, and me, if he were to find out."

"We were just having dinner together after a tough day." A green distance sign flashed by. Three miles to Amicable.

Rhonda looked down to her lap. "Those are the little lies that become half-truths which grow to be large distractions. That's what my husband says. I can never lie to him."

"That must be good, right?" Stedman felt the conversation spiraling away from where he wanted, but she needed to get something off her chest.

She snorted. "It's impossible to lie to him."

"Why is that?"

"Because he has a gift. He's a human lie-detector."

Two miles to Amicable.

"What, you mean he's perceptive?"

"You could say that." He waited for her to continue. "Okay, he's a man who can look at you, and within a moment, he's got a full read of who you are, where you've been and probably where you're going."

A cold, sinking sensation flooded Stedman's veins. Putting two and two together, his mouth dropped. "Your husband's a butcher, isn't he?"

Head down, she nodded into her chest.

One mile to Amicable.

Chapter 12.

Well, Stedman thought, *this has certainly taken a hairpin turn.* "It's hard for you to live with that kind of pressure, isn't it?"

A few tears dropped from her eyes. "You have no idea."

Entering the 'city limits,' Stedman slowed the car. "I don't know where you live."

"Over by the school."

Flicking the blinker upwards, he turned left next to the Casey's and moved towards Winslow Park. Suddenly, Rhonda reached her hand out and grabbed his forearm. "Stedman, you can't drop me off at the house. How would that look?"

"I suppose you're right." He slowed the car and pulled off to the shoulder of the road. "Where would you like me to take you."

Looking to her left at the park, she nodded. "This will be fine, thank you."

Taking a risk, Stedman put a hand over hers. "Thank you for the night. I really appreciate it." Electricity sparked at the touch of their skin. Letting his hand linger for a millisecond too long, Rhonda's Figment almost devoured her. His face was just near hers. Those lips that she had stared at. The luxury car in which she'd had a taste of the good life was around her. Would it be so hard?

Suddenly, a semi used its air brakes behind them, a roaring, contrary sound which shredded the intimate moment. Startled back to reality, Rhonda pulled her hand from under his.

"From now on, Stedman, everything is professional."

"Of course," he said with a cat-like smile.

Opening the door, Rhonda exited the car and began to walk home. Stedman watched her momentarily and then made a U-turn and drove back to Peppertree.

Emboldened by the thought of destroying the butcher, Stedman grinned malevolently as he drove past the ruined elevator and back to his rental house. *Professional. Sure thing, Mrs. Butcher.*

Chapter 13.

Rhonda stood in front of the mirror, noticing already her puffy eyes and blotchy cheeks. They'd had a fight. Butcher, by nature of his gift, had never been a jealous person - he had never needed to be - but when she had returned home at 10:30 on Tuesday night, he had, for the first time, wondered about her whereabouts. Although she had told him the half-truth, that she had been encouraged by the town council to bring goodwill to the insurance adjuster, just as he could sense the little white lie, she could read in his face a wariness to believe her.

Butcher was waiting for her in the living room. He had risen early, as was his practice, showered and dressed in his black suit and tie. He only had one suit and one tie, and he had only worn the outfit once before - to their wedding. They woke the children; Georgie did not understand why she was being pulled from bed. J.T. thought they were going on an adventure.

"Dad, why are you wearing that?" J.T. stood alongside his father in his pajamas.

"We're going to church today."

"But it's not the right day, is it?"

"No, it's not the right day. Something very different is going to happen."

"What is it?"

"Uncle George is going to be buried today."

J.T. frowned. He wasn't quite sure what this meant. The little boy had buried all sorts of things in the back yard: Matchbox cars, his sister's Barbie doll, little green army men and, when he thought his parents weren't looking, he tried to bury all the canned peas in the house. J.T. hated peas. Burying Unca Dorge - that sounded weird. J.T. didn't think Dorge would like to have all that dirt on him. Really, there were a lot better things to do with Unca Dorge, like going for a walk, playing cowboys and Indians, throwing marshmallows at each other - anything - but burying him. That was just plain dumb.

"I don't get it." J.T. rested his hand on his dad's arm.

Chapter 13.

"John Thomas," Butcher's voice broke, "just give me a minute."
Butcher stood up and moved to the kitchen sink. At that moment,
Rhonda emerged wearing a stunning black dress. She had pulled her hair
up away from her neck. A cross hung in the crevice of her throat.

"Mommy, what's wrong with Daddy? And why is Unca Dorge
going to be buried? I want him to come back. Where did he go? I want
to play cars…"

Why? Where did he go? – These questions broke her heart anew.
Fresh tears squeezed from the corners of her eyes. Unlike her husband,
she allowed her son to see her sorrow. J.T. ran to his mother and threw
his arms around her legs squeezing her knees. They weren't yet sure if
J.T. or Georgie had Butcher's gift, but the little boy was, even at a young
age, very perceptive.

"Mommy, Unca Dorge died, didn't he?"

"Yes, Sweetie," she said as she knelt beside him. "Uncle George
died and went to be with Jesus."

"But, but," J.T. tried to connect the dots, "I didn't give him any
of my cars so that he can play with Jesus."

Rhonda laughed through her sob and hugged the little boy.
Georgie appeared and pulled out a chair. After climbing into the seat, she
announced that she was ready for her breakfast. Butcher, without
speaking, fulfilled the request. Immediately, Georgie began to dig into
the cereal, spilling drips on the table in front of her and stringing milk
pearls on her chin. Rhonda looked up at her husband to catch his eye,
but he averted his gaze.

Rhonda stood and smoothed her dress. "As soon as the kids
have finished their breakfast, we'll have to get them dressed and get
moving."

"I know."

"Are you okay?" She asked.

"I'm fine."

"Can you please look at me?"

"Yes?"

"I know you're not fine. You haven't been fine all week. There's
a lot of pressure, I know, but things will get better. Once George's
funeral is out of the way…"

Butcher's jaw clenched.

"What? What do you want to say?" Rhonda moved closer to him, reaching out for his hand.

"George's funeral is not going to get anything out of the way. You may be able to put his death behind you, but not me."

"That's not what I meant." Rhonda could feel her cheeks flushing, the argument resurfacing.

"Getting ready to put all this behind you, move on to new life…"

Rhonda scowled. "I'm not sure I like what you're insinuating."

"At least I'm staying home with the kids at night while you're dallying with the enemy," he covered his mouth sarcastically, "oops, I meant delaying Stedman Boswell."

"Oh, Leo, how could you?" Georgie covered her ears with her hands while still chewing her soggy cereal. "I'm trying to fix everything. The council has asked me to smooth the waters with him; I'm trying to take care of my fam…"

"Oh that's rich! Smooth the waters? Is that what you're doing? And taking care of your family. Which night have you been home this week?" Butcher took Georgie's unfinished cereal bowl from underneath her face and dumped the remnants into the sink, causing the little girl to cry. Then, picking her up, he took her to her room and began to get her ready for the funeral. Rhonda followed them and stood in the doorway while he pulled a white lace dress over her head.

"We'll talk about this when we get home. I don't want to get worked up any more before the funeral."

Butcher shook his head and muttered as his wife left the room. *She doesn't want to get worked up. Poor thing…*

As the Jensen family walked down the steps, they met Connie who was waiting for them at the end of the sidewalk. As they walked west past George's house, each one of them glanced deliberately at the front porch and the window leading into his living room. The grass was freshly mown by local youth. It looked and smelled like he was still there.

Walking past the school beneath the boughs of oak trees, leaves billowing and waving glad tidings to the mournful travelers, they saw students playing on the playground. Young children, dressed in jeans and t-shirts, threw their arms in the air as they cascaded down slides, pulled themselves up the monkey bars or raced across the very safe rubber-topped pavement. Their exuberance for the day was in stark contrast to what was happening just outside the fence.

While the Jensen family trudged towards the church, they were joined by other black-clad families. It was as if the streets of the town were veins, the people, blood cells merging from capillaries into greater vessels towards the heart. A few whispered greetings, but for the most part, Amicable walked in silence. As the school children's screams faded behind them, the Jensen family saw that a few high school students were walking to the church also. Butcher noticed Demetrius and Aaron walking side by side.

The doors of St. Clements were thrown open; the church expressed a slow, mournful sob. Light shone through the stained glass windows, but it seemed muted, dulled by the fact that a saint had died. Most everyone would agree that one hundred and three years was a double overtime for someone's life, yet most wished that somehow the old man could be revived.

The undertakers, dressed in black, stood beside the open casket greeting mourners as they paid their last respects. Rhonda had been dreading this moment since the day George had died. Even though she and Butcher had been the first ones to find him, she still wasn't prepared to see him in the coffin. Even from a distance in the line, Rhonda could see that he was wearing his dark blue suit with dark blue tie. His thin white hair was parted to the side. Liver spotted hands were folded on his chest and his face made up to hide the pale thrall of death. The mortician had done a good job of making it seem as if George was sleeping rather than dead. Georgie jumped the queue and quickly made her way to the casket, where she held onto one of the handles. Looking back at her mother, the three-year-old motioned to Rhonda for her to hurry.

"Can't see, Mommy. Wift me." Rhonda apologized with her eyes to the people she had passed and then with shock, she beheld her second best friend lying in the coffin. Lifting Georgie, they both studied George's corpse, noticing every detail for the last time.

"Why is Unca Dorge sleeping in front of everyone?"

Rhonda shook her head as the first tears pushed out of her eyes. "He's not sleeping, Georgie. He's gone to be with Jesus."

"But he's not!" Georgie argued. "He's wight thewe. I can see him. He's sweeping." She leaned towards George. "Unca Dorge! Unca Dorge! Wake up! Evwyone is watching you!" When he didn't respond, Georgie's eyes looked puzzled and she spoke more quietly. "Unca Dorge. It's time to pway. When you wake up, the Bawbies are having a tea pawty, okay?"

"Okay?" Georgie questioned softly. "Okay, Unca Dorge?" Rhonda was unable to hear the bewilderment any longer and, with a short sob, she turned to take Georgie up the steps and into the sanctuary.

Minutes later, Butcher found them at the back of the church, huddled together in a corner. Connie stood silently, dabbing her eyes with a handkerchief. Half a dozen women gathered with them, speaking softly as if somehow the noise might seem disrespectful.

The next three-quarters of an hour passed with excruciating slowness. Rhonda wanted two things to happen: firstly, that the funeral finish quickly - she couldn't handle much more grief - and secondly, that she wouldn't have to make small talk with anyone else today. Rhonda simply wanted to crawl into bed and sleep.

At nine o'clock, the undertakers discreetly gathered the Jensen family who would walk in behind the casket. George Hendriks had no living relatives. His wife, Mabel, and both of his children had died years before. Rhonda, Butcher and the children were his closest friends.

The casket was closed. A wreath of roses and a crossed thatch of pine branches, George's favorite tree, adorned the wooden frame. Underneath the decorations, an American flag draped the coffin.

Jim the Organist/Mailman (whose mail route was being filled by a substitute), launched into the first hymn (chosen by George, of course). Rhonda and Butcher filed in behind the mortician and his associate, an intern whose name escaped everyone on that day, and most importantly, George. Georgie had buried her face in Rhonda's shoulder while J.T. solemnly held onto his father's hand. As the music played, they slowly filed forward to the front of the church where John Deakins stood.

The Jensens sat in the front row on the right while the undertakers positioned the casket in the center aisle. After readjusting the arrangements, the undertaker and his understudy resumed their solemn position at the back of the church. Photos of George were stationed on easels around the coffin, but none of them were of a solitary George: all of them were pictures of him with other people. The largest was from fifty years ago when he and Mabel, and their children, stood knee deep in Lake Ikmakota peering out over the western edge to a setting sun. Mabel stood with hands on her hips; George, with an arm around his wife, looked on happily while the children were caught in mid-splash. On one side of the coffin sat a smaller photo - George with the Jensen children, and on the other side, George surrounded by a mob of teenagers at the bowling alley.

As Rhonda's eyes fell on the pictures, she felt her heart break. Tears of sadness, sorrow, hope, joy and love spilled over her cheeks and onto Georgie's back. Butcher, sensing but not seeing his wife's tears, attempted to remain stoic, but his lower lip trembled.

John Deakins' voice quivered. "Welcome to the celebration of the life of one of Amicable's great men, George Douglas Hendriks." John Deakins forged his way through the obituary. Moving on to the Bible readings was a relief for John. For him, the Bible became a lifeline of hope thrown out into the depths of grief.

"Most of you have come to farewell a good man, but in reality, George wasn't a good man." Reverend Deakins paused to see the mourners look up quizzically.

"He was an extraordinary man."

John threaded together the hope of George's faith and wove it into a tapestry of love spanning over ten decades. Although he didn't strand himself long on George's military record and his Purple Heart, he knew that George's own heart was much more precious to those in attendance than anything a President, or anyone else, could pin on him. What took up the majority of Reverend Deakins' words was the narrative yarn of the last six years in Amicable: George's compassionate hope for the youth of the town and reminding the community that they were a village of encouragement.

"It's a good thing that we have a heavenly Father," he said, "because it feels like we just lost our earthly one." John stepped down from the pulpit and leaned over the casket, and after bowing deeply, he kissed the wood.

"Goodbye, George. We'll see you later."

Communally, Amicable succumbed to the weight of its collective grief. From every corner of the sanctuary, sniffles and cries began to resound from the pews. Here a stifled sob, there a groan and hitched breath. Like a giant net thrown over a drowning man, the gathered were dragged to the depths of their sorrow. John stood, tears streaming from his face, and saw Leslie, who held her mouth in her hand, weeping. Without thinking, she rose from her seat, left her children and moved quickly to his side, where she embraced him.

As they wept together, John felt another set of arms surround him, then another and another and another and then after looking up, he noticed that the entire congregation was moving forward to circle around the fallen, extraordinary man, George Hendriks.

Together, they mourned, even those who had not moved from their seats. Finally, emotions spent, Reverend Deakins sent them back so they could finish celebrating George's life. Ultimately, smiles replaced sobs, but glistening cheeks were a reminder that loss of life carried both joy in remembering and sorrow in regretting.

John opened the mic for stories to be shared. One by one, most keeping their memories to a minute or two, Amicable shared its appreciation for George. Tracey Thomas, escorted by Derek Peterson, shared her first experiences of recognizing the power of the community in the bowling alley.

Finally, Reverend Deakins nodded at Rhonda. "Our last speaker is Rhonda Jensen, George's best friend. She would like to share some of George's last words with the community."

Rhonda stood slowly and moved to her right and out into the aisle. As she made her way to the lectern, she averted her eyes from both casket and pictures. She needed to look above them, beyond them, past her grief.

"Most places don't care much for old people," she started. "Once you reach a certain age, or a certain decreased productivity level, you get quickly shuffled off to the nursing home." She looked at Gavin Edwards, the director of the Amicable Rest Home, and smiled apologetically. "No offense, Gavin, but I think if given the option, everyone would like to die as George did: in his own home, surrounded by photos of his family and living next door to his best friends."

"Butcher found him," Rhonda continued after clearing her throat. "Butcher, the outsider, the interloper from God knows where," this brought slim laughter from the congregation. "Butcher would be the one to befriend him like no other - even me. He knew him…" At this point, Leopold Jensen inhaled sharply.

He had forgotten. Butcher had forgotten to love.

"But even Butcher couldn't possibly know that George's gift was even greater than his own; George's gift to the town was like… like…" she struggled to find the right metaphor, and then raised a finger when it popped into her mind. "He was like a defibrillator. George's love shocked us back into life." Rhonda's voice trembled and she swallowed waiting for the spasm to pass.

"Butcher found him and then came to get me. George wrote a letter to me, to us - Butcher and I - maybe to all of us - the night he died, and I want to read part of it to you."

She unfolded the piece of paper in front of her and began to read.

Dearest neighbors,

It's late, or should I say early - 2:29 a.m. to be very exact, and I can't sleep. Rhodie, you and I had a discussion not too long ago about the fate of this remarkable small town. I believe I Butcherized the future and pretended to know something about it that may or may not happen, but either way, it's a future that won't have me in it. I can simply fade into the past and be taken to a worry-less place. Don't think that I won't think about you even as I go; it's just that the end of life has a way of taking the edges off what I used to think was important.

Enough of the fatalism.

A voice spoke to me after you left - don't worry, I'm not going that senile, but I am open minded enough to think that there are angels poking around in places that nobody expects. This particular angel seemed to be urging me to add one last sentence to my prophetic vision from earlier in the day.

Baker

> *When all is said and done, and it seems as if Amicable is about to breathe its last:*

One voice, and one voice alone can save this town.
You will recognize the voice when you hear it.

> *I'm realistic to know that I will not be around to hear the voice. But you must, Rhodie. You must. If you don't, Amicable will be no more.*
> *No pressure.*

Rhonda folded the paper up. "He was writing his last will and testament to all of us – to Amicable. You see, we were all his neighbors. We were all his friends. We were everything that he had and all that he wanted, and during his last moments on earth he wanted us to know that the town can and will be saved. Did you hear that?" She paused to let the words sink in. "*When all is said and done, and it seems as if Amicable is about to breathe its last, one voice and one voice alone can save this town.*" She looked around. "Which one of you will that be?"

Letting the power of the moment set in, she sensed that each one of them hoped that they might be the one about whom George had prophesied.

"We don't know when this voice will come, but if our faith is strong, and our hope is enduring and our love is continuing, we'll be ready." She placed her hands on the lectern in front of her.

"George would have wanted it that way." She smiled and tapped the podium once before making her way back down to her seat. After pausing at George's coffin, she whispered something, something so soft that no one else heard it. She returned to her seat next to Butcher. Her heart jumped as he reached out to touch her hand. At that moment, she knew everything was going to be all right.

Rhonda turned. In front of the latecomers was Stedman Boswell who, after watching Rhonda Jensen's eulogy, caught her eye and waved. Strangely, the same feeling she felt for Butcher surged through her, but it was different. It was not the deep throb of shared history, but the feeling of disorientation. She looked away quickly.

152

For Rhonda, the rest of the funeral service passed in agitation. Instead of paying attention to the words, Rhonda flitted back and forth between the profile of her loving husband and her children to the image imprinted on the back of her brain, that of a handsome young man of means. Her mind uncontrollably played out various, polarizing scenarios from punching Boswell in the face to taking the children with him to Kansas City, far, far away from the troubles and meddlesome small-townedness of Amicable. Then, here was Boswell moving to Amicable, where he became part of the community. She, Butcher and Stedman become good friends. Rhonda shook her head. There was no way any of those outcomes would happen.

Finally, and mercifully, the wall-mounted screen flickered at the front where a video montage, one that she and Butcher had produced, began to play. Although George had planned most of his funeral and paid for it all ahead of time, it had been the Jensen's idea to create the video. As the images began to play across the screen, the face of Amicable's town hero flashed humbly on the screen. Behind the photos, Frank Sinatra sang George's favorite song - *You'll Never Walk Alone.*

Rhonda wasn't quite sure when the tears began, somewhere between the end of the storm and the appearance of the golden sky, but she knew that quite possibly she'd never felt this kind of grief in her life. George's death was an anvil on her chest. The hammer pounded, striking with unbelievable force echoing in her very core. Heart thumping, breath heaving, Rhonda watched George's beautiful face transform through the ageing process. From a bouncing baby dressed in knickers and cute little hat, through his high school years, George was an all-American boy. He was a basketball star (like Rhonda) at Amicable High School, then to the military looking excitable and dashing as he headed off to Europe. Then, images appeared of a sad-eyed, loving man who had lost his wife and children.

"Well," Deakins said as he ascended the pulpit again, "I think George would say, 'Enough of that. Let's get bowling.'" Grateful laughter resounded. "I'm not joking," Deakins said, spreading his arms. "The bowling alley will be hosting the funeral party - that's what George wanted - and through the generosity of the bowling alley, there is free bowling for the rest of the afternoon and night." He laid a hand on the casket. "George will be with us at the bowling alley for a few hours before we'll leave for his interment at the Amicable cemetery."

Deakins raised his hands in blessing. "Now may the peace of God which passes all understanding, guard your hearts and minds in Christ Jesus. And," he added with smile, "may you walk with hope in your heart knowing that you'll never walk alone."

As the casket led the way, the Jensen family walked closely behind. The pews emptied mourners spilling into aisles flooding backwards, a rush of humanity longing to be anywhere but in the tomb of their grief. The undertakers, still at their posts by the back door, ushered the attendees out into the bright sunshine, pointing to the bowling alley where the doors were thrown open. The sign above the front door read:

LAST GUTTERBALL FOR GEORGE HENDRIKS. MISSED, BUT NEVER FORGOTTEN.

The undertakers, with the help of the pallbearers, crossed the street and hoisted George's casket up the front steps and through the door. Once inside, the traditional sounds of a bowling alley greeted the mourners. The humming of the ball retrieval machines, the tinging and pinging noise of the arcade games. All of this seemed like business as usual except for the strange sight of the coffin near the front counter. What could have been morbid seemed strangely appropriate.

When Tracey and Derek entered through the front doors, Tracey noticed her father standing with other members of the town council. Tracey was worried about her dad. His brown eyes looked tired and harried as if he hadn't been sleeping.

A group of Amicablean women were seated in the shoe-changing area furtively glancing around to see if anyone was watching them.

"Come on, Derek," Tracey said, as she noticed the women, "let's go to the bar."

They wound their way through the milling crowd nodding and smiling at the cliques of gathered people. The group nearest the coffin seemed indifferent to the fact that they were talking about corn prices while George's body lay two paces away.

Turning into the Greedy Pecker, Derek spotted Shania who smiled and waved to them. Her motion caught the attention of the other person standing at the bar - Stedman Boswell. Even though there were roughly two dozen smartly dressed Amicableans in the bar area, they all stood in pairs or small groups consciously avoiding the outsider.

"He's here," Derek said and stopped short.

"Come on," Tracey said resuming her pulling, "he won't bite. And if he does, I'll protect you."

"I'm not worried about his bite," Derek said, "I'm worried about mine."

She laughed. "You're just a teddy bear."

"Oh really?" He said raising his eyebrows. "That sounds like a challenge."

"No, not a challenge. A reality."

Derek and Tracey pulled out two bar stools and sat down. Shania approached and set out two coasters in front of them. "What can I get for you?"

"I'll have a cola," Derek said. "I've got to get back to work yet today. Dad's manning the shop and he'll be itching to get out."

"He didn't go to the funeral?" Shania pushed the button on the wand, which spurted the cola into a glass.

"He did, but *this* isn't his scene."

"Ah, and you, Tracey?"

"I'll have a glass of water."

At that moment, Derek looked over Tracey's head and froze. Boswell had approached.

"Some nerve showing up here, Boswell," Derek said.

Stedman shrugged. "Is it always like this?" He took a drink and motioned with his glass at the Amicableans. "When there's a death, people head out to the party."

Derek gritted his teeth and noticed Tracey slightly shaking her head in warning. He cleared his throat. "No, just a celebration of a good man."

"It's kind of creepy bringing a corpse into a public space like this. There's got to be some violations broken somewhere. Health laws or something."

"And you'd be good at making sure the authorities would know about the violations, wouldn't you?" Derek sniffed.

Stedman raised his eyebrows. "This country was founded on rules, Mr. Peterson. Rules that have to be followed or people get hurt."

Derek stretched his neck muscles. "Or more importantly in your case, corporations could get hurt. Lawsuits suck, is that right?"

"Insurance is the response to a society that revels in, how shall we say, a certain penchant for litigation." Boswell smirked as he lifted a finger to Shania to order another beer.

Derek's face turned red. "I just figured out why I dislike you so much."

Boswell's eyes narrowed and his hand shook slightly. "Oh yeah? Why is that?"

"Because you're an arrogant, self-absorbed asshole."

Stedman felt a surge of pleasure that he had wedged himself under Derek's skin.

"Okay, boys," Tracey said, "Maybe it's time we go to our corners and cool off." She pulled on Derek's arm.

"It's all right, babe," Boswell said, "eventually you'll get tired of your hayseed boyfriend and get yourself a real man."

Tracey snarled. "Wow, you really are a dipshit."

Boswell noticed that much of the bar was watching them peripherally. Stedman raised his glass to Derek and Tracey and then exclaimed in a loud voice, "Thank you for your hospitality. Y'all have a good day now, y'hear."

Derek's face turned red because it seemed like Boswell got the last word. All eyes in the room focused on Derek and Tracey then back to the exiting insurance man, who strutted out of the room.

Tracey put a hand on Derek's chest. "You did a good job," she said, "my knight in shining armor."

Chapter 14.

Both groups, the town council and the Angels, watched Stedman Boswell swagger out of the bar with a smug look of self-satisfaction. Boswell's eyes completed a circuit of the bowling area catching the looks of curious onlookers. Whistling as he walked past George's casket, Stedman left the bowling alley.

"What do you think that was all about?" David Thomas asked.

Mayor Stensrud shook her head. "He sure seemed pleased with himself."

Elvin Meier chimed in. "I agree. Something is definitely up."

"I thought everything was on track," Dave said.

"I thought Rhonda was supposed to soften him up a little bit. Does anyone know how she's doing?" Elvin added.

"She met with him a couple of times this week," Janice responded. "Supposedly, he's been examining the elevator records and the maintenance history." Janice fidgeted with the red plastic soda cup in front of her.

"So what does that mean?" Dave asked. "Do we just sit around here and wait?"

"Maybe," Janice said quietly, but the words were drowned out by laughter behind them.

"Okay," Linda said confidently, "it's time to press forward." She looked around at the circle of eight women all who were dressed in black, but each dress was drawn from decades past. Most of their dresses had shoulder pads and pleats. Leona's had a small bow positioned at her waist. These women were not prone to spending exorbitant amounts of money on occasional clothes. That was the Amicablean way.

Penny frowned. "I understand in theory about this 'Phase II' thing, but I fail to see how this is going to work. I mean, what if we just make him angry?"

Linda returned the frown. "Chill, Penny. I think we've got him right where we want him. After the next phases of the battle plan, there's no way that he will want to stay in Amicable. He'll be hightailing it like a whipped dog back to Kansas City before you know it."

"Oh, don't say that," Jeannie said. "I can't handle animal abuse. It makes me shiver."

Penny's eyes widened. "Do you realize we killed two birds in the last 'battle plan'?"

"Well, yes, anyway, there's a difference between murdering spare pigeons and beating a defenseless dog."

Angela's voice rose over the din. "To be fair, killing those birds was not necessarily my idea."

"No one's blaming you, dear," Anne Johnson patted her arm. Her walker had been placed to the side where it contained all of her necessities including purse, tissue box, makeup case and her antiquated cell phone, her 'dumbphone,' as she called it.

"I just want to set the record straight that I'm not a bird killer."

"Which," Linda said exasperatedly, "is *so* far beside the point we really don't even need to talk about it."

"So what's the next step?" Connie asked.

"It's a 'phase,' Connie," Leona corrected. "A step would signify only one thing at a time, but 'Phase II' is a carefully orchestrated and covert attack on Satan."

"If we could please refrain from referring to Mr. Boswell as 'Satan,' that would be greatly appreciated." Penny's mouthed pursed in distaste at the term.

"We have to stay impartial," Leona countered.

"But it's… dehumanizing."

"Try and keep up here," Linda said. "This is for the good of Amicable."

"Anyway, back on task…" Donna leaned into the circle.

"Yes, thank you, Donna. Now, as you all know, the *enemy* has a sports car. The car gets it first. This is called 'hitting him where it hurts.'"

"I thought that was a man's balls." Jeannie scratched her head.

"Yes, Jeannie, that literally is what it means, but my assumption is that you aren't going to raise your hand to be the one to kick him in the groin."

"Goodness no, that wouldn't be nice." Jeannie's face blushed at the thought.

"So we hit his car, his Porsche," Linda pronounced it *Por shuh*, "which will hurt him just the same."

"We're not going to kick it in the tailpipe, are we?"

"Aaagh! Jeannie! Follow the metaphor trail!" Linda's outburst caused the others to lean back. "Phase II. Angela, do you have more ammo?"

"Uh, yes." Angela had taken the cake decorating bags home and washed them thoroughly. There was no shortage of ammunition, though.

"Tonight is the Amicable football game - it's a home game. Angela, we'll need some more chicken poop and..."

"I'm out for tonight. Demetrius is playing, and I want to watch him."

Linda sighed. "Well, then, can you keep one eye on Sata...," she corrected herself, "the enemy, while you watch the game? That would be greatly appreciated."

Angela shook her head. "No, I'm sorry. I want to focus on the game. He's only got a few left."

"Can you at least gather some more chicken poop?" Jeannie tittered.

"Yes, okay." Angela relented. "Where do you want it?"

Leona raised her hand. "I'll take it. But make sure you put it in a container."

"I can watch Stedm... I mean, the enemy," Jeannie volunteered. "I mean, I've got my binoculars."

"Thank you, Jeannie, for your dedication to the mission."

"And what shall I do with the poop?" Leona asked.

"I've already contacted Liam about access to the garage on Peppertree. He said he didn't want to be involved in any 'law-breaking,'" she used her fingers for quotation marks, "but he might 'accidentally' leave the garage door open for inspection. You and..." she looked around the circle and pointed, "...Connie will meet there. Connie, can you bring a bottle of dishwashing liquid?"

"Sure. What for?"

Linda leaned in and spoke so that only the women could hear. "Leona, you're going to splatter three or four large droppings of bird crap on his front windshield. Connie, you're going to replace half of the enemy's windshield wiper fluid with an entire bottle of dishwashing liquid. When he turns on the wipers to get rid of the splatter, he's going to be looking through suds for weeks."

Jeannie giggled. "That will be really funny."

Anne frowned. "Isn't that relatively infantile?"

"Of course," Linda responded, "but we can't be too blatant."

"How is that not blatant?" Donna asked.

Linda looked around the circle. "Am I the only one here who sees the bigger picture?"

"I see it," Jeannie said. "It's beautiful."

"Next," Linda said loudly, "his vanity."

"Uh oh," Donna said under her breath.

"While Connie and Leona are in the garage, Carley and I will be inside the house."

"We can't break into his house," Anne said.

"Of course we're not going to break into his house, but if stopped, we could say that we heard some 'strange noises' and felt it would be the neighborly thing to do to investigate."

"That might be going a little too far."

"Look, I hear your worries about the legal ramifications regarding a little… breaking and entering. We're not breaking anything, really. But once again, for the sake of Amicable…"

"Ooh, this sounds so exciting," Carley clapped her hands and then covered her mouth. "And dangerous. What do I have to do?"

Linda looked around and opened up her purse. She produced a bottle that looked like nasal spray.

"What is that?" Angela asked

"It's called, 'Liquid Ass.' Supposedly, the odor is likened to what the inside of a colon really smells like. Medical colleges use them to simulate the smell of someone who has crapped the bed."

Carley burst out laughing. The bray caused most of the bowling alley to look towards the group.

"I have a friend, Anji," Connie smiled, "who is a doctor and she says that in the hospital, when someone craps the bed, they call it a 'Code Brown.'"

More hoots of laughter.

"Ooh, I love it. I love it." Carley clapped her hands excitedly. "What do I do with it?"

"You're going to go into his bathroom, open up his cologne and put two or three drops in." Linda handed the bottle to Carley. "Do not, under any circumstances, let any get on your person or your belongings or we might be implicated by scent."

Carley laughed again and saluted. "Aye, aye, Captain."

"Does it seem to anyone else that we might have a fecal fetish?" Donna asked with a laugh, but the thought of Phase II was really starting to grow on her.

"What are you going to be doing?" Leona asked.

Linda pulled another bottle. Veet. Hair removal product.

"Oh my goodness," Jeannie giggled into her hand.

"While Carley is administering the Liquid Ass, I'm going to put this in his shampoo bottle."

"Now that's evil," Penny's eyes glinted malevolently.

"Remember," Linda said with a wink, "I'm the angel of death."

"It feels like we're kind of straddling the line of harassment," Angela questioned. "I mean, what are we taking next? His masculinity?"

Linda's eyes narrowed and she smiled malevolently. "Phase III, Angels. Phase III."

Chapter 15.

Angela Chandler checked her watch.

She knew that she was supposed to be watching the game, but two things conspired against that actually happening: first, the Amicable football team was losing badly. The second, though, was far more concerning. Angela had found an old set of headphones and was listening to the conversation taking place across town on the beautiful Midwestern September evening.

Jeannie sat next to Angela looking through her binoculars. Excitedly, she tapped Angela. "There he is! On the visitor's side of the field!" Jeannie pointed in front of her binoculars as if this somehow would help Angela see him. Jeannie had mentioned multiple times that it would be neat if she had only one ear bud in, like the kids. It made her feel like a Secret Service Agent.

"That's nice, Jeannie," Angela responded. The lackluster crowd clapped, as the first half mercifully came to an end.

Jeannie held her walkie-talkie up to her mouth. "Satan occupied with minions. Operation Armageddon set for go. Repeat. Armageddon, go."

Jeannie smiled at Angela, who had pulled her earphones away from her head. "Do you think you could say that any louder? I don't think the announcing booth heard you." She motioned above them.

"I'm sorry," Jeannie whispered. "I'm excited."

"Copy that," a staticky voice replied. "This is Azrael, we are in place. Do you copy, Archangel?"

Leona's voice came through. "That's a copy. Ammunition ready. Waiting for deployment."

"Stand by."

Angela watched Jeannie stare at her device. "Don't you think it's a little weird that Linda and Leona are communicating by walkie-talkie when they're ten steps apart?"

Jeannie shrugged. "Come on, Sourpuss. Live a little. Turn that frown upside down and grow a smile."

"Uriel, do you copy." Silence. "Uriel, this is Azrael, are you there?"

Another ten seconds passed. Finally, Anne's voice broke through. "Sorry, ladies. I was pushing the wrong button down. These things are just plain stupid."

"Uriel, are you in position?"

"Yes, I'm at the corner of..."

"Uriel, do not give away your position!" Linda commanded.

Anne's aged voice came back on line. "Yes, you're right, the CIA is probably pinpointing our location. I'm in Florida drinking a daiquiri. Is that better?"

"Affirmative," Linda responded. "Much better."

"Azrael, this is Archangel, are we go for mission?"

More dramatic silence. Linda's fallback method. "Affirmative, Angels. We are go for Armageddon. Move out."

"Okay, then," Anne said. "I'm just going to sit here and drink on the beach."

Angela rolled her eyes.

Seven blocks away, four figures slinked through Stedman Boswell's rental property on Peppertree Lane. Each one of them wore black pants and black shirt. For good effect, they had applied lampblack on their faces, also.

Leona and Connie broke off crouching towards the garage. Linda used hand signals to move them. She pointed to her eyes and then to Carley whose own wide eyes were filled with excitement and terror. As Linda moved towards the house, Carley stayed behind. Linda repeated the hand signal to 'move out.'

"I don't know what that means," Carley said into her walkie-talkie. "You keep pointing at your eyes and doing things with your fingers. What does that mean?"

Linda ran back to Carley. "We're going to enter the house now, Carley."

"Oh, that's good." Sneaking across the yard, they were two stumbling figures, one hunched and looking around furtively, the other giggling.

Moving to the backdoor, Linda watched Leona and Connie creep into the garage through the unlocked door. Thankfully, Liam Wilson had not forgotten to leave a key under the garden gnome. "Seraph, Cherub, we are in. Raguel and Archangel, are you in position?"

"Affirmative, Azrael. Dropping bombs now. Deploying into the fluid container now."

"Copy, Archangel. Good work." Linda held the back door open for Carley who entered the shoe removal area. They turned on their headlamps and made their way through the house towards the bathroom.

Sparse in decorations, Boswell's house was a second-hand store in a newly built house. A recliner and non-matching sofa were positioned on the edge of the living room facing a console television. A tacky painting was hung on the wall to the right of the TV, while on the other side, an old brass lamp sat on a coffee table. Even though the house smelled of new carpet, it seemed dusty.

Moving from the living room down the hallway, they passed Boswell's bedroom. The women noticed that Boswell was fastidious in his organization. His collared shirts were hung neatly in the closet and his shoes were arranged in even rows on the floor. The bed was made with military precision.

"Wow," Carley said, "I wish he'd come give Peter some lessons."

"Focus, Carley," Linda said. "Stay on target."

"Aye, aye, Captain," she saluted and spoke into her walkie-talkie even though she was standing right next to Linda.

"What was that?" Anne asked loudly into her mouthpiece. "I missed it."

Jeannie chimed in first. "She said, 'I, I, can't bean.'"

"What the heck does that mean?"

"I don't know. Maybe she can't be... Who said that and what did you mean? Are we okay?"

Linda stopped and spoke clearly annunciating her words. "Listen to me, everyone. Stop talking! Don't say anything unless you have to. Does everyone understand?"

Carley and Linda made their way into the bathroom and flicked on the light. Carley almost screamed when she saw herself in the mirror, and then snorted with laughter.

"Don't I look sexy?" She posed in front of the mirror.

"Carley. Please," she implored. "Put the Liquid Ass in his cologne." Linda moved towards the shower where she opened the door and entered. Reaching up onto the shower rack, she grabbed the bottle of shampoo. "Head and Shoulders. Nice." Carefully, she unscrewed the cap of shampoo so as not to dribble any onto the floor. Then, reaching into her pocket, she retrieved the bottle of hair remover and emptied half of it into the shampoo bottle. After placing the cap back on the bottle, she decided to pour the other half into the conditioner bottle for good measure. Glancing down, she was pleased to see a bar of soap sitting in the holder. A few curly hairs were stuck in it, which caused Linda to curl her nose. Her own husband, Dick, left the soap looking like a perfumed chia pet and it drove her insane. Coating the outer layer of the soap with Veet, Linda looked around to see if she had left any trace. Satisfied, she turned to close the door behind her.

Instead of doing the job assigned to her, Carley had watched Linda work methodically to apply the hair-removal product.

"What are you doing, Carley? You're supposed to be… you know… helping! Put it in the cologne."

Carley jumped and turned towards the cologne bottles. Opening the first, (*Creed Aventus*, she had never heard of it before), she took a whiff. "Ooh, that's nice."

"Carley," Linda warned.

Reaching into her pocket, Carley opened the plastic bottle and squeezed the rubber end of the eyedropper. As it sucked in the Liquid Ass, a whiff of the contents reached her nose.

"Oh my God!" She shouted and almost dropped the bottle. "That's horrific. Have you smelled this stuff? Oh, hello!"

"Just breathe through your mouth!" Linda said.

"Are you kidding? Why would I want to embed that smell there?"

"Just do it, Carley! We have to move."

The walkie-talkie made a noise. "Hello Guardian Angels this is Urine, uh, what's my name again?" She paused and remembered. "Oh yeah, Uriel. I'm still in Florida and have moved on to margaritas, but

---

Baker

Satan is walking up the street and he's about to pass me on his way back to hell. Maybe you should get a move on."

"Crap," Carley said and turned back to the problem at hand. She took a deep breath and put a dropper full of Liquid Ass into the *Creed Aventus,* and then did the same with the *Vert Malachite.* "Isn't this a beautiful bott…" Carley held it up to Linda and then took another whiff of the Ass and gagged. "Never mind," she said, and placed one more dropper full into the other bottle.

"Okay," Linda said. "Good enough." She lifted the CB to her mouth. "Angels, this is Azrael, Armageddon is complete. Fall back. We are flying out. Over."

"Roger," Jeannie looked at Angela. "See, I know the lingo now."

"I think you're supposed to say, 'copy,' Jeannie."

"Dang it!" Jeannie exclaimed and then depressed the button again. "I mean, copy!"

Just as Carley was about to screw the lid back on, she turned and the unthinkable happened. Linda's elbow, which had been extended to speak into the walkie-talkie, bumped Carley's hand and the Liquid Ass flew into the air. In slow motion, both women attempted to catch the bottle but only succeeded in fumbling it between them, sloshing Liquid Ass onto both of them. Simultaneously, both Angels began to retch. As bile filled Linda's mouth, she knew that she was about to vomit. The same thought crossed Carley's mind, but as she brought her hand to her mouth to stem the flow of puke that was coming, she ultimately realized that the Liquid Ass was all over her hands also.

Both women knelt at the toilet at the exact same time and emptied the contents of their stomachs into the porcelain bowl.

"I hope everyone is out of the house now," Anne said. "Satan is picking up speed."

"Negative! Negative!" Leona said. "They're still in the house!"

"Azrael, this is Cherub! Where are you?"

Linda reached for her walkie-talkie. "Oh God, I've got Ass all over me." She retched again and pulled Carley, who was still gagging, to her feet. "Come on. We've got to get out! Now!"

Somehow, Linda managed to flush the toilet and the two scrambled from the bathroom. Moving quickly across the living room,

166

they exited the back door and ran past the garage, across the front yard and over the street where Leona and Connie were waiting for them.

As they approached, the smell followed them.

"Oh, heavenly beans," Connie exclaimed and plugged her nose. "What happened?"

Linda's eyes were full of frustration. "Mission accomplished," she said and then bent over to vomit once again.

Tom Busman couldn't stop laughing.

Making his usual trip from Omaha to Minneapolis, he generally zoned out for most of it. Occasionally, he would call out on the radio for someone to keep him awake, but tonight, this was something else.

The girls were back up to their antics. Previously, he followed their discussion as his own imagination filled in the blank spaces. What they were doing from the top of a building, he didn't know, but he enjoyed their banter. He pictured lively young women, perhaps in their thirties, maybe forties. Of course they were attractive, lonely women having some fun. Tonight, though, it sounded like one of the women had to be older - the one in Florida.

Either way, he laughed uproariously when the Floridian said 'Satan is picking up speed!' 'They're still in the house!' (What could they possibly have been doing?) Then his favorite, 'Oh, God, I've got ass all over me!'

Tom burst out laughing and reached for his CB. At first, he thought about contacting some of the other truck drivers to see if they had heard the same conversation, but instead, he decided to contact them directly. Good clean fun.

"Azrael, this is Big Tom Tom heading west on Highway 30. Sounds like you're having some good times tonight."

He waited. "Repeat, Azrael, Big Tom Tom here. Just checking in on the Angels." He remembered that each one of them had a different angel name the last time.

Nothing.

Just as he was replacing the handset, a voice crackled. "Uh, Big Tom Tom, this is Archangel. Can you tell us who you are?"

He smiled. "Tom Busman, truck driver heading back from Minneapolis. I was cruising past you earlier last week and I overheard some of your shenanigans, but tonight I thought I'd talk to you directly, over."

"That's real nice of you," Leona said pulling a fake southern accent. It seemed like the appropriate thing to do. One never heard truck drivers speaking in a Northeast accent, or even a Midwestern one, for that fact. It seemed like in all the movies, truck drivers came with the twang.

"And...?"

"Well," Leona said, "Lin...er... Azrael can't come to the phone right now. She's... uh... ill disposed."

"So I heard," Tom said, "something about getting ass all over her. Interesting, over."

"Big Tom Tom, you git your brains otta the sewer. It's nothing like that." Tom could hear her giggling into the handset. "She got some Liquid Ass on herself, over."

"What?" Tom began to laugh so hard he almost swerved to the other side of the highway. "What is Liquid Ass?"

"Well, Tom Tom, it's a chemical that smells like the world's worst fart."

"Why in the world would someone want to bottle that?" Tom took off his cap and scratched his head.

"I guess I don't know the original intention."

"So what are you using it for?"

"Uh, Big Tom Tom, that's classified." Static then silence. "Um, over."

"What are you, CIA? Classified, my Liquid Ass."

"I wish I could tell you, Big Tom Tom, but you'll have to drive all the way back to Omaha scratching your head and wondering what these good old ladies in Amicable are doing." Again silence. When Leona pushed the button again, there was shouting in the background. "I mean, in... Clancy."

"Sure, Archangel. Okay, well, if you ever need anything, just let me know. I'm on the road a couple of times a week making the run..."

"Will do, Big Tom Tom. Y'all have a good night now, y'hear?" More shouts in the background. *Why are you talking like that? You sound like a moron!*

"Thanks, Archangel. See you in heaven." Tom returned the handset to the mount above him. *Liquid Ass*. He shook his head and continued barreling down the road back home to Omaha.

Stedman Boswell jingled the keys in his pocket. As he traveled the last block to his house, he enjoyed the fresh, country air. Since he had arrived in Amicable, he had noticed how much better his lungs felt and his skin shone with a coppery glow. Not only was he feeling better physically, but his emotions were stimulated by the game afoot. The interaction with the Peterson boy tonight was enervating. The dance with the Butcher's wife filled him with excitement. The thought of winning the insurance game made him happy.

Stedman had always been a fighter. Perhaps this came from the chasm of indifference opened by his parents. He had to cross the void by arguing, or fighting, or destroying their arguments with good reason.

At the front sidewalk, Stedman stopped and sniffed. Something did not smell right.

Whoa, that's rancid. What is that? Sewage?

Approaching the house, the smell seemed to fade. Boswell chalked up the odor to normal farm reek. Thankfully, the breeze tended to carry the smell away as he approached the house. Unlocking the front door, he stepped inside. The smell hit him like a two-by-four across the nose.

"Holy shit!" Dropping his keys onto the front desk, he moved into the main area where he sniffed once again.

"What the...?"

Wondering where the stench was coming from, he moved toward the back of the house. Approaching the bathroom, the putrescent odor overwhelmed him. He pinched his nose shut.

"Oh, man." Bile rose into his throat. Grabbing the air freshener, he sprayed lavender around the room coating the carpets and walls. Moving into the living area, he spritzed it also. Uncovering his nose, he found that the air was at least passable now. He returned to the bathroom.

He sniffed. *Bad, but not too bad.* Lavender mixed with the smell of feces was still better than the scent of feces alone.

He checked his watch. 10:11. Still early.

Early enough for a shower.

After turning the taps, he undressed. Checking himself in the mirror, he noticed that he had put on a few pounds. A few miles of jogging would take that away. As he glanced at the counter, he noticed a black smear. He rubbed it off with his fingers and smelled it. *What was that?* It didn't have a smell, and it didn't seem like grease. He shrugged. Just one more mystery for the night.

Boswell's nose had mercifully adjusted to the lavender/fart mixture and he began to whistle as he stepped into the shower. Wetting his entire body, he grabbed the bar of soap, lathered up and washed all the parts that men normally wash - face, underarms, crotch and chest. His mind wandered.

The game had been thoroughly uninteresting. Amicable's football team was ploddingly slow, uncoordinated, and lacked any kind of killer instinct. Even the big kid what was his name? Chandler - the boy was a moving mountain, but he couldn't seem to get out of his own way.

Stedman reached up for the shampoo, and pumped some into his hand and lathered his hair. His thoughts turned towards Rhonda Jensen. At the funeral, her eyes lingered on him. She looked gorgeous in that tight black dress, her tall, slender form filling it out nicely. She had aged well.

Stedman put his head back under the showerhead and rinsed out the shampoo. Then, he repeated the process with the conditioner, rubbing it into his head.

After rinsing the conditioner, he flung back his hair and turned off the spigots. It was then, after looking down, that he noticed something odd. Reaching for his pubic hair, he was mortified to see it was coming out in clumps. *What the hell?*

Like plucking a chicken, the hair kept coming out. "Aaagh!" He stepped out of the shower and looked into the mirror. Wiping his hands on the towel to clean the curly hair from his hands, he noticed that his chest hair was thinning also. Not only his chest hair, but his underarm hair looked six inches long. Lifting up his arm, he saw that he was molting. Taking a towel, he vigorously dried himself, but to his horror, he noticed all of his hair was sluffing from his skin.

Then, he touched his face. One of his eyebrows moved. "No, no, no, no, no, no!" Gently, he reached up to touch the hair on top of his head.

With great relief, he felt his pelt stay in place.

What was wrong with him? What happened?

After drying, Stedman's stomach roiled with fear. He went directly to WebMD and checked his symptoms. Swallowing, Dr. Google diagnosed him.

I've got alopecia areata, he thought. The stress had been too much. He used his finger to underline the important information on the screen. *My body's immune system is attacking my hair follicles.* "DAMMIT!"

Stedman's mind precipitously fell to worst-case scenario: from zero to some rare form of cancer in seconds. Death was closing in. He hadn't done enough in life! He hadn't travelled as extensively as he wanted. He wanted a Lamborghini, maybe a big house in Aspen like Baker's. His heart pounded in his chest. That must be the cancer eating away at his veins already.

Stedman lay down naked on his bed and threw an arm across his face.

Oh, the horror. Dying young...

Chapter 16.

By the time the Jensen family returned from the interment, the children were exhausted; both of them needed a nap and, frankly, so did the parents. As they entered the house, Rhonda took J.T. while Butcher gathered Georgie in his arms and they carried them to their separate rooms. After undressing them, they tucked the children in and watched them fall asleep almost instantaneously.

Rhonda smiled at Butcher as he closed Georgie's door behind her. They walked down the hallway to their own bedroom, where Butcher allowed her to enter first.

"Can you help me with this?" She asked Butcher, as she revealed her neck to him so that he could unclasp the necklace.

He finished taking off his shoes and walked over to his wife who was lifting up her hair. The skin of her neck was soft, made of buttery white chocolate. Unclasping the necklace, he took it from her neck. As he turned back to take off his shirt and get into more comfortable clothes, she stopped him.

"The zipper too?" She had remained in the same place, stationary, hair still raised. Although Rhonda's question was not spoken provocatively the casual intimacy stirred Butcher.

"Of course," he said softly, and undid the clip at the top, then pulled the zipper down carefully so as not to catch her sensitive skin. The ritual was common, an everyday occurrence for the couple, but the choreography never seemed to grow old. She smiled, thanked him, and shrugged out of the dress one strap at a time. His gaze lingered upon her shoulders, back to her neck, then down again, lower.

"Are you checking me out?" She asked playfully.

"I think so."

"How about we check back later. I'm really tired, aren't you?"

Butcher smiled. "Not that tired."

Rhonda laughed and turned towards him. Her curves called out to him, but he stayed focused on her face. She placed a hand on his chest. "I just wanted to say that I'm sorry for any stress that I've caused you in the last week."

He looked away. "I… I… me too."

"I should have told you what I was doing from the beginning."

"Yes, that would have been helpful."

"Thus," she said as she unclipped the bra behind her back, "I'm sorry."

Butcher turned away from her to take off his own clothes, to collect his thoughts and not be distracted. "I'm just in a weird space," he spoke into the space between them. "All those years of reading people, and then I trust you. Everything changes. It's hard to trust people implicitly."

"Welcome to the ways of the other seven billion people on the planet." She smiled.

He smiled wanly. "I know, I know, but when I see you with him, it makes me… I don't know… pissed off."

"Ooh," Rhonda said as she put on her t-shirt and shorts, "my big bad Butcher is a little bit jealous, then?"

Butcher ground his teeth. "Be that as it may, I can read Boswell and he's got designs on you. I promise you this: I'll kick the shit out of him if he starts."

"I remember when George said that to you." She pointed a finger into his chest, and then felt a pain at mentioning George's name.

Butcher could see this in her eyes and moved in to encircle her. "I'm sorry, Babe." She nodded into his chest, but she had no more tears to cry. His scent, masculine, rough, still that familiar hint of sanitizing agent from the butchery, brought back all the memories of their time together.

"It's okay," she spoke up towards his chin. "Everything is going to be okay."

"Just promise me," Butcher said, "that if Boswell makes any untoward movements, you'll let me know. We've invested far too much into Amicable to let some moronic insurance adjuster blow it all up."

She smiled painfully. "I promise."

When the children woke, the family cooked dinner together and reminisced their own George stories. Taking their meals out onto the porch, they settled in for a night of watching Indian Summer fireflies flit and float in the last gasp effort to hold onto the sun. Soon enough, the cold would settle in and blanket the Midwest with only golden memories.

There were very few things better in life than sharing a meal with one's family.

When dinner had finished, J.T. and Georgie did their part to clear the table. After a bath, the little ones, with wide yawns, were tucked back into bed. Just as Rhonda and Butcher were also about to retire for the night, there was a knock at the door. Rhonda glanced at Butcher. "Who could that be?"

Rhonda flipped on the porch light and opened the door.

It was Donna Humphries.

"Donna?" Rhonda said as Butcher appeared behind her over her shoulder. "Is everything okay?"

Donna looked around the house. "I think so, but..." she swallowed hard enough that her throat muscles could be seen working, "...do you think that we could talk?"

"Sure, sure," Rhonda said and moved outside.

"I think it's best if we were inside, if that's okay," she said quietly.

Rhonda nodded. Butcher spoke up behind Rhonda. "Do you need me to go?"

Donna looked down ashamedly and shook her head. "No, you'll need to hear this too."

Butcher waited for Donna to look up and then...

Oh, crap. Connie. Instantly, Butcher could read what Connie and the others had done - no, were doing - something regrettable. As he stared into Donna's eyes, he noticed that she was unconsciously touching her hip. Too big for a phone.

"Donna," Butcher said, "what is that?"

Rhonda looked at Butcher as if she had somehow missed the joke; Donna's shoulders slumped and she reached for her hip and produced the walkie-talkie. She held it up.

"Why do you need a walkie-talkie?" Rhonda asked.

"It's for communicating over distances."

"I know what it does, Donna, but who are you communicating with?"

Donna looked up at Butcher pleadingly. "Come in, Donna, have a seat and you can tell us what your group is doing." She slunk through the doorway like a whipped dog.

"Can I get you something to drink?" Rhonda asked.

"No, no thank you."

The three of them sat at the table. "Now," he began, "what in the world is Connie doing?"

Donna's eyes widened. Rhonda's head snapped toward Butcher. "What?"

"It's all of them, but your mother is in on it, isn't she, Donna?"

Donna nodded.

"What is it, Donna? Tell me." Rhonda's greatest fears resurfaced. Her mother had come so far. She'd been doing so well.

Donna held up the walkie-talkie.

For the next twenty minutes, Butcher, Rhonda and Donna listened with mute horror, amusement, astonishment and a solid dose of disbelief. Donna gave them a rundown of what Phase I and II had been. Butcher, against his will, laughed aloud at the idea of putting the Liquid Ass into Boswell's cologne. But what they'd done wasn't *exactly* legal. Their hearts were in the right place but their brains had been displaced.

"Any questions?" She asked meekly.

"Of course we have questions," Rhonda said with a nervous laugh. "What's with the names?"

"We're all supposed to be some kind of avenging angels - like we're taking care of the Lord's business. What we're really trying to do is to get Sata..., er... Mr. Boswell to go back to Kansas City so that someone else will come, someone who might have a little more... empathy for the town. Isn't that right, Butcher?"

Rhonda looked questioningly at Butcher.

"Well, Donna..." he stammered.

"That's what you told Linda, Leona and Jeannie, or at least that's what they said."

"Leo?" Rhonda was perplexed.

"I... well... I didn't mean that you should all take it literally, like we're purposely trying to get rid of him..."

175

"I can't believe you!" Rhonda exclaimed as she pushed back her chair. "And I thought I was the one keeping secrets from you!"

"Let me explain, Hon…"

"Don't you 'Hon' me. When were you going to tell me about commissioning these impressionable women for their… what did you call it?"

"Armageddon," Donna filled in.

Rhonda lifted her eyebrows. *See?*

The stammering continued. "I… well… they're highly logical, er, at times… I mean, certain moments."

"Linda and Leona? Highly logical? And my mother? What's next? Is she going to start watering his grass with Roundup? A few marbles on his front steps? A little Ex-Lax in his morning cup of coffee?"

"Of course not," Butcher's hackles were up. "I merely said that it would be *better* if Boswell was no longer on the case."

Donna looked uncomfortable. "Maybe I should go…"

Rhonda glanced at the woman. "Of course, Donna. Please realize that none of this is *your* fault."

"Okay, then," Donna responded, rising quickly. "I'm so sorry for bringing this to you."

"Wait a second, Donna." Rubbing her face with both of her hands, Rhonda felt the frustration emerging even more. "Why did you come here tonight?"

"I was worried. I keep thinking that they're going to do something worse."

"Why would you think that?"

Donna worried with her hands. "When we were talking, Linda says to the whole group, 'This is not a step; it's a phase. In steps there is only one action occurring at a time. But a phase is a coordinated attack.' And then she kind of got this weird look in her eyes, like she's crazy or something, and she says, 'Welcome to Phase II.'"

Butcher felt his stomach drop. "You mean you've already had Phase I?"

Donna nodded. More shame. She explained the bombing.

"Oh, God," Rhonda whispered.

Clearing his throat, Butcher rose from his chair. "Um, Donna, how many Phases are there?"

"That's the problem! I don't know! With Linda, she won't stop until she gets her way. Remember with you?" Donna pointed at Butcher. "She was going to keep going with you until you left, but fortunately, you stayed."

"I see," he said.

"So what should I do, Rhonda? I mean, your mom is involved, Penny Reynolds, even Anne Johnson, for gosh sakes!" Eyes widened with fear, Donna clapped her hands on her cheeks.

Rhonda rose from her chair. "It was the right thing for you to come and tell us." She passed a look to Butcher, communicating an assortment of negative consequences. "We'll have a discussion after you leave, but the most important thing you can do is to stop Phase III. Do you think you can do that?"

Donna nodded tentatively. "I'll try." She turned to walk out the door when the walkie-talkie went off again.

"Azrael, this is Big Tom Tom…"

"Who the hell is that?" Rhonda asked.

Donna shrugged her shoulders and headed out into the deepening night.

Rhonda and Butcher settled in for a lengthy discussion before Rhonda's mother arrived home.

Chapter 17.

As expected, Stedman Boswell slept fitfully. Every fifteen minutes, he would check the previously hairy parts of his body to see if any was growing back or if more was falling out. Like any other malady, humans are quick to hope that the body will fix itself quickly. A slightly swollen lymph node is more often than not a sign of infection. But, once it is noticed, a person keeps touching it, often making it swell even more. This increases anxiety which, in turn, inflames imagination. The person with a swollen armpit nodule has already envisioned bouts of chemotherapy, lymphadenectomies and a grieving family attempting to pick out the perfect casket.

Enter Stedman Boswell on that Friday night in September. The unfortunate usage of WebMD caused Boswell to imagine the worst, and then reimagine it every few minutes afterwards. Although his 'symptoms' were quite minor in retrospect, it did not stop him from getting up at midnight to re-check the internet to see if he had, in fact, misread the diagnosis regarding his rapid hair loss.

As the clock chimed twelve, he was appalled to see that he had shed not only his armpit hair, chest hair, and three quarters of his pubic hair (what a spectacle that was), but his right eyebrow was missing also. He cringed.

Alas, there was nothing he could do about his death from shedding, so he cocooned himself under the covers and prayed, or what he approximated praying to be.

"Dear God," he spoke aloud, thinking that verbal prayers would be answered quicker, "please don't let it be cancer."

As the night wore on, his skin began to itch and burn. *Rapid-onset cancer,* he thought. Not, *allergic reaction.* At 3:24, he went back into the bathroom to investigate his skin and he was appalled to see that the rash was spreading. In that instant, he thought about calling the ambulance. Perhaps they could do something with his condition. Maybe they could extend his life for a few more months - he'd even take an extra week or two, party, maybe finish his life on a vacation.

Chapter 17.

From the time between 3:24 and 5:48, Stedman Boswell pondered the meaning of life, its brevity, and all the things he should have done. Nowhere in his thought process did he think about Amicable or his job. Nothing about connecting an illegal Cuban immigrant to an explosion in the small Midwestern town. Whether this was theological bribery or merely a pondering of life, he genuinely felt bad about the life he was leading. Alternatively, he imagined himself a 21st century Albert Schweitzer; he could remain with these natives helping them to look beyond their ignorance to see the bigger world. Maybe he could teach them a thing or two about the wonderful benefits of wearing nicer clothes…

Finally, at 5:48, as the sun made an extraordinary Saturday appearance on the eastern horizon, casting its rays up, up and over the shell of the grain elevator, Boswell made a vow to a God he didn't believe in that he would do his very best to be a good man. *Just give me a reprieve on death.*

Finishing his prayer, Stedman groggily pulled himself from bed. Entering the bathroom for the third time in the last six hours, Boswell pulled a brush through his hair. Breathing a sigh of relief, he was happy that his mop was still connected to his scalp. If he was dying, he might as well look good doing it. Choosing a pair of khaki pants and a green striped golf shirt, he straightened them in the mirror. His teeth looked fine. His jaw, though missing hair, was sharply defined. The only off-putting detail was the half-a-right-eyebrow thing. Licking his thumb, Boswell attempted a modified eyebrow comb over, but to no avail. *That was the way it had to be.* With careful deliberation, he chose his favorite cologne, Creed Aventus, and sprayed some into his hand and wiped it on his cheeks and collar.

"What the…?" Immediately, he began to retch. His mind changed gears into overdrive.

It was another symptom of the cancer.

He'd read somewhere that when people have cancer of the brain, it affects their senses. Twice in a night? This was definitely a sign of brain cancer.

He had barely raised the lid of the toilet before he emptied last night's meal into the porcelain receptacle. Even as his head was pressed against the seat, he still couldn't get the stench from his nose. Suddenly, he worried that he'd be breathing out of his mouth the rest of his life.

Groaning, he pushed himself away from the toilet, flushed, and wiped his mouth with the bath towel. Another whiff.

Am I being punished because of Amicable?

Dragging himself to the living room, he grabbed his keys, his wallet, his phone and his watch. Throwing open the door, he stepped into the fresh air and breathed deeply, but to his horror, he found that the smell was following him. No matter where he went, the cancer was going to affect his sense of smell. The thought of lifelong feces brought tears to his eyes. Finishing in the house, he locked the door behind him and went to the garage. Opening the side door, the darkness reminded him of a tomb.

The musty smell mercifully took over, and briefly, he inhaled the odor of oil, dirt, dust and... a dead rodent... *Maybe I'm not going crazy.*

Stedman opened the door of his Porsche, climbed in and slammed the door. In the confined area, he waited. For a second, he didn't smell anything, but then realized he was holding his breath. Taking a cautious sniff of the air, he was immediately greeted again by the overwhelming scent of fecal matter and cologne.

"SHIT!" He screamed.

Stedman, forgetting the garage door was manual, pounded the armrest and got out of the car. Opening the garage door forcefully, he was blinded by the sunlight. Muttering, Stedman reentered the car. The smell hit him again and he ground his teeth. Looking up, though, he noticed that his morning was about to get worse.

The windshield was splattered with monstrous bird droppings. It looked as if an ostrich had used the glass for its toilet. Putting the car in reverse, he backed out of the garage. But in his haste, he hit the frame and pulled his mirror off.

"AAAAAAAAGH!"

He looked in the rearview mirror at his reflection: the other half of his right eyebrow was hanging near his nose and his face looked like a blotchy tomato. He needed to get to a hospital. The nearest one was in Clancy.

In order to clear the windshield, he pulled back on the lever, ejected wiper fluid onto the glass and started the blades in motion. Whatever was wrong with his wiper fluid was making his windshield looking like a Bob Ross painting. *Happy little clouds here and there. Isn't that a nice pine tree?* Stedman pounded the steering wheel. He pulled back on the lever again with the same result, except this time, the fluid foamed. Happy little fecal clouds.

"What else can go wrong?" Stedman glanced in the rearview mirror. At this unfortunate moment, his left eyebrow dropped like a furry caterpillar into his lap.

Stedman Boswell put his head onto his hands on the steering wheel and began to cry.

A minute later, while Stedman Boswell sat in his driveway bemoaning the fates of the universe, there was a knock on the window. Rhonda Jensen.

Stedman ignored her. She was the last person he wanted to see, especially in this condition - puffy eyes, red blotchy cheeks, no eyebrows. He put his head back on the steering wheel.

"Stedman," Rhonda said through the glass. "Are you okay?"

"Go away."

"What's wrong? Get out of the car so we can talk."

"No. I can't."

Rhonda tried to open the door, but he had locked it. She looked at the front windshield. When she gazed back through the driver side glass, she was amazed, and deeply thankful, that he still had a full head of hair. "Open the door, Stedman. We need to talk."

"I don't want to… not in this condition."

"What condition?"

"I said I don't want to talk about it!"

"I need to tell you some things, Stedman. Open the door."

Stedman sat up and looked at Rhonda, whose eyes registered surprise and revulsion at his appearance

"I know!" He shouted. "I'm hideous! Something's happened to me! I think… I think I'm having a stress reaction. I looked it up. I might have cancer."

"Stedman, turn off the car. You don't have cancer."

"I'm going to the doctor. Tell the town council I'll be in touch. I need to get this figured out." He put the car in reverse and began to drive backwards (the only direction in which he could see) down the lane.

Rhonda chased him. "We need to talk! I can explain everything!"

The words were lost on him. Stedman Boswell pulled back into the street, narrowly missing a Ford Escort, and then put the car into drive. Rolling down his window, Stedman stuck his head out like a dog. Tearing down the street, he was at least pleased to note that the wind seemed to take away the smell.

Rhonda watched him drive west on Peppertree and turn right. She thought she heard his tires peeling off onto Highway 10.

"Well, there goes that." She said to no one in particular. She sniffed the air.

Crap.

Chapter 18.

Hours later, the town council waited patiently in Janice Stensrud's office for the last two members to arrive. David Thomas had planned for a day off, but the emergency session required that he forfeit the last nine holes of his golfing round. Needless to say, he was displeased. Tony Culbertson, yawning, staggered through the door at seven minutes after eleven. The Saturday had not started well for any of them.

Janice called the meeting to order. "Thank you for coming in," Janice said. "I realize that many of you had plans this morning, but it was essential that we gather. Rhonda has some information that will… change our direction." She nodded towards Rhonda.

Rhonda took a sip of her coffee. Careworn and sleep deprived, she smiled ruefully. "Thanks, Janice. Last night, information came to me regarding unbecoming activity of some of our Amicablean citizens." Murmurs of surprise.

"During the football game last night, a number of citizens took it upon themselves to attack Stedman Boswell."

Gasps.

"What are you talking about?" David asked.

"Although well-intentioned, the citizens did damage to Mr. Boswell's property and body. As we speak, he is at the Clancy municipal hospital."

"Oh, gosh," Burton Wilson, Liam's father exclaimed. "Is he okay?"

"As far as we can ascertain, yes. I met with him briefly this morning, but since then, he hasn't returned my phone calls. When he left for the hospital, he said that he would not be able to keep his appointment today."

"What are we going to do?" Jim asked. "If he finds out what happened, he may well sue the town."

"Dang it, Rhonda! What happened?" Steve Evans was beside himself. "I thought we were all on the same page?"

Rhonda sighed. "I can't tell you exactly what has happened, but when we do meet with Mr. Boswell, you will notice changes in his appearance."

"They didn't beat him up, did they?" David again.

"No, no. The assault took a much different form."

"Come on, Rhonda, you have to tell us. You have to prepare us."

"I'm sorry, Steve."

"Do we need to go to the hospital? Should someone send flowers?"

Rhonda looked around the room. "It's probably best that I go. I'll figure something out."

Propped up in a hospital bed, Stedman Boswell's paper-thin gown splayed across his legs. His hands, restless and fidgety, worried in front of him. For the umpteenth time, he wondered about the lack of hair on his fingers and the patches of missing hair on his forearms. It was not the first time in his life that he had felt lonely, but as he sat in that hospital bed sheltered by a plastic shower curtain divider, he had never felt so utterly alone.

When he had arrived at the emergency room of the Clancy hospital, his eyes were wide and his hair was windblown. At 6:30 in the morning, the nurse at the front desk was not used to patients entering in that condition. Regular hypochondriacs at least got a decent night's sleep before they paced nervously outside the automatic doors before choosing to come in. When Nurse Simpson glanced up to see the wide-eyed young man stumble through the doors, she was startled. As he approached the desk, she noticed multiple strange things at once.

The man had no eyebrows and his facial hair seemed to be spotty at best. A shaving accident gone bad? *Forrest Gumped it,* as the nurse called it - *stupid is as stupid does.* This man didn't look like stupid, though. He looked like a terrified man who had parachuted into the hospital.

"Can I help you?"

Stedman approached the desk. "I hope so," he said, his voice breaking.

At that moment, she smelled something awful. Or, as she reflected with cringing mirth, *offal.*

"What is it that I can do for you?" It was a special kind of challenge not to react to his smell.

"My hair." He pointed to his arms and his eyebrows and looked briefly towards his nether regions. "I'm losing my hair."

She waited for the 'emergency' part of his problem. In general, hair loss was not considered a phone-the-doctor-on-call kind of drama.

"I don't think you're hearing me," Stedman said more forcefully. "I've lost all my hair."

"Have you had an allergic reaction to something? Chemotherapy?"

"No, no, none of that. I went home tonight after a football game, took a shower and all of the sudden, I...I... was shedding hair. And that odor. Can you smell it? Please, tell me you can."

Controlling her expression the nurse said, "Yes, yes, most certainly, I can smell it."

"Do you think it's me?"

"Uh, sir, it's definitely you. Have you had any issues with diarrhea tonight?"

"What? No, of course not."

"You didn't have any flatulence and... a little bit escaped?"

Stedman recoiled. "Don't you think I'd know if I crapped my pants? I think I'd know if I'd crapped my pants."

She shrugged. "You're the one who asked me if you stunk."

"It takes such a load off my mind to know that you can smell it too."

"Sir," Nurse Simpson stood from behind her desk. "I can admit you and you can wait in a room until the doctor makes his rounds." She checked her watch. "That is in about half an hour. Or, I suggest that you go home and take a shower."

"But... but... what about my hair loss? What could have happened that all my..." he pointed southwards, "hair came out tonight?" He leaned in and said quietly. "I look like a frickin sphynx cat down there."

Nurse Simpson crossed her arms. "Okay, Okay, I'll admit you. The odds are it's just a reaction to something. Have you been through any stress recently? Any shocks to your system?"

"Not any more than normal. I mean, my job can be stressful, but it's not that. I'm an insurance adjuster. You see, I've been sent to Amicable, you know with…"

"Thank you for the extra information sir."

"If it's not stress, what else could it be?"

"I can't really make any other guesses sir, but the odds are you've had an allergic reaction."

"Could it be…" he paused and lowered his voice, "cancer?"

"Sir, it would be very rare, but alopecia can be a sign of… you know what, never mind."

"Alopecia?" Stedman's voice raised a notch. "What is that? It sounds serious."

"It's just a fancy name for hair loss and you haven't lost any hair on your head, so let's focus on allergy, shall we?" She shoved an admittance form onto the shelf between them. Stedman quickly filled it out. Shortly afterwards, she led Mr. Boswell down the hallway toward his new and unexpected home.

"Do I have to share a room with someone? I'd rather not."

Sighing, she said, "I'm sorry sir. If you have to stay for any length of time, you might be transferred to a private room."

Hours after his admission to the hospital, Stedman checked his watch. The doctor was supposed to have made his rounds at 9:00, but now it was almost 11:30. What if the nurse had told him her fears about his hair loss? What if it was a symptom of a rare kind of cancer? He Googled his symptoms again on his phone and was dismayed and horrified to find out that he *must* have Hodgkin's Lymphoma. Reaching under his arms to the recently-made-hairless pits, he pressed his fingers into the places where the screen told him he should find lymph nodes and sure enough, he felt them. They didn't seem too big, but there were lots of lymph nodes around his body. He moved his hand under his gown and pressed his fingers into his groin region - probing. The cancer cells must be around…

"Am I interrupting something?"

186

Boswell jerked his hands out from underneath his gown. "No, of course not. I was just feeling my lymph nodes."

"Hmm." Rhonda controlled her smile.

"No, really…" His face turned red.

"It's okay." She pulled up a chair and sat down next to him. "How are you doing?"

Stedman flopped his head back into the pillow and closed his eyes. "Not so good."

"Talk to me."

"I can't. I mean, I don't want to."

"Trust me."

Closing his eyes, he mumbled. "The doctors haven't ruled out cancer."

"What!" Rhonda almost fell out of her seat. "Are you kidding? I mean, it's just hair."

"So you noticed," he opened his eyes to see hers on his face.

"Yes, of course, but…"

"Don't say any more." He reached out his hand to Rhonda. "If this is cancer…" his voice caught, "I have to rethink how I live, how I treat people."

Rhonda, strangely moved by the younger man's epiphany, took hold of his hand. She knew that it wasn't cancer, but something inside her told her to let this new scenario play out. Rhonda pulled the plastic curtain around them creating a cell of perceived aloneness. "Talk to me. What's going on?"

Boswell felt the smoothness of her hand; the strange, out-of-place intimacy between strangers was disconcerting for both of them. Not for the last time was he envious of the butcher.

"All my life I've been treating people as stepping stones, or maybe like stairs. Always climbing higher. Never caring about other affected lives or stories. In the last couple of hours, I've really had second thoughts about my selfishness. When I ultimately stopped to take a look at the surroundings of my own 'dream,' I recognized that I wasn't climbing, I was walking downwards.

"Okay," Rhonda said slowly.

"So, that's what I feel like. Am I going up or down, you know what I mean? Now that I'm confronted with my mortality like this, I'm just reevaluating a few things."

"Stedman..." Rhonda interrupted.

He held up his free hand. "Just hear me out. I know that the Amicable explosion was an accident. I know that there should be nothing impeding the insurance payout. But the way of the corporate world is always about money. Money. It's a hard world, I know. People are stupid about insurance, though. They buy it and don't think about it."

The comment riled Rhonda, but she kept her mouth shut.

"But the money is a shell game. Baker pays me to stretch out the investigations. Eventually, I'll find a loophole so that the company doesn't have to pay the entire amount. I always do."

"What are you saying? Amicable is not getting its insurance money?" She pulled her hand away from his.

He dropped his head in shame. "There is no way that Baker would allow that to happen. I'm sorry."

"But... but... we've paid the premiums all these years! We've done everything that we should have or could have! The explosion..."

"I know," he said quietly and deliberately, "it doesn't matter. Baker sees Amicable as an easily manipulated mark."

"That's infuriating."

"I'm sorry," he repeated.

Rhonda knew deep in her heart that he was right. Amicable was not just a nice town, it was a town built on bootstrap tugging. The hard working farmers, laborers, business people, teachers - everyone - would, after the announcement of the claim's refusal, shrug their shoulders and say, 'This is the Lord's will,' and get on with life. Her mind flashed to the school children who would not be there next year because of jobs lost. She thought about Human Beans shutting down. *Where would they go for coffee? What about the grocery store and the bank?* All excellent people and wonderful employees sacrificed on the altar of corporate greed.

Rhonda projected her anger from Baker directly onto the shrinking shoulders of the man in front of her. "How much will the town actually receive?"

Stedman's eyes closed again. "My guess? One quarter. At the most, one third."

"Holy crap," Rhonda muttered.

He nodded. "This is why I need to make amends. When the doctor finally tells me what's going on, if I'm going to need chemotherapy, radiation…" his bottom lip puckered and quivered.

For the very first time, Rhonda saw him for what he truly was - a lonely, young predator caught up in a carnivorous world. A man who never had a childhood, and yet, ironically, a boy who could never grow up. As Rhonda's eyes were opened, she may have recognized what Butcher felt all the time. It was an improbably strange feeling to see someone physically, and then to see them psychologically. Stedman's teary eyes tugged at her heartstrings, but she hardened her heart at the knowledge that this man was the linchpin to Amicable's survival. He had openly admitted that the insurance company was going to screw them out of their livelihood. If she told him now that his hair loss was a result of a few zealots bent on saving the town by any means possible, he would back off from his confession. If she didn't tell him the truth, the implicit guilt on her would drive her insane.

"Thank you for your time, Stedman." Making a quick decision, Rhonda stood abruptly and pulled back the plastic shower curtain that separated them from the rest of the room. Pausing briefly at the door, as if about to say something, she turned without speaking leaving Stedman Boswell in shocked silence.

Moments after her departure, Boswell's phone rang.

Theo Baker.

"Hello sir."

"Boswell," Baker shouted into the phone. "I need an update on that little town, whatever it's called."

"Amicable," Stedman responded as he noticed a doctor coming down the hallway. His blood pressure increased exponentially.

"It doesn't matter what the name of the town is, I need to know if you've found the information we need."

Boswell swallowed. "Uh, I think so, sir."

"Well…?"

"It's not a good time, Mr. Baker. I… I'll have to call you back."

Stedman could tell that Baker was barely restraining his fury. "You listen to me you little pissant. There is a lot of money riding on this, and unless you're dying, you'd better tell me what's going on."

"Mr. Baker, I'm at the hospital."

"Are you dying?"

"I don't know, sir."

"What do you mean, you don't know? How can you not know? What's the problem?"

Boswell held up his hand to the doctor. "Look, sir, I'm going to have to call you later. The doctor is waiting for me."

"You listen to me, Boswell, if you don't tell me what's going on right now, I'm going to drive to Asshole, Iowa and sort this out myself. Do you hear me?"

Boswell hung up the phone. There was no way that Theo Baker was going to drive to the middle of nowhere to check out an insurance claim. Had he ever done it before? Stedman understood his superior's anger, but this point in his existence, as he was about to hear the death sentence or life sentence, he didn't really care if Theo Baker had a hissy fit or not.

"Hello, Doctor," Stedman lifted a hand, "I'm sorry to have kept you waiting."

"The apology belongs to me," the doctor said, "I'm a little bit late this morning, but things have been pretty busy in Clancy."

"A veritable triage."

The doctor's mouth set firmly. "Yes, well, there are many others to see in different wards around the hospital. I'm on call this morning…" he said as if that would appease the patient's frustration. "My name is Doctor Ditmore. You can call me Tim if you would like."

"Okay, Tim. I'm Stedman."

Doctor Ditmore looked at the chart. "Nice to meet you, Stedman."

"So…?" Stedman raised his eyebrows as his heart raced.

"Well," the doctor said slowly, as he leafed through to the second page of the chart and then looked at his watch, "it's hard to say."

"Just give it to me."

"That's just it, I don't know." Doctor Ditmore put on rubber gloves and touched Stedman's face, neck and hands. "It says here that you've had a spontaneous loss of hair on various parts of your body, including your genitals, is that right?"

"That's right," Stedman flushed.

"Have you had any sudden stresses? Any shocks to the system?"

"No."

Doctor Ditmore took off his gloves. "Strange. If I had to guess, I'd say you had an allergic reaction to something, but that would affect the hair on your head also, but I don't see any of that. And this odd smell…"

"What about… what about… lymphoma?"

The doctor held Stedman's gaze. "WebMD?"

Stedman dropped his eyes.

"The odds of you having Hodgkin's or anything like it would be extraordinarily rare, especially, as I said, because the hair on your head is still intact."

Stedman breathed a sigh of relief. "So you don't think I have cancer?"

Ditmore shook his head. "No, but we can do some blood tests if you like. We won't find out the results for a few days. Do you want us to do that?"

"Yes, that would give me some peace of mind."

Ditmore wrote on the chart and then took a pad of paper out of his jacket pocket. "Okay, we'll have some blood drawn. I'll write you a script for some steroid cream just in case this is an allergic reaction to something." Stedman nodded. "I'm sure this is just a result of something you've come into contact with. In a week, maybe two weeks, this should all clear up and the hair will start to grow again."

"That's a relief."

"But," Doctor Ditmore said, "if you have any changes, especially if the hair on your head starts to come out, then make an appointment. Okay?"

"Okay, Doc."

Later that day, Boswell was in his Porsche driving back to the Casey's gas station to scrub the rest of the bird dung from his windshield. Oddly, the windshield kept making bubbles. It didn't matter. He just wanted to get home and take a shower again.

Chapter 19.

"And…?" Butcher, Leslie and John Deakins were sitting in Human Beans, waiting for Rhonda to explain what had happened.

"I don't know. It was so weird. He implied that he was a changed man and that this brush with 'death' was going to cause him to change his life."

"According to you," Leslie interrupted, "his close brush with death has nothing to do with cancer, but with the exercise group adding some chemicals to his soap."

"I know. I know. And, I feel particularly guilty on that point. But, when he told me that Baker was going to hold out on Amicable, I couldn't tell him the truth. It was like… I don't know… it was like I wanted him to suffer like we are. How much of a sinner am I, John?"

He shrugged. "You had to make a choice. You didn't reveal the entire truth to do a greater good, even if it caused one person to suffer a little bit more," John said.

"And," Butcher added, "one who probably deserved to suffer."

"Then what happened?" Leslie asked.

"I think he regrets being a corporate pawn."

"Until he finds out what happened." Butcher's gaze moved back and forth between John and Leslie.

"Yes, well, I suppose we'll have to make sure he doesn't find out. Those ladies have to stop, though."

"So now what?" Leslie asked.

Outside of Human Beans Café, it seemed as if Amicable was taking a large breath, inhaling the present and exhaling the past. External pressures were pushing on the walls of everything. Strangely, though, no one was waving to each other. On the walk to the coffee shop, John and Leslie even heard someone tap their horn! The horn was only there to signal to your spouse to come open the manual garage door on the Morton building - never to signal impatience. That would not be nice.

A few people strolled on the far side of the street, shopping bags swaying with groceries, feet hurrying along without pause. Even the afternoon lunch crowd didn't stop to chat. Shifting eyes, guilt, fear, the worst of imagining a future without each other. Already, many citizens were subconsciously wondering if Amicable's disease would be an incurable cancer, metastasizing into every arena of life.

Rhonda's voice broke the reverie. "I'm going to talk to Linda, Leona and Jeannie." John was about to say something, but Rhonda stopped him with her hand. "I know what you're going to say: 'It could just spur them on,' but I think I can convince them to lay off."

"Then what?" Butcher asked.

"At this point, we have to figure out how to keep Stedman's mind on a helpful trajectory." Butcher looked up sharply at Rhonda. In using his familiar name, he wondered if she was losing her objectivity. Once again, he cursed his inability to read her.

"How?"

"I've got an idea, but…"

"But what?"

Rhonda's eyes moved around the small circle and then outside as she prepared to get up. "It's going to require some extra people."

"Who?" Leslie asked as she followed Rhonda's movement.

At that moment, those extra people entered the café.

Stedman Boswell pulled his Porsche into the parking lot of Wilson's Garage. The decrepit garage door, badly in need of paint or even restoration, was raised and a 2009 Toyota Camry was lifted up on a hydraulic lift. In the pit beneath, Liam Wilson, clad in oil-stained overalls, peered up into the underbelly of the car, squinting underneath the engine. Liam had become increasingly aware that his usefulness as a mechanic was ending. In all these new cars and pickups, computers talked to computers, not to people. He longed for the days when the cars used to talk to him, sang to him, coughed to him, screamed at him to be fixed, not plugged into a computer which told him what to do. Classic domestic cars were examples of the way things should have stayed: well-made, solid, dependable, and eminently fixable. Midwest built cars. If he had to look at one more foreign car, with their fancy little displays and abilities to park themselves, and, God forbid, a hybrid car (totally un-American if you asked Liam), he'd bite one of his fingers off and spit it into the drain. He sighed, as a car pulled into the lot behind him. By the sound of it, not domestic.

"Hello, Liam…?"

"Yuh," he shouted without looking.

The smell of gasoline, oil, rubber, exhaust and a tinge of fresh pine scented mirror hangers clung in Stedman's nose. Along the far wall, a row of tires was stacked three deep. Red tool chests, most of the drawers lolling open like panting dog tongues, were scattered throughout the shop. A smeared water cooler stood by the office door, but the plastic was so streaked with grease, it was difficult to see the water within. As Stedman peered through the darkened garage, he saw Pennzoil magnets covering the ancient curvy refrigerator.

"Are you busy?"

Liam rolled his eyes. *No, of course I'm not busy, Dipstick. I'm working on a Saturday; I've got seven cars needing oil changes and brake checks.*

"Nope. I've always got time for the common public." Wiping his hands on the already stained rag, Liam exited the pit and parked himself across from Stedman. "What can I do for you?"

"Something happened to my car."

Wilson waited for him to respond. He had no idea what the ladies had done, but he hoped that they hadn't put water in the gas tank, or something worse. Even though he didn't like foreign cars, he hated to see a beautiful machine like Boswell's Porsche punished for its owner's arrogance.

"When I got up this morning, I went out to the garage and found that some stupid birds had crapped all over my windshield, and when I tried to clean it off, something happened with the fluid. It just started foaming up and smearing. I had to drive to Clancy with my window down so I could see to get there."

"So you want me to look at the windshield wiper fluid?"

"Could you?"

Liam looked at his watch. "Yeah, I guess, but I've got to finish up a few other jobs first. Can you leave the car here for the afternoon? It's Saturday and I'd like to leave at a decent time, but it sounds like your job might not be too difficult."

"You can keep it for the weekend. I won't be using it."

"All right, then." Liam looked over Stedman's shoulder at the car glistening in the sun. Wilson felt a twinge of jealousy for the man's car. The sleek lines, big engine for the little car, even the leather interior, was foreign in Amicable, where the cars (or pickups) were known for their blockiness, engines that grumbled, and the interior made from fabric or synthetics.

"Do you need a ride home then?"

"No."

Liam scratched his nose. "Can I ask you a question?"

"Yes."

"What happened to your eyebrows?" The only people Liam had ever seen remove their eyebrows were old ladies who penciled blue ones on. It never ceased to surprise him that when he arrived at church, the older ladies had purple color by number eyebrows and hair.

Unconsciously, Stedman touched his forehead. "I, uh, I don't know."

"What do you mean you don't know? They were stuck to your head, weren't they? It's not like they had a vote to secede from the union?" Liam snorted and smacked his leg.

"I'd rather not talk about it." Stedman folded his arms.

"Okay, you have a good day now."

Stedman walked away, but he still heard the mechanic mumble under his breath, "Weirdo."

Boswell felt his blood boil. *You'd think these people would figure it out. They're back-country hicks living in a cesspool - swimming in it! They don't even recognize the smell. It...* Taking a deep breath, he summoned the old Stedman Boswell. Enough of feeling sorry for these people; enough of sinking to their level of intelligence.

Weirdo. I'll show them weirdo.

Stedman crossed Highway 10 skirting the skeleton of the grain elevator. The county safety supervisors had erected orange fencing around the entirety of the property with 'No Trespassing' signs. Without understanding why, Stedman felt sorrier for the building than he did for the people. The elevator had done nothing wrong. Now it was a rubbled mess, a shell of its former self. Sharp pieces of concrete, rebar and even the scattered seed lay strewn around the grounds. Caged, the grain elevator seemed to be a corpse in an orange casket.

And, he was the undertaker.

"Hi guys," Rhonda said, greeting the couples. "Come and sit with us. Can we get you a drink?"

"That would be nice," Tracey said.

"Who's buying?" Derek asked.

Rhonda smiled and pointed at Butcher.

Derek rubbed his hands. "In that case, I'll have an extra-large hot chocolate and," he checked with the others, "maybe we should get some hamburger sliders while we're here?"

Nash laughed. "What a great idea."

Rhonda shook her head and smiled. "You two never change. Go sit down and I'll order."

Moving to the tables, Butcher and John stood and helped the boys grab some chairs so that the eight of them could sit together.

"What's happening?" Derek asked.

"We're just having a discussion about the future of Amicable and you all figure prominently." Butcher responded

"Why do I feel suddenly uneasy?" Tracey asked.

"Look," Butcher continued, as Rhonda took the seat next to him, "the old guard has to start taking a step back, passing the baton, if you will. It's time for you guys to start running the next part of the race."

Derek put his head down. "Uh, I think I can speak for everyone here, Butcher, that whatever you're planning sounds like old-people stuff. If running with the baton means lots of meetings, and budgets and taxes and road maintenance…"

"And sewage," Nash added.

"Yeah, and sewage, then no thanks."

"Okay," Butcher said, "what's going to happen to Amicable then?"

Tracey leaned back while Derek put his arm behind her on the chair. "Someone with those talents will step up."

"What talents?" Butcher pressed.

"I don't know, organization, you know, looking towards the future and mapping stuff out," Tracey answered.

"Who is going to do that, Tracey? Give me some names of people your age or younger who are good at looking towards the future, mapping it out."

"Jeez, Butcher," Nash said, "no reason to get snippy."

"Sorry," he apologized. He ran a hand through his hair. "I'm just wondering how Amicable is going to survive. We need a plan, and if good solid citizens like you four, who are probably not moving away any time soon, are not willing to commit to the future, we might as well start packing up right now."

Rhonda agreed. "We need your voices."

"But there's got to be other people…" Shania insisted. "We can't do this by ourselves. No one has taught us how to be leaders."

"And," Derek interjected, "we're allergic to commitment. It's a thing, really."

"No it isn't, Derek," Butcher retorted, holding Derek's gaze. "I've worked with both of you, and you are the most committed young men I've ever met. You guys run the business. You both do everything, not just cut meat, but the finances, clean up, marketing, management, customer relations. You don't even think about it - it's just what you do."

"And you, Shania, manage the Greedy Pecker. You might think that's insignificant, but you don't even realize how much influence you have in Amicable. People know you by name. They trust you. They know that you won't judge them. You take care of them. Do you see?"

John put his voice forward. "Tracey, you have a college education, and even though you might believe that's not a big deal, not everyone in Amicable has that kind of 'foreign' knowledge. You know how things are done in other places; you have the ability to write and to influence people with your words."

"But most importantly," Butcher said, "you have each other."

"I don't know, Butcher," Nash was doubtful, "it's a different story leading a town. There's so many old people that wouldn't support our ideas…"

"Nash," Leslie chastised, "George would be ashamed to hear you say that." He reddened. "Have you not learned anything from the last five years? Every person in this town has taken a role in shaping you for this moment in time. Amicable needs youthful leadership, new ideas, combined with old wisdom."

"This sounds like a pep talk," Derek said.

"Maybe that's because it is," John said. "Maybe it's your turn to get off the bench and take the game into your hands."

"But… but… what about those who are in leadership now? The mayor? The council? My dad? Won't their feathers get a little ruffled?"

Butcher leaned in. "I can guarantee that if you, as a group, approached the town council and told them that you'd like to take an active role in the future of leading Amicable, all of them would be willing to mentor you."

"Okay, assuming we agree. How do we begin?"

John smiled. "As I said, we'll help you."

"You guys are serious?" Shania said incredulously.

"Absolutely," Rhonda said, "but there's one thing that I need Derek to do. And it won't be fun."

Derek held a hand to his chest. "Me? Why me?"

"Because you are the key to this whole thing…"

Chapter 20.

Stedman tentatively opened the door to his house and sniffed. Nothing. Grateful, he shut the door behind him and dropped his wallet and watch onto the front stand by the door. The front living area was quiet. The only sound in the house was the humming refrigerator and the tick-tock of the clock in the kitchen. Walking through the living room, he shed his shirt and unbuckled his pants. After throwing them into the laundry, he walked towards the bathroom where the scent of sewage increased.

After entering the bathroom, he knelt by the drain in the floor and sniffed hesitantly, but it did not stink. Leaning over the toilet, he did the same: nothing like what he'd experienced the night before.

Rising, he moved towards the sink where he bent over to smell that drain. The odor did seem stronger. Like children playing the game 'Hot or Cold,' Stedman followed the scent with his nose until he rested directly over his cologne bottles. *Strange,* he thought. Picking up the bottle of Creed Aventus he put his nose to it.

He sprayed a little bit into the air. His gag reflex sent him back to the toilet where he dry heaved. Once in control of himself, he returned to the cologne stand and grabbed the Vert Malachite spraying a large stream into the air and over his body. He swore loudly.

Turning the shower on, he stepped inside the cubicle and reached for the Head and Shoulders. Pumping madly, the white shampoo filled his hand. Because the Veet had now made its way up the straw and out through the pump, the chemical reaction began. Stedman rubbed the shampoo vigorously into his hair, lathering and foaming.

Why? What was going on? Did someone...? He looked down as the drain was clogging up.

"What the hell?"

He leaned down to clear whatever was clogging the drain and then realized that it was his hair. And, a lot of it. Quickly reaching up to touch his head, he found that his scalp was almost naked.

"No! Not happening!"

Horrified, he stopped the shower, soap still clinging to his body and head. Dripping his way across the bathroom, he stood in front of the mirror, aghast at his reflection. There were still a few tufts of hair sticking up in the front, a clump near his right ear, a thimble full on the back of his skull. He touched the one by his ear and it began to slide down the side of his head.

"Oh, my God," he muttered, aghast at his appearance.

Walking back to the shower, he reached down to the drain. A scream rose from the inner depths of his being, and he wailed as he pulled up the remnants of his thick, previously luscious, but now decidedly unattached hair. All the visions from the night before hurtled back to the forefront of his mind: perpetual baldness, cancer, chemotherapy and, ultimately, a very slow and painful death. He carried his hair out into the living room like a recently deceased pet awaiting burial.

Naked as a jaybird, Stedman Boswell made his way into the kitchen. For what reason, he was not sure other than to dump the remnants of his hair in the trash. He needed to get rid of it. He needed to have it out of sight. Like Lady MacBeth attempting to eliminate the stain of blood from her hands, Stedman Boswell dumped his hair into the wastebasket and proceeded to pick individual hairs from between his knuckles.

Frustratedly, Stedman rubbed at the hairs still sticking to his hands. He could feel tears come to his eyes. Unaware that he was going into shock, Stedman began to tremble.

Suddenly, there was a voice at the front door.

"Hello, are you in there Boswell? Are you okay?"

Stedman froze. He was unprepared, obviously, to have someone enter the house, especially at this sensitive time.

"Uh, yes," he called out from his hiding place in the kitchen, "can you come back some other time? I'm… busy."

The sound was moving towards the kitchen.

"I heard screaming outside and I just wondered if everything was all…" When Derek Peterson saw the naked insurance man positioned by the wastebasket, his jaw dropped. "What… the… fabric?"

Both men froze. For the longest five seconds of either man's life, they stood facing each other, jaws hanging slack.

Finally, Boswell broke the impasse. "Do you mind?"

Derek shook his head. "Oh man, oh man, I'm really sorry, I didn't know you'd be doing that…" Derek hustled out of the room.

"I'm not doing *that*!" Stedman shouted with embarrassment. "I'm throwing away my hair!"

"Call it whatever you want, man, I'm sorry for interrupting you. I was just seeing if you were okay." Derek's voice diminished, but Stedman did not hear the front door open. He was still in the house.

"Go away, Peterson. I need a few moments."

"We need to talk."

"I don't want to talk, especially to you!" Stedman looked around the kitchen and found a dishtowel, which he used to modestly cover himself, and walked to the kitchen doorway. Peering around the corner, only his head showing, he saw that Derek Peterson was staring out the window facing away from him.

"I appreciate your concern, but you need to leave. I have to get dressed and then I'm going back to… the hospital."

"The hospital?" Derek did not turn around.

"My… condition… is being monitored."

Derek paused and Stedman could see him take a deep breath. "That's what I wanted to talk to you about. I know why you've lost all your hair."

"Rhonda told you." Boswell took a step out into the living room.

Derek nodded. "Yes."

"It was a shock to me too. I'm pretty young for this to be happening, but I'm going to fight it."

"They didn't do this because you're young."

The words didn't compute. "What? What are you talking about? Who's 'they?' The doctor told me about Hodgkin's Disease. I have all the symptoms."

"You don't have Hodgkin's Disease. Your hair loss is because of Veet."

"Veet? I don't understand."

Derek gestured with his hands to the window, still unwilling to turn around. "Hair removal product. Some zealous town members broke into your house and put the product on your soap and in your shampoo."

The information floored Stedman. "But… but… how is that possible? When did this happen?"

"Friday night while you were at the football game."

Stedman's mind reeled. Was it possible? He did take a shower that night… "But why, then, did the hair on my head fall out only after the second shower? If the hair removal product was in there on Friday night, I should have lost my hair then."

Derek shrugged. "I don't know."

"You're lying, Peterson. You don't want me to go to the doctor. You want me to die!"

Derek turned around, flinched, but then forced himself to keep his eyes on the bald man's face standing ten feet away holding a dishtowel over his private parts. "That's ridiculous. This town might be crazy, but we're not murderers!"

"You can't fool me. I'm going to the doctor, and when I get better, I'm going to raze this town just like that old piece of crap elevator." He started to gesture with his towel hand, but thought better of it.

Subconsciously, Derek moved his hands to cover his own groin, but stopped short of cupping himself. "How can I prove this to you? If I can show you what they did, can we sit down and talk?"

"Okay. If you can prove it, we'll sit down and talk."

"Excellent," Derek said.

"If it is as you say it is, then take a shower and wash your hair… If you lose your hair, I'll believe you."

"Oh, no way. That is not how this is going to play out."

"Oh really? You just admitted to me that a number of Amicable citizens have committed a laundry list of crimes against me. If that's true, I think the press will have a field day about how this little town of dimwits tried to interfere with an investigation."

Baker

Dangit, Derek, you dipstick! Caught between a rock and a bald place. Derek's mind raced for alternative solutions. "Look, I'll just put some on my arm, or legs. You can still see the hair come o…"

Boswell grinned malevolently. Now he knew that Peterson was telling the truth. "Nope. All or nothing. You become like me."

Derek's mind raced. The embarrassment. The staring. The gossip. Nash was never going to let him live this down. What about Tracey? Things were going so well.

"Okay. Okay. I'll do it. But if I do this, you can't go to the cops, no on-line posting."

"Whatever you say, Peterskin."

"Oh, hell no, Stedwoman."

"Come on, let's get you out of those clothes and into the shower." Stedman's derisive laughter was almost too much for the younger Peterson twin, but he checked himself. *Taking one for the team.*

"That's the grossest thing I've ever heard in my life," Derek said as he walked past the gesturing insurance adjuster to the shower.

"You're welcome."

Summer Teichman drove Baker's Lamborghini, while Theo sat in the passenger seat, idly thumbing through his social media pages.

"How much longer until we're there?" Baker asked without looking up.

Summer checked the navigation device, which Baker easily could have seen. "About fifty miles yet."

"Do you think you could speed this up? I'm pretty tired of the scenery and I'd like to get out of the car for a while and stretch my back. It's been a long ride already."

Looking over, Summer willed herself not to react to Baker's infantile whining. "We're making good time. I'm still doing sixty-five on the backroads. There might be a cop out here. And, because we're driving this," she tapped the steering wheel of the sleek, yellow vehicle, "we might be a little more prone to radars."

Baker sniffed. "They couldn't catch us anyway."

Chapter 20.

"Maybe you should drive then." Summer touched the brakes to slow down.

"No, thank you. You're doing a great job. I'm working."

She chanced a look at his phone. Candy Crush.

Figures.

Summer couldn't understand how a man his age, with his experience and responsibilities, could consistently act so childish. All of his toys, his phone, his car, even his clothes, bespoke someone who couldn't quite grow up.

As her thoughts ran on autopilot, a large, monarch butterfly committed suicide on the windshield leaving a resinous yellow splotch right in front of Baker's face. Summer thought that he would complain, but he didn't even notice.

She left it there.

"Okay," Derek said, "you can leave the bathroom now."

"I want to watch you do this."

Derek frowned. "Don't be ridiculous."

"Screw you. Leave your underwear on. I don't want to see your peterskin anyway."

Shaking his head, Derek raised a closed fist to Stedman. "When this whole thing is over, you and me, we're going to have words."

"Bite me."

Derek turned on the shower and stepped out of his clothes except his underwear. Heart beating rapidly, he put his hand into the shower's flow gauging the temperature but also leaving time for procrastination. "Dammit, be reasonable."

Stedman smiled. He had put on his clothes and now the roles were reversed. "Reasonable? Are you going to ask the same thing of your crazy friends?"

"Yes! Yes! I'll tell them. It won't happen again!"

"Damn right," Stedman responded. "Now, start lathering."

Derek sighed and stuck his head under the shower feeling the water flow over his feet. Derek's upper lip curled in revulsion. There was still quite a bit of human hair clogging the small holes of the drain.

"Come on, Derek. Pump away."

Without looking, Derek reached up and pumped the Head and Shoulders into his hand. Staring at the white pool, he glanced out through the shower door at Stedman, who stood, arms crossed, smiling. Slowly, he raised the shampoo to his hair and, with trembling heart, worked it into his hair.

"That's a good boy," Stedman derisively encouraged.

As the water washed over Derek, the effect was not instantaneous, but still quick. Tufts of hair began to appear in his hands. "There!" He shouted. "Are you happy now?"

"Not yet!" Stedman shouted back. "Conditioner. Condition the crap out of those goldilocks!"

"You buttmunch!" Derek reached up and filled his hand with the conditioner. Like a man about to jump from a cliff, he quickly put it in his hair and scrubbed. "AAAAAAAAAH!" Hair sloughed off in clumps and landed on the floor of the shower. Derek could feel the smoothness of his scalp.

The hair in the drain was beginning to clog and the water was rising quickly. "It's done. All right! Can I get out now?"

Boswell's joy was almost compete. Knowing that he had been given a new lease on life, no cancer, just a hairless existence, Stedman felt happy. At the same time, Peterson's abasement was cause for happiness. "Not quite. You've still got hair left!"

"Where?" Derek felt his head. "Where. It's all gone."

"Not there," Stedman said malevolently. "There." He pointed at Derek's underwear.

Derek blanched. *I'm going to kill Butcher.*

Summer slowed as they approached Amicable. When the shattered remains of the elevator appeared on their rural horizon, Summer gasped. Finally, Theo Baker looked up.

"Will you look at that?" Baker mused.

"How horrible."

Baker shook his head. "I know. That building right there is going to cost the company millions of dollars."

Summer looked at him sharply. "The remains of that building have cost many their livelihoods."

Frowning, Baker surveyed the rest of the town, while Summer slowed and stopped outside the orange fence barriers encircling the destruction. Much of the damage surrounding the building had been cleaned, but the broken concrete, rebar, rock and sand laying at the base made the building look like a construction site.

"Well, isn't this town a little slice of hell." One citizen spotted the Lamborghini and pointed at them, which gave Baker a thrill of self-satisfaction.

"It's quaint, Theo. These are probably really good, nice people."

"They're country bumpkins, Summer. They should be pitied, yes, but not for what happened. Just where they live."

Summer wasn't sure if she'd ever detested a man more than him.

"Now, let's take a spin down that street over there," he pointed to Main Street where gawkers had gathered to stare at the car. "We need to see what we're up against. Then," he said looking over his bifocals at the navigational device, "we'll head to 184 Peppertree to find Boswell. We're going to have a little discussion." Baker's voice rang with rancorous glee.

Stedman handed Derek a towel. Derek had done an excellent job of washing the entirety of his body hair into a pool of water at the base of the shower, and as he emerged, a bouncing baldy, he looked up balefully at Boswell, who was smiling at him.

"Now, that wasn't so bad, was it?"

Behind Stedman, Derek could see the reflection of the back of Boswell's head and the front of his. They looked like twin aliens.

"You're still a putz, you know that?"

"Yes," Stedman said simply.

"You can stop watching now, pervert."

"I will," Boswell responded, "but I think there's one more thing that will make this morning be even more glorious."

"What's that?"

Looking down at the counter, Boswell's vengeful gaze rested below him. "I think you might need a spritz of cologne."

Derek froze. *Oh crap.*

"I figured this one out, too."

"No, you don't have to do this!" Derek held up his hands, still naked from the waist up.

"Uh, yeah, I do."

Squirt, squirt.

Summer and Baker lapsed into a disagreeable silence. While circumnavigating the town, Baker snobbishly nitpicked. To her chagrin, he had taken photos of people staring at them. She felt embarrassed, not just to be riding around town in the ostentatious car, but to be seen with this arrogant prick who was making fun of people in their misery.

The navigation device announced *Arrived.* Both Baker and Summer gazed at the small two-story house surrounded by beautiful maple and ash trees. The front sidewalk was well-manicured and led directly to a three-step porch replete with a black mailbox on the right and black handrails on both sides.

184 Peppertree appeared to be a new house, which seemed strange because all of the other houses they'd seen in Amicable appeared to be at least fifty years old.

Baker pointed to the house. "Is that it?"

Summer rechecked the GPS. "That's what it says."

Theo ducked down looking under the trees. "I bet Boswell is enjoying living in this hole."

"I think it looks nice," she retorted.

"You would," Baker mumbled.

Summer was about to respond when the front door of the house flew open and two figures exploded from it. One was dressed in khaki pants, a collared shirt and socks; the other wore only pants. Oddly, both humans were hairless.

"What the…?" It looked like both were simultaneously vomiting in the grass.

After they had finished emptying the contents of their stomachs, the two hairless apes faced off against each other, but as they moved in for what seemed to be a fight, they began retching again.

"Are they drunk?" Summer asked.

"I don't know, but this is pretty weird." He looked at the address again. "Are you absolutely sure this is the right place?"

"Why don't you go ask them?"

"Not me," Baker said, "they could be having a lover's quarrel. That's the last thing I need to get involved in."

Summer ground her teeth.

"You do it. Go talk to them."

"Me?" Holding her hand to her chest, Summer then pointed to the vomiting men. "I'm not going over there."

"Why not? You're a woman. They won't hurt you."

"You're such a pig."

"Sticks and stones. Sticks and stones. Get out there." He reached across Summer, flipped the Lamborghini door upwards and pushed her out.

"You owe me for this," she spit back at him.

"I pay your salary. That's enough." He responded, and closed the door behind her.

Fuming, Summer straightened her dress, took a deep breath and walked towards them. As she approached, she smelled feces. She turned around to see Baker motioning with his hands pushing her towards the scene.

"Excuse me," she shouted.

Both sets of eyes turned towards her. Stedman looked confused. "Summer?"

Summer's mouth dropped open in shock. "Stedman?"

Nodding, Boswell wobbled towards her. "Yeah, it's me."

"What... What happened to you? Who is that?" She pointed at Derek. "What's going on here?"

He held up his hands. "Have you ever had a nightmare before?"

"Of course, but what does that have to do..."

209

"Okay," he interrupted, "now add every Freddie Kruger, Jason, the Saw and mix them into that dream, and then wake up and find that it's not a nightmare but reality. That's my life right now."

She gasped and then choked. "What in the world is that smell?"

"I can explain it all later, but right now, I'm kind of busy. Can you come back later?"

"But… but…" she pointed at his head, "what happened to your hair?"

"Summer, take Baker and go get a cup of coffee. There's a café on Main Street, Human Beans. I'll meet you up there in about an hour."

Shaken, Summer nodded and began her retreat. "But I wouldn't drive that thing up there?" He motioned towards the expensive car.

"Why not?"

"Strange things happen to nice cars in Amicable."

As he finished the statement, he heard, before he felt (or smelled), the onrush of Derek Peterson behind him.

WHAM! Derek tackled Stedman Boswell and drove him face first into the ground. Screaming, Summer wheeled away from them and stopped at the end of the sidewalk. "Stedman! Do you want me to call the police?"

"No!" He grunted from beneath Derek. "Go! I'll find you later! I can… take… care… of … this."

Going back to the car, Summer found Theo Baker's face pressed against the window. She smacked it and he jumped.

"What's going on out there?"

"We're getting a cup of coffee."

Exhausted, the two young men retreated, back to Stedman Boswell's rented living room. Both were scratched and bruised. Their tussle, vented frustration and tension, had been necessary and helpful. Although they both itched mercilessly from the dirt and grass on their naked skin, there was a different feel in the room.

Stedman had a bloody nose. The pile-driving tackle had caused it. At least he couldn't smell Liquid Ass now. Derek had a cut below his eye, which was already beginning to swell. Both felt that they had won the fight.

"Okay," Stedman said through plugged nose, "I'm ready to talk."

"I bet you are."

"Actually," Boswell continued, "I'm ready for you to talk. Is everyone in Amicable completely insane?"

Launching into the rehash of the last two weeks, Derek reminded Boswell of Butcher's gift. Derek told him about Butcher's lapse of judgement and the unfortunate moment when he had let his reading of Boswell spill over into the public sphere, where a few members of the willing (and gossiping) public had run with it.

"What did he say about me?"

"He said that you had no intention of helping Amicable to rebuild the elevator, and that the best course of action was to... find a way for you to leave so that we could get someone here who was eminently more... empathetic to our cause."

"And he figured this out how?"

"You saw him in the Butcher shop. He can do that with anyone."

Stedman shook his head. He winced. "That's ridiculous. Nobody can read the future."

"Was he right?"

Boswell's mouth moved, but no words came out for a moment. Then, he stammered. "I'm... well... I'm just trying to do my job."

"You're not going to deny it."

"That's not what I'm saying. I get paid by Baker to investigate bogus insurance claims. It's my job to make sure that doesn't happen."

"You aren't even looking at the facts here in Amicable.".

"Look, Derek, I'm just a pawn..."

"Don't give me that crap! Every person has free will to act ethically."

"Oh! Oh! Hypocrisy in action!" Boswell pointed at Derek. "What about your little underlings in Amicable assaulting me? Didn't they have ethical and moral obligations? What about them? I was an outsider just doing my job." His anger simmered.

Derek sighed. "You're right, Stedman. Absolutely right." He paused. "On behalf of Amicable, I apologize. I'm sorry."

Stedman's eyes squinted quizzically. Derek Peterson, similarly, was just a pawn in the recent chess game. All of them had been moving pieces in the game, manipulated by kings and queens of fate. If somehow he could take the butcher, Rhonda and the reverend, he would have knocked over the king, queen and a bishop and the game would be his - or, Baker's. This revelation, that he really wasn't fighting his own battle, but for his own black king, Theo Baker, was a shock to him. Stedman had never wanted to be a pawn in anyone else's game, but here he was, fighting the same fight, no longer against his mother and father, now with Baker.

"Who was that woman outside?"

Even though the car was no longer there, Boswell's eyes moved toward the window. "That was my boss's secretary, Summer."

"She's gorgeous."

"Yes, she is."

"How does that happen?" Derek asked. "Beautiful women and rich old men…"

Stedman shrugged.

"Do you have a girlfriend, Stedman?"

"No," he said. "I haven't had a girlfriend for a long time."

"Why not?"

Stedman shrugged. "I haven't found the one, I guess."

Derek sighed and grinned. "This is better, don't you think? You're almost like a human being, other than your hideous haircut."

Boswell smiled and winced then pulled himself from his chair.

"Where are you going?" Derek asked.

Boswell inhaled. "Come on. I have to introduce you to the real Satan."

Chapter 21.

The western light glittered above the wall of Carley's X-Er-Size studio and reflected off the shiny black tables of the café. Sitting near the window, Baker and Summer sipped coffee and stared morosely outwards at Main Street pondering the bucolic, small-town drama as it played out on the Saturday afternoon. A few older women, handbags draped over arms, floral dresses billowing slightly in the breeze, walked southwards. Were they stopping at the grocery store or the shoe shop? Would they stop and chat with people along the way? The mailman would know the ladies by name, of course: Gladys, Dorothy, maybe even a Martha thrown in - old lady names - and then pass them their packages or parcels. They would buy stamps (because people still sent letters in small towns) and complain, *Ooh it's getting so expensive to send letters nowadays*, but the good-natured postman would shrug.

Across the street, a shop door opened. Summer squinted to see what was written on the window.

X-Er-Size.

A group of women walked out carrying bags and towels over their shoulders; none of them seemed particularly sweaty. They gabbed madly and noisily. Summer thought they looked very much like hens, pecking here and there, clucking, clucking.

The last person out the door was a chubby, full-faced cherub in black stretch pants and fluorescent pink tank top. Pointing across the street at the café, she said something and laughed, then locked the door behind her. The chickens crossed the street together, clucking, clucking. A pickup truck paused patiently in the middle of the street, waiting for them to cross. One of the women near the front smiled and flipped him the bird.

"Mr. Baker," Summer tapped the table. "That lady, see the one at the front? She just flipped off the driver in that pickup truck."

"So?" he responded absentmindedly. "What about it?"

"The truck driver didn't even beep his horn. It's like he was expecting it. Isn't that weird?"

"Mmm."

The women finished crossing the street and entered the café.

"We'll have the regulars," a middle-aged woman exclaimed as soon as she walked through the door.

Summer was fascinated. The scene was well-orchestrated, like a symphony or a ballet. Oddly, Summer felt a mystifying sense of envy. *What would it be like to have time to spare for yourself and for others? What would it be like to walk in the door and somebody already knows what your 'regular' is?*

After sitting, heads bowed closely over the table, the women spoke quietly. Summer wondered what the secret was. Then, the chubby one giggled into her hand and said the words, "Phase III," which prompted shushes from the others and cautious glances around the room to see if any of the five other patrons were listening.

"Did you ever wonder what it's like to live in a small town, Mr. Baker?" Summer's eyes remained on the women in the middle of the room, as the waitress brought out their coffees and doughnuts.

"No."

"I think it's a fascinating social experiment. Put a bunch of people in the middle of nowhere, give them all similar jobs and similar outlooks on life…"

"Don't forget inbreeding."

Summer ignored the remark. "…theoretically, it should be survival of the fittest. The weak falter, the strong survive. But look at them. It's like they're all on the same team."

"Summer, enough," Baker responded impatiently. "Just shut up until Boswell gets here. You're talking is giving me a headache." He finished his espresso and looked out the window. "If Stedman is not here in the next twenty minutes, we're driving back there to pull his skinny, bald ass out of the house, to fire him."

Summer, angered, stood up. "You know what, Mr. Baker, you're a real pain in the …." she stopped and found the café's attention was fixed pointedly on her.

Baker leaned forward menacingly. "Summer," he lowered his voice, "you are one continued sentence from also being fired. Do you understand?"

"I'm going for a walk," she said through clenched teeth.

"What about Stedman? Don't you want to be here for this?"

214

"Not really," Summer responded and moved towards the door. Opening it, she melted into the moving shadows.

Linda stared at the man in the corner of the café. She had never seen him before. He did not fit in, not with his expensive pants, designer shirt and fancy-schmancy leather shoes. He was like a geriatric version of Boswell. A large gold watch sagged loosely about his right wrist. A gaudy ring encircled his wedding finger. Sunglasses, resolutely positioned on top of his head, reflected the café's lights. They did not appear to have been bought from a spinning sunglasses rack at a gas station.

Angrily, the man watched the gorgeous young woman stomp from the café. Linda wondered if they were lovers. She'd watched enough soap operas, *The Bold and Beautiful* being her favorite, to know what a lovers' quarrel was like.

The man turned to stare at her. At first, she wanted to turn away, but instead, she held his gaze. His blue eyes were pale enough to be grey. His cheeks showed a dark shadow. He had a strong jaw, high cheek bones and a full head of greying hair. He looked like an intimidating man. Linda, a woman who had been married over thirty years, was resigned to the casual and comfortable love that she had with her husband, but a man like this could be very dangerous.

One side of his mouth curled up. Unsure whether to smile or sneer, she hoped for a smile and returned it. His eyes strayed across her body. Men always did that with her. When his eyes made it back to hers, they were cold, calculating. She shivered.

He broke their connection and checked his loose watch.

At that moment, there was a commotion outside of Human Beans. A crowd across the street had stopped to stare at the entrance of Human Beans. Something was happening. Something gossip-worthy.

Opening the door of the café for Stedman, Derek tried to ignore the stares. Unused to the baldness, he grimaced at his reflection in the shop window. As they entered, all conversation stopped. Derek tried to close the door behind him, but a stream of Amicableans suddenly felt a strong urge for a cup of coffee at 4:58 on a Saturday afternoon.

Terri Landis' jaw hung loosely, unhinged. As the owner of Human Beans, she was quite sure that she knew every single person in Amicable. But these two, two aliens, one who looked very much like one of the Peterson twins, the other, the insurance guy, were hard to recognize. They approached the counter and ordered two coffees.

Stedman immediately strode to Theo Baker. "Mr. Baker."

Baker looked up shocked, but he controlled his surprise. "Stedman." His eyebrow raised. "You're late. Do you know how boring this place is?"

Stedman looked around at the milling café patrons who were attempting polite, distracted and quiet conversation. "Actually, sir, it has been anything but boring."

"Whatever. Tell me about the case. Are we on track...?" Both men noticed that all conversation in the café had ceased. Terri had lowered the volume on the radio.

"I think it's best if we chat somewhere else."

Baker's jaw twitched. In an attempt to intimidate Boswell, Baker stood. "Look, Boswell, you don't have to worry about them," he growled and jerked a thumb at the Amicableans. "Simple people."

Unfortunately, for Theocrates Baker, the simple people of Amicable had very good hearing. Faces hardened, jaw muscles tensed, and frowns arose from nowhere.

"Sir," he whispered, "I must insist. I think it best if we go somewhere else."

"What's wrong with you, Boswell? I send you here for a couple of weeks and what happens? You lose your hair, you walk around town - where the hell is your Porsche?" This elicited a snort from Carley, who then pretended to fan herself and asked Donna about the weather.

"And then... and then!" Baker stuck his finger up in the air, "you make me sit here without any indication of what's going on. You called me from the hospital, in God Knows What Hole-In-The-Earth, Iowa, telling me that you've got cancer, or something ridiculous..."

"Mr. Baker!"

Stedman Boswell's voice carried far above the silence and froze it into that moment in time. Theo Baker had never had anyone shout at him before - not parent, teacher, wife, boss – no one, and here was this little pissant, Boswell, raising his voice. Baker, shocked, narrowed his eyes to slits, and growled.

"You better tell me what's going on."

"If you would be so kind as to follow me outside, I think we can speak reasonably. Please, Mr. Baker," Stedman said indicating the way with his hand.

Baker relented. As they left, Leona's coffee mug was suspended in midair beneath her mouth; Jeannie's eyes were wide with excitement. Angela looked at Linda who was touching her hair. Derek Peterson watched impassively knowing that the fulcrum of the town's existence was either being built, or destroyed at that very moment. Everything pivoted on this discussion.

Baker and Boswell left the café. Boswell cast one last glance at Derek and raised what was left of his eyebrows.

"Well," Leona clapped her hands and added, "wasn't that fun?"

"It seems as if there is a new front to the war," Linda said theatrically. Her eyes strained to catch sight of the two departing men.

"What do you mean?" Jeannie asked.

"That man," she pointed to where Theo been sitting, "wants nothing to do with restoring Amicable. Boswell was one thing; but this guy... Butcher's head would explode if he got near him."

A few of the women looked at Connie, but she said nothing.

"What are we going to do?" Angela asked, attempting not to bite her nails, but failing miserably.

"Phase III," Linda said simply.

"What is Phase III?" Derek asked, overhearing the women from his position at the coffee bar.

Linda studied his new hairless look and blinked rapidly.

"I know," he said, "I'm bald and it's your fault."

"But... but..." Jeannie stammered.

"You planted the hair removal product in his shampoo and conditioner bottles, but the pump action delayed the product. Unfortunately," he continued, "that same difficulty didn't occur in the cologne bottles. What in God's name is that stuff?"

"Liquid Ass," Carley answered. She really enjoyed saying 'ass.'

"Whatever it is, the smell made me puke."

"Tell me about it," Carley nodded sagely to her friends.

"How did you get your black eye?" Connie asked.

Derek gave them a brief rundown. "I get that you wanted to help out and you did the best that you could, but that's not the way to stop the insurance company. The owner, Baker... from what Stedman told me, is bad news."

"Back the truck up for a minute," Linda said. "What, are you guys friends now? Because I thought you hated each other."

"We won't be the Best Man at each other's wedding, but we've reached a truce."

"I'll say."

"It's the price I've been asked to pay."

"Who asked you to pay it?" Penny asked, engaged in the story.

Derek's mind flashed to Butcher and Rhonda. "It doesn't matter, but what does matter is what you are going to do next. Back to the original question: what is Phase III?"

Linda closed her eyes and breathed deeply through her nose. "Emasculation."

"What?"

"You heard me." Linda's face was dreadfully serious.

"You can't cut off his... his..."

"No," Linda responded as she touched his arm, "we're not going to cut off his asset, but we may make it difficult for him to, shall we say, appear in public."

"From experience, I don't think that's such a good idea."

"Please, Derek, you said the man is up to no good and wants to destroy Amicable. We might only have this one chance to save the town."

"But what is *it*?"

Linda looked around and then pulled up a chair for Derek. "You'd better sit down," she said.

Chapter 21.

"All right Boswell, what in the world happened to you? What's going on? Has everyone gone insane?"

"Yes, in a way, Mr. Baker." Stedman related his time in Amicable, withholding only a few details. He did tell his employer that his shampoo bottle had been violated.

Baker's eyes widened. "Why aren't you pressing charges? These people should be behind bars, or at the very least getting some serious professional help."

Stedman shook his head. "They don't need professional help," he said quietly. "They need assistance from their insurance company."

"Oh for God's sake, Stedman, don't tell me you've fallen for their sob story. I mean, really, I expected more from you."

The rebuke hurt Boswell and he winced.

Baker continued his diatribe. "You've fallen for the oldest trick in the book. Let me guess, a woman?" Stedman didn't say anything. "Good heavens... Okay, so you've fallen for a girl, she's stripped you of your senses, and somehow they've helped you see the luminous, altruistic light from the sky." Baker changed the tone of his voice to baby talk. "We're a small town full of really nice people and our main source of revenue blew sky high. Help us. Cheep, cheep. Feed us. Give us a free handout. Cheep, cheep."

Infuriated, Boswell saw in Baker's attitude a mirrored reflection of his own.

"Sir," he said firmly, "these people are good people, and they've been paying their premiums..."

"SHUT UP, BOSWELL! I'm not paying you for empathy, I'm paying you to do what you're told do. I've told you to find the loophole. You said you'd found it. Some Mexican with an axe to grind, is that right?"

Townspeople gathered on the street to watch. As they stood, mesmerized by the verbal confrontation, Summer approached them.

"Yes! Yes, I found a crack in the story of the elevator." Stedman responded, motioning with his hands. "But, he might have just been in the wrong place at the wrong time. It could have been an accident. Who knows? But the whole employee vs. employer vengeance angle isn't going to help anyone."

"Is that right?" Baker asked. "No one? What about our shareholders? Are you finally getting it through your thick skull, Boswell?" He grabbed Stedman by the arm.

"Theo!" Summer's voice rang out behind them. "Let go of him. You're making a scene!" She pointed across the street where townspeople were staring.

"I don't give a flying fart who sees or hears what I'm doing. I've got about twenty-four more hours in this cesspool and then you're going to drive me back to Kansas City as fast as possible."

Summer glared at him.

"Now," Baker released Boswell's arm and he straightened his shirt, "Boswell, if you know what's good for your career, you're going to supply me with your notes and then," he poked a finger into Stedman's chest, "I'll take it from there." He annunciated each word carefully with individual pokes. "When you are done providing me with said information, you will then pack up your belongings and drive back to Kansas City, where you will unpack your Porsche, turn on your television set, and pour yourself five fingers of scotch to forget this massive screw-up in Dumpyville, Iowa." Baker's eyes drilled holes into Stedman's, who turned away.

"Are we all on the same page?" Baker spoke through gritted teeth.

"Yes," Stedman and Summer mumbled simultaneously.

"I didn't hear you!"

"Yes!" They shouted together.

"Good!" Baker pushed past them to cross the road. "We're staying in Clunky, or Clanky, or whatever the name is of that shit-heap town fifteen miles from here. I'll be back in the morning for my information." He stopped. "Hey!" He shouted at Summer. "Let's go!"

"I'm staying with Stedman to help him get everything ready," she responded gloweringly. "You can drive yourself."

"Suit yourself!" Baker yelled, stalking back, not slowing to break through the ever-growing crowd, which had gathered to watch the confrontation. "Out of my way!" He stalked to the Lamborghini where, after unlocking it, he pulled up the door and climbed in. Within seconds, he peeled out onto the street. Turning left, he gave Summer and Stedman the evil eye and accelerated away from them. Not stopping at the stop sign, he roared past St. Clements and the high school. By the time he reached Fourth Street West, there were flashing lights behind him.

Chapter 22.

Some Sundays, Demetrius might have vetoed going to church, but not this one. He did not want to miss it.

Demetrius pulled the phone out of his desk drawer and checked his social media.

"Apparently," Wendy Mercer wrote (the word 'apparently' was used in almost every sentence), "this insurance guy from Kansas City showed up and totally was, like, sup, and he weirded out in front of everyone."

Robbie Carson answered. "Supposedly, like, you know one of those butchers, the twins, showed up as a skinhead."

The last message in the conversation ended at 3:48 a.m. when Dennis Toddman *apparently* wanted to have the last word. "I am a hundo p. that I need to do some adulting to y'all and tell you to go to bed. We can gasbag in the mon."

"White people..." Demetrius muttered.

After dressing in a nice pair of shorts and a large t-shirt, Demetrius plodded downstairs to the kitchen. Opening the door, he found his mother furiously cooking pancakes, while his father was doing the dishes.

"Good morning," his father said. "Sleep well?"

"Yup."

Demetrius approached his mother, towering over her, and leaned in to kiss the top of her head. "How did you sleep, Mom?"

"Oh," she said jumping slightly. "I'll be fine with an afternoon nap. Just need to stop the wheel from turning over." She pointed to her head with the pancake flipper. She was already in her church clothes, but the apron protected them.

"What's wrong?" Demetrius asked, and his father paused to look over at her.

"Nothing that you should worry your young head over."

"Does it have to do with that insurance guy?" Demetrius took seven pancakes to the table, buttered them, and slathered syrup over the golden tops.

She looked sharply at him. "What did you hear about that? Have your friends been making up stories?"

Confused, Demetrius paused his eating. "Supposedly the insurance man's boss turned up at Human Beans and he started going off at Boswell and this other lady."

Angela Chandler turned off the griddle and, without looking at Demetrius, put the spatula into the sink. "Yes? Anything else you heard?"

"Were you there? Wasn't that right after your exercise group?"

Angela nervously glanced at her husband. Her eyes were fearful. It was just too hard to deny being somewhere. Someone was always taking a video, a photo, or just opening their mouth.

"Why, yes, I was there. I thought you were… talking about something else."

"So, what happened?" Demetrius ate half a pancake in one bite. Syrup dripped down his chin, which he wiped with the back of his hand.

"Boswell's boss was waiting with this woman, she was gorgeous. She was wearing this beautiful black dress, tight around the waist, lacy shoulders and these pump black shoes. I am not one for coveting, but…"

"Mom," Demetrius interrupted, "you were telling me what happened, not what the woman was wearing."

"Sorry. They were obviously frustrated with each other. We could only hear a little bit of what they were saying, but…"

"Who's we? Is that the rest of your exercise group?"

She nodded. "But things didn't really get out of hand until Stedman and Derek walked in."

"Together?"

"Yup." Her lips made a popping sound on the 'p.'

"Don't they hate each other?"

"That's what I thought too, but then Derek's holding the door for Boswell and well…" Her voice dropped, gossipy, "…both of them had shaved their heads."

"Then what happened?"

"This Baker guy goes after Boswell and the woman with the *really* nice clothes, and they go outside, supposably to get out of our

223

earshot…" Demetrius also let the word 'supposably' pass. It was something Aaron said all the time too. "He gives them an earful and gets into his yellow car, a real nice one, too, like a Corvette, but fancier even. It had doors that actually folded up!" She used her hands to signal the engineering.

"You're kidding!" Demetrius exclaimed. "A Lamborghini!"

"Or some other kind of pasta." His father's dad joke was ill placed. They ignored him.

"So then he gets into his… that car you were just talking about…"

"The Lamborghini…"

"Mmmhmmm, yes, but then he went squealing his tires down Main Street and turned towards the school. I think Louise caught him on the outskirts of town."

"Did she arrest him?"

Angela leaned against the counter. "You bet she did."

"Is he in jail?"

"That's the word on the street. Supposably, a night in Amicable's pokey probably did a world of good for his supersized ego."

Demetrius finished off his seventh, and last, pancake and wiped his mouth one more time. Pushing back the chair, he moved to where his mother was leaning. He rinsed his plate and put it in the dishwater in front of his father who began to wash it.

"So, are we ready to go to church?"

His father looked up at Demetrius, surprised. "You? Excited to go to church?" Feigning amazement, his father put a soapy hand to his chest.

"Whatever, Pops, I'm always ready to go to church." Demetrius pushed off the sink to put his shoes on.

"Okay, then," Angela said as she took off her apron. "I guess we'll get a move on."

Deakins scanned the items surrounding him, icons and relics of a previous, spiritual age. On one shelf was a picture of Jesus in various states of emotion: the 'Laughing Jesus' (which drove Deakins insane) and the 'Almost Naked and Dying Jesus' hanging on the cross, hands and ankles bloodied by wonderfully clean, straight nails. The cross itself seemed to be handcrafted by the best artisans, beautiful squared lines, probably American oak if you'd ask any of the Amicableans - Jesus would have wanted it that way.

Above the artwork were the brassware, plates, paten, chalices, and all the finery that Jesus *should* have employed at the last supper. When he put the wafers (gluten-free included - couldn't be too careful in this day and age of universal allergies) onto the tray, he wondered if Jesus could have said with a straight face, "This," as he pointed at the perfect wafers with a *chi* and *rho* crossed, "is my body broken for you."

What in the world? Deakins thought to himself. Have I missed something? Why are they so noisy this morning?

Deakins looked at his watch. 9:25. Jim should be beginning the prelude now, but he definitely didn't like conversation occurring while he was playing. During Jim's practice, John would sometimes sit in the back pew and listen to the ancient echoes, reverberations of faith calling people to worship. Closing his eyes and breathing deeply, he would wonder where it all went wrong. Eventually, his eyes would focus on the cross and he would be deeply grateful, that in the end, it was all going to end up all right.

It was just a matter of how they were all going to get there.

John nodded as the organ started. Blessed Assurance. In the past week, he'd changed the words to 'Blessed Insurance' in an unconscious hope to manipulate God into changing the insurance man's heart. Pharaoh could just let his people go.

The buzz continued through Deakins' frowning. Finishing one last short prayer, he stood, adjusted his tie, and walked out the door of the sacristy to the chancel. As he descended the step between the sides of the altar, he scanned the congregation. Jim, the Organist/Mailman was not pleased and played even louder. This, in turn, caused the congregation to increase the volume of the conversation over the music. Deakins looked up to the balcony where Jim was furiously playing his 6/8 time, but even *he* could not bring peace to the assembly.

Deakins eyes fell to the nave where he saw what the buzz was about.

Two women were sitting next to two bald men in the front row. Not just bald - barren. No hair from the crown of their heads to their chinny-chin-chins. Deakins squinted and tilted his head slightly. Visitors?

Oh, Good Lord.

One of them was Derek. But the other, Stedman Boswell!

Jim finished with a flourish but the sanctuary was filled with voices.

"Good morning and welcome. Is everyone all right?"

Nervous chatter.

"Wow. You'd think someone just got engaged or something."

Laughter.

"So, let me in on the secret. What's going on?"

The congregation, used to Reverend Deakins' relaxed style, waited for any one person, one brave soul, to break the back of the question.

Aaron Carlson answered courageously. "Pastor J., haven't you heard? There's a new sheriff in town."

"I did hear something about that." He raised his eyebrows.

"Yeah, like, there's this guy and he's driving a Lamborghini," more tittering, "and he shows up at Human Beans with…" Aaron's eyes move towards the front where the bald young men were staring back at him. Derek was smiling; Stedman was not.

"Never mind," Aaron finished the sentence.

"No, really, it would be good for us to talk about it, don't you think?"

Angela Chandler cleared her throat. "Maybe it's best if we chatted after worship?"

Groans.

"Yes, well, maybe that's a good idea."

It was not a good idea at all, actually, because only half a dozen worshipers paid any attention to what was happening in worship that day. More than a few times, people checked their watches during the sermon; the hymns were sung with less gusto and with a sense of impatience. The scriptures were read quickly and without inflection. Prayers were intoned rapidly – *Dear God, you know what we need, please make it happen.*

Chapter 22.

Reverend Deakins felt an ambient pressure to push through his sermon regarding God's wrath on the faithless Israelites who didn't put their trust in him.

As the last chord finished and the triumphant descant floated into the ether, voices hushed in expectation. Eyes peered over red hymnals at the pastor who checked his watch. "Amazing," he pronounced sarcastically, "we've set a world record. Forty-two minutes. Congratulations." A few young people in the back began clapping, but were stopped quickly by frowning parents.

"Okay, maybe we should all adjourn to the basement where we can have a cup of coffee, sit around some tables and have a discussion." No one moved. "Or," Deakins said alternatively, "we could all stay here and talk it out."

"I think that's a good idea," Dennis Bradford, a fifth generation Amicablean, said settling back in his pew.

John's eyes scanned the congregation.

"I think we should start off by welcoming some guests in our midst…" He let the sentence trail off. Stedman and Summer did not move.

"I see." He folded his hands in front of his black suit coat. "Is there anyone who would be willing to speak first?"

Tense seconds passed. John was about to breathe a sigh of relief when a voice broke through the back corridor. It was Steve Evans.

"I wanted to remain silent, but I just couldn't." Steve walked halfway up the aisle, far enough to be seen by the congregation. "Look," he wrung his hands near his silver, seed-company belt buckle. "I understand that we're all trying to be good and 'Christian' here, but if I read my Bible correctly, we're supposed to tell the truth, and sometimes the truth has some tequila in it."

"Go ahead, whatever that means," John's voice fell off to a mumble.

"Well," he said, after much more hand wringing, "in the last couple of weeks, I've listened and watched as Mr. Boswell there has entered our town, and I've tried my best to give him the benefit of the doubt, and even more, I've tried to give him the benefit of my faith, but…" Steve Evans was doing his best to be nice but couldn't find a way to be nice and honest. "... But Mr. Boswell seems hell-bent on doing us, and by us, I mean Amicable, in."

A collective gasp arose from the gathering, whether it was from the word 'hell' in church (even though it played a relatively prominent role in some congregants' theology), or calling out a visitor in their midst, wasn't clear. This was most certainly *not* nice.

Sweat beaded on his brow and moistened his palms. "I'm sorry to say this, Mr. Boswell, but I believe that the people of Amicable have the right to know what you're doing."

Steve glanced at his watch, and continued. "When you first arrived, Mr. Boswell, we assumed that the insurance investigation would be fair and unbiased, but as we probably could have guessed, insurance companies are about as fair and unbiased as Fox News." His attempt at humor elicited a few chortles from the handful of Democrats in the crowd, including Tracey Thomas, who was sitting next to Derek. "But we never imagined that Baker would sink so low as to besmirch the reputation of a dead man."

The congregation collectively leaned in. This was new information.

"Enrique Fernandez was a good and hard-working man. Through many trials and tribulations, he made his way across the United States to our beautiful, small community of Amicable. Enrique was unafraid to talk about his extraordinary crossing of the Caribbean, his path through the underbelly of the drug culture in Miami and north to us. We Amicableans have no concept of his difficult life, but we welcomed him, like we do with so many others, with open arms."

"Amen!" a voice shouted from the back, followed by a chorus of assents.

Steve pressed his advantage. "Okay, so Enrique's documentation was in limbo. We know that he wasn't 'legally' a citizen of the United States, but he was a hard worker, a kind and decent human being who was thriving in Amicable."

John Deakins nodded, but frowned. "I'm not sure where you're going with this, Steve. What does Stedman Boswell have to do with Enrique Fernandez?"

Steve swallowed and then pointed at Stedman. "This man was about to use the lack of citizenship of Enrique Fernandez as the primary source of denial for our insurance claim."

Gasps. Murmuring. The congregation sounded like an angry mob.

"We have it on good authority that Boswell's compilation of speculative safety inspections, record keeping and, especially, filling in blanks in Enrique's background by labelling him a terrorist..."

Someone shouted from the back. "Enrique's not the terrorist - it's Baker. They're the ones spreading terror. Greedy basta..., er... jerks!"

Things were going to get ugly soon. John attempted to quiet the crowd again, but frustration had been building: joblessness, fear of the future and a realization that Amicable would be changed. A few women and men, in their Sunday finest, faces gathering like an onrushing storm, stood to point fingers and shout unintelligible things.

Steve waved his arms. "We needed to do something from the beginning. Butcher tried to warn us, but we, the council, decided that the best thing that we could do was to hope that in the investigation Boswell would warm to the town. But, we were wrong. He called his boss, Theo Baker, who arrived yesterday with... her..." he pointed at Summer, whose eyes were wide with fright "... and they arrived in a," he snorted with derision, "a Lamborghini. I mean, how stupid can you get? Do I really think Baker has our best interests in mind? Hell no!"

The congregation/mob was threatening to get out of hand.

From the back of the room, a figure emerged and the voices hushed one row at a time as he passed.

Theocrates Baker. His clothes were in disarray; both shirt and pants displayed uncharacteristic wrinkles for a man of his status, and his hair, neatly positioned yesterday afternoon, stood up at the back of his head.

"It's just as I thought!" Theo punctuated the air with a finger. In his hands he held a sheaf of papers. "I've been to Stedman Boswell's house to pick up information and yes, I found his report." He held up the folder. "Through no coercion from Baker Insurance Corporation, Stedman Boswell wrote an exhaustive report on the explosion of the Amicable grain elevator. It leaves no doubt in my mind that Enrique

Fernandez was a terrorist and thus, the leadership of the elevator was at fault."

The crowd booed. Baker waited for their shouts to diminish. John Deakins had crossed his arms and was frowning at the front.

If Baker could have crawled inside Butcher's mind, even for a tense few moments, he would have seen malevolent hatred and unfiltered disgust for him. Stedman Boswell leaned forward, his bald head resting on his hands, which was holding the modesty guard in front of him. Summer's hand was on his back, but her face was perplexed and fearful. As she looked around the room, she understood for the first time the incredible emotions involved in insurance disputes.

Butcher, though worried about what was going to happen, smugly sat back in his own pew holding J.T. and Georgie in his arms. They both covered their ears because of the noise. Rhonda, like so many in the room, felt helpless.

"So!" Baker shouted above the roaring crowd, "I will do my best to help the people of Amicable, but there are legalities. It will take some time to work through them."

"What a load of crap!" A voice shouted from the back. "Insurance companies don't care about people!

Theo Baker could not restrain his smile.

"How much is Baker going to give back to the community so we can start rebuilding?" A shrill voice penetrated the uproar. The number would either incite a riot, or quell the fears of the town.

Baker crossed his arms. This was the part that he relished the most - seeing the expectant faces of hopeful policyholders, transformed into hollow shells. Deep down, he knew that he should be working for the good of his clients. They paid their money, followed the rules, but technicalities were important. A long time before this confrontative moment in Shitville, Iowa, Theocrates Baker had hardened his heart and inured himself to the reactions of those slighted. For him, this was the game. Winning was all he cared about.

"I've done my best," he said with faux empathy, "but the best we'll be able to repay is forty percent. If you only…"

The rest of his statement was lost in the uproar. Furious faces, threatening words, raised fists.

"That's only twenty million!" Steve said as he quickly calculated what they'd need to rebuild. "That barely gets us off the ground! You've killed us."

Baker raised his hands as if surrendering. "Look, I know that's not the news that you wanted to hear, but Baker has a responsibility to the rest of the policy holders not to reward people or groups for incompetence."

Nothing Baker could have said would have riled the crowd more than the word 'incompetence.' From the get go, Amicable had been raised on competence, doing the job well, accurately and finishing on time. Whether Liam Wilson the mechanic or Burton Caskins, a farm implement dealer, if the customer wasn't satisfied, these business owners would keep going until they were.

James and Naida Thompson trudged to the exit carrying their crying son. Others sat back disconsolately in their pews, arms and jaws slack with bewilderment and disbelief that the Amicable's obituary had just been written.

Carl Johnson walked forward passing the pulpit with its green vestment picturing a white lamb speared by a nail and dripping blood into a cup beneath. His eyes focused first on Reverend Deakins and then on Theo Baker. Deakins was aware that there was something dark and desperate in Carl's eyes, something that might spill over into regret if Carl wasn't careful. At the last moment, Carl stopped ten feet short of Baker but aligned with the row where Summer, Stedman, Derek and Tracey were seated

"You…" Carl pointed a finger directly at Baker's face, "… and you," he said through clenched jaws, transferring his point from Baker to Boswell, "ought to be ashamed of yourselves. More than that, you should be begging God for forgiveness. God says that he will stand for those that have experienced persecution and injustice." He wagged his finger at both of them. "Just you wait."

Baker rolled his eyes. "Is God going to strike me down? A bolt of lightning? Worms running through me? Plague, pestilence?" He looked up at the ceiling. "I'm ready, God! Take me now!"

Deakins' righteous anger arose. "How dare you blaspheme!"

231

"Me! Me?" Baker responded incredulously, leaning forward towards both Deakins and Carl Johnson. "Where is the 'Christian' spirit? I spent last night in the Amicable jail because I ran a stop sign. Do you know how demeaning that is? I've lived in Kansas City my whole life, a few tickets... but to be arrested? This vendetta you have against big city people is not just intolerant it's... it's... prejudiced!"

He pointed around to the crowd, continuing. "You call yourselves Christians, but my friend," he said slowly, "Stedman Boswell, arrived under perfectly good pretenses to do a job that, to be honest, very few want to do because it requires looking at reality, not this pseudo-communal nicety that you call Amicable. The reality of this life is that you make do with what life gives you - this is not lemon into lemonade, but crap into fertilizer. Stedman did his job. And so it's come up snake eyes for you, what are you doing to do about it?" He folded his arms. "I'm sorry to say, there's nothing you *can* do about it."

Miserable silence. "I don't make the rules; the government does. You purchase insurance for the unthinkable, but it happened. I truly am sorry that you've had to go through this, but that's no excuse for how you've treated poor Stedman."

Each time Theo mentioned Stedman's name, Stedman wanted to sink further into the pew. Everything Baker had said struck a chord in him. Although he was aware that Summer's hand was still on his back, he felt conspicuously alone. Yet, something new was stirring in him. The mere fact that Derek Peterson had taken the time to come to his house yesterday, even if under false pretenses, spoke of the power of this community. Even more than the anger he felt about his car, his body and, perhaps, his spirit, Stedman recognized a growing sense of admiration and respect for this community which wanted to take care of their own against incredible, and probably insurmountable, odds.

"Stedman," Baker said, "I just want you to know that this isn't your fault. Come on, let's go."

The congregation heard Baker's words. They sounded like a father, albeit a bad one, reaching out to his prodigal son to bring him home.

"What are we supposed to do?" Carl asked to everyone and no one in particular. "Without the elevator, Amicable will die. We will lose our jobs, our homes, our... history."

Baker defiantly held Carl's eyes.

Deakins wondered if he should say something. Butcher desperately wanted to crucify Baker. Reading him quickly, Butcher knew that he could destroy the man. Janice Stensrud wanted a plan C. Every person in the pews wanted to do, or say, something, anything that would dispel the gloomy silence filling the church. No one moved, though. No one breathed. Until finally, one voice spoke. One voice, small and tremulous, a youthful, hesitant and hopeful voice in the darkest pit of Amicable's despair.

Tracey Thomas.

At first, she didn't stand, she simply spoke towards the altar and the cross above it. Her eyes fixed on the scene carved into the wood: thirteen people, one of whom would betray Jesus with his actions, the others with their words and inactions. Tracey didn't know why she was speaking, only that she felt compelled to do so. Yesterday, when the eight of them had settled into Human Beans for their own Last Dinner of cheeseburgers and cups of coffee, she understood her own value. It was one thing for your parents to tell you that you are loved and that you are special and you have both beauty and giftedness, but it was another thing altogether when community leaders encouraged it.

Oddly, Baker's revelation had awakened something different in her. She knew that the town, if reimbursed, could rebuild and go back to normal. Strangely, her heart dropped at the thought of a return to business as usual. Life would continue, the community would begin to smile again, the school would produce and reproduce good and healthy graduates who would move on from Amicable to go to college and build lives in other places. If the insurance company didn't fully fund the rebuilding though, there was another way. It came from a dream.

This dream required intense courage.

Thus, her one, solitary voice, courageously stopped the death knell.

"Last night," she began, "I had a dream."

All eyes focused on her.

233

"In my dream, I saw Amicable die."

A stifled sob echoed in the back. Tracey felt it more than heard it so she decided to stand up. Pushing past Derek, then Stedman and finally Summer, Tracey moved into the aisle in front of Deakins, Carl and Baker. Amazingly, she found that she was not nervous.

"It was not the death of the town as much as it was the death of Amicable's lifestyle."

Tracey's statement was met with quizzical looks.

"For all of our town's existence, our lifestyle has been about hard work, respectability, and an unstoppable faith that somehow Amicable will make it through whatever comes, hell, hail or high water, if you will. We've treated Amicable as if it was a person, and that person is dead." She swallowed. "But Amicable is so much more than a singular identity, it is us - we who live here and love each other now. We are Amicable. Even though the elevator lies in a heap at the center of the town, we are still alive. Even though Mr. Baker believes he is writing our obituary, we still live."

"We are not dead, not even close, but the days of relying on big companies to be our insurance against ever-present tragedies are over. Now, we must rely on our own wits, our own power, our own justice, our own God-blessed love for life, liberty and the pursuit of so much more than just happiness. We, as Amicable, can transform this tiny little town in the middle of the Midwest, surrounded by oceans of green, the lifeblood of this nation, from open hands receiving government regulated insurance handouts, to clasped hands working together to build a new future. We can't rebuild the past."

Tracey's eyes, now lit with a furious hope, searched the crowd. A hand shot up from the back. Leona Simpson. "But how? We need the elevator."

Tracey nodded. "You're absolutely right. We do. And we'll rebuild, but not on the hopes of back-breaking financing, loans that will never be paid off - we're not Washington D.C., you know…"

Theo Baker began to unfold his arms. He was beginning to feel uncomfortable.

"Thankfully, the plan, as it came to me last night, takes into account no real assets from corporations or handouts. We…" she lifted her hands to the assembly as if in blessing, "we rebuild."

"But, you still haven't answered how." Leona's voice of reason took the wind from the sails.

"Let me explain to you what is in my mind. Mr. Baker," she said as she moved towards him, causing him to take a step back, "I think you accomplished what you came to do. You forced the hand of the people, but what you intended for bad, God might soon use for good."

Baker looked around at the crowd. He felt a desperate need to escape. He turned on his heel and walked with his head snobbishly held high.

After he had left all eyes moved back to Tracey, who smiled at her fellow Amicableans.

"Here is an opportunity…"

Before Tracey could continue, Rhonda Jensen arose and approached Tracey. She motioned for John and Carl to take a seat before she hugged Tracey. There were tears in Rhonda's eyes, tears of hope and faith, yes, but also pride, a communal pride that this young person was about to lead them to the Promised Land.

Rhonda turned to face the congregation. "This is what George was talking about! Don't you remember? George's letter!"

One voice, and one voice alone can save this town.
You will recognize the voice when you hear it.

I'm realistic to know that I will not be around to hear the voice. But you must, Rhodie. You must. If you don't, Amicable will be no more.

"It's Tracey's voice!"

With a true sense of wonder and marvel, the congregation gasped. As much as the congregation members believed in the Bible as the source and norm of their existence, it was still difficult to *actually* believe it. Ancient prophets, prophecies of death, burial, redemption, visions into the future - these were sources of admiration for the people, but to actually have a prophecy come true in Amicable two or three thousand years later would have been unthinkable. George Hendriks as a prophet, especially on his dying day, was also not easily imaginable, and yet it had happened. Now it was up to Tracey to deliver the prophet's vision.

"I… I… don't know about that," Tracey flushed. "But I know that this idea can work."

Rhonda placed a hand on her shoulder. "I'll be right there beside you. We all will."

Tracey took a deep breath. "Okay then. Here is where we begin…"

Stedman watched the young woman lay out her plan. It was amazing. Then, he glanced at Summer and Derek who were both smiling at Tracey. How quickly things change.

Newfound empathy for Amicable stirred in Stedman Boswell. He felt a strange connection with the community.

"Baker insurance company," she smiled broadly, "has publicly promised forty percent which, if Mr. Evans' calculations are correct, is about twenty million dollars."

"Isn't the cost of the rebuilding supposed to be about fifty million?" A voice queried from the side.

"According to estimates, that's correct," Tracey said, "But I've been doing some calculating this morning, and I think we can shave off at least ten million dollars from that."

"Come on, Tracey," Jim Olson, a loan manager at the bank, spoke out, "we love the fact that you are looking outside the box, but let's be realistic. You don't know anything about finance. We're talking about a massive project well beyond the scope of a dream."

"Let her talk," another voice shouted from the other side. It was her dad.

Tracey's eyes welled up with tears. She could sense the pride in his voice. "Ten million minimum - maybe more." She had their attention. "Let's think logistically. Over the next couple of years, what will be the first costs?"

Hands raised and she pointed at them. *Clearing. Big machinery. Labor. Administration costs. Materials. Architects.* With each continued point, she wrote them on the back of her bulletin with one of the blunt, half-chewed pew pencils.

"Now all of you are thinking, 'Where will we get the money to pay for *those* things?'" Nods. "Well, instead of thinking in terms of money, why not think in terms of resources? Time, labor, knowledge." She pointed them off on her fingers.

"Clearing – yeah, we have a lot to clean up. Fortunately, most of the materials from the old elevator - the rubble, gravel, even rebar - can be recycled or reused. Think about the clearing itself - why not engage the high school students again? With proper supervision, we could do this."

The high school kids liked that idea. Demetrius stood up. "I'll volunteer to be part of that group. Maybe," he said looking around the church at other young men and women, "the football and volleyball teams can use the clean up as part of our training?" Kids nodded.

"Okay, that's manual labor. I also know that there are an extraordinary amount of handy men and women around here, farmers, with the best practical engineering minds in the country. Combine that with loaning out some of the big machinery, semis or tractors, backhoes and such, that would really help."

"But architecture? That's expensive."

She smiled. "This is where the entire community is transformed." She got goosebumps at the thought of what she was proposing. It was life changing. Mind altering.

"We all suppose that we'll have to hire outside architects, outside tradespeople, outside minds. What would happen if we brought people in to teach us how to do it ourselves?"

"I'm proposing that even the curriculum at Amicable High School be altered slightly." Tracey looked at Principal Moganan who was frowning. Some of the teachers were catching on to where Tracey was going. "Why don't we, as a school, train our students to run the town, rebuild the elevator and pass on opportunities of responsibility to them? We kill many more than two birds with that stone. First, they learn a trade; second, they practice that trade here in Amicable; third, we help them to understand that this town, is a place to stay, not a place to flee."

"What exactly are you proposing, Ms. Thomas?" Mr. Moganan asked, his perpetually red face even darker than normal. His mustache twitched like a cat's tail.

"Our mathematics classes are focused on practical applications of rebuilding the elevator, clean up, materials, resources needed, human-power required. Those numbers are given to our future architects in twelfth grade. Maybe a competition for architectural plans, not just for the elevator, but for other buildings. Meanwhile, those not interested in mathematics, drafting, or even engineering sciences can be trained to work in the trades: electricians, plumbers, builders, garbage collection, restaurant leadership, civic planning, human resources, entertainment, education…" Tracey's eyes glowed with excitement. "Don't you see? Every student in Amicable, male or female, can graduate with a degree in Community Life. We'll be the envy of every town in the Midwest!"

Tracey could feel the hope surging, but Mr. Moganan raised his hand again. "Not to be a wet blanket here, but we don't have the teaching staff for that."

"No, we don't have the teaching staff for that… yet."

"But there is no room in the budget for more teachers. We don't even have enough students for what you're proposing."

"Here is the genius of my plan, if I do say so myself." She produced a piece of paper from her pocket.

She spread her arms, letting them take in her words. "Truly, when I say this, what Baker meant for bad, could turn out to be the best thing ever for this community. By actually refusing sixty percent of the funding, we can play on the heartstrings of America. Through social media, we, the good people of Amicable, do not spread a blanket of public shame on the insurance company, but we actually speak in these terms:

Dear public, we want you to hear the strength and pride of small town America. A month ago, in tragic circumstances, our grain elevator blew up. We lost beautiful people in our community. Unfortunately, in the midst of this tragedy, we have been denied full compensation by our insurer.

Chapter 22.

We, the people of Amicable, are not overwhelmed with fear. We are
emboldened to make a new start to embrace an entirely new future,
which we'd never imagined. We, Amicable, want to rebuild not only the
elevator, but reconstruct our society as a blueprint for others here in
Iowa.

Here is what we ask of you:

1. Do not pity us. We are unimaginably strong.
2. If you would like to donate to the effort, we have a pathway for this to
happen.
3. We welcome all talents from anywhere and everywhere to help rebuild
our town.

Lastly, we know the cost of those who help us will be dear, but Amicable
is one of the most hospitable places on the earth. We will welcome you
with open arms, open houses and open hearts.

You'll even get a free t-shirt.

If you look deep inside yourselves, you will recognize that in every
community, big or small, there is a little piece of you that recognizes we
are all the same.

We are all Amicable.

 Tracey looked out over the congregation, where a few of the
attendees were wiping their eyes. Stedman Boswell stared at her in
wonder. Was this actually possible?
 Through it all, Tracey had an incredible sense that there was a
recently deceased one-hundred-and-three-year-old man who was wildly
clapping also.
 The exercise group started a standing ovation.
 Linda leaned down to Jeanie. "I need to get the walkie-talkies."
She was grinning from ear to ear.

Chapter 23.

Theo Baker was furious. For one of the first times in his life, he had been publicly humiliated. His assessment of the insurance claim had been correct, even though slightly skewed. They should have thanked him for his generosity. Forty percent was a lot of money.

At the Motel 7, Baker surveyed the ground-floor only accommodation. He wrinkled his nose. Never had he stayed in anything like this

After pulling his Lamborghini into the 'Visitors' car slot, he opened the door, making sure he didn't scratch the paint. Entering the motel, the window marked by paw prints, Baker walked into the lobby. Brochures of the local sights, restaurants and 'tourist destinations' sat in tepees on the desk. A trade-a-book section stuffed full of romance and mystery novels took up space in the entrance. There was a smattering of books about Amish women, which Baker thought decidedly appropriate.

"Can I help you?" The woman asked, her voice as harsh as a rasp. Baker wanted to clear his throat on her behalf.

"I'm not sure whether to say yes or no."

The woman frowned.

"Yes, I need a room for one night, and one night only."

"We've got a deal on if you stay for two or more nights in a row, we can get a free glass of wine delivered right to your room."

Baker's face could not hide his disdain. "As tempting as it might sound to receive a glass of your finest boxed wine, I think I'll forego the second night and keep it to one."

"Suit yourself. That'll be forty-nine dollars, cause it's a weekend. Normally it's only forty-five dollars."

"Well, lucky me," Baker's sarcasm echoed in the room.

The woman hacked as she turned to find a metal key hanging on a board behind her. "Will you need room service?"

Baker followed her gaze to an adjacent room full of four-chair tables sitting on top of worn carpet. Red lampshades hung low over the tables and a lonely buffet was dimly lit in the middle of the room. A few sorrowful travelers stared morosely at each other without speaking.

"Does the food come from there?" He asked pointing to the dining room.

She frowned. "Like, where else would room service come from?"

"I'll pass, then."

Handing him the key, the woman pointed out the door and to the left. "Room thirteen. Halfway down on your left."

"As opposed to the right where there are no rooms?"

"Huh?"

"Never mind."

After driving his car to park in front of room thirteen, Baker opened his car and extracted his expensive leather suitcase and travel bag. Grabbing them, he felt angry that Summer had not accompanied him. By next week, both she and Stedman would be fired. He would make sure of that.

Walking to number thirteen, he inserted the key and unlocked it. A blast of incredibly bad air, sweat, tobacco, a twist of urine and a hint of vomit greeted him.

"Oh, my God!" He exclaimed as he covered his mouth with one hand. Backing up to his car, he reached into his pocket and grabbed a stick of gum. Putting it into his mouth, he chewed madly. Inserting a finger into his mouth, Baker rubbed the finger on his upper lip creating a scent-deadening barrier. Hopefully, after time, the smell would diminish.

Throwing the paperwork onto the table, Baker went straight to the bathroom to take a shower.

A two minivan, one pickup motorcade thrummed down the highway from Amicable to Clancy. Driving one of the minivans, Angela Chandler looked to the passenger seat where Connie was smiling, and behind her, Anne, who was not.

Penny, Donna and Carley rode in the pickup behind them. As the plan transformed, Phase III had shifted monumentally from Stedman Boswell to Theo Baker. Surprisingly, the idea had not originated with Linda, but with Jeannie. Satan had been replaced by Lucifer.

Baker

In the final minivan, Linda, Leona and Jeannie, rode excitedly. Linda drove, of course; riding shotgun, Leona. Jeannie sat in the middle row, sans seatbelt, her head poking between the front seats. She bounced on the seat in restless anticipation.

Jeannie looked at Linda and laughed. "You look funny."

Without turning her head, Linda glanced peripherally at Jeannie. "This is how prostitutes are supposed to look."

"I don't know." Leona was unconvinced. "You might have overdone it a little bit. I don't think they wear that much makeup." Linda's face seemed clownish: bright blue eyeshadow, overdone rouge, thick, crimson lipstick. A bobbed wig sat slightly off center.

"Trust me, I know men. There is no way he can resist this." She sat up straighter, her cleavage became even more prominent.

"But don't you think the nurse's costume is a little bit, I don't know, cliche?"

"Are you kidding?" She changed her voice, raising it a few tones and adding more air. "Excuse me, sir, I've been told you need to have a bath... Oh, you are dirty..."

This sent the other two into paroxysms of laughter.

When Leona finished laughing, she wiped her eyes with her palms.

"Let's run through the plan one more time," Jeannie said. "It's just pure genius."

"Okay," Leona said, "we pull up to the Motel 7, but not too close. Then, Linda is going to get out of the car and walk to Baker's room. After she enters to 'show him a good time...'"

"Which does not include anything physical..." Linda added.

"Like, duh," Jeannie said.

"Then, then..." Jeannie said clapping her hands, "while you 'service' Baker, we service his car."

"Very good." Linda reached for her walkie-talkie on the dashboard. "Angels, this is Azrael. Do you all know what you're supposed to be doing?"

"Copy, Azrael, this is Gabriel. We are ready to go."

Linda was nervous *and* strangely excited.

242

Chapter 23.

At five o'clock, Human Beans opened up for a special meeting. Ted Winke took notes: Tracey Thomas, Derek Peterson, Nash and Shania Peterson, Butcher Jensen and, incredibly, Stedman Boswell and Summer Teichman.

"Thank you for coming," Janice began the conversation from the head of the makeshift conference table. "I realize that it's a Sunday, but these are extraordinary times. Thank you to our guests for coming."

"As we begin the meeting, it's important for us to know why Mr. Boswell and Ms. Teichman are here."

Tracey opened her mouth to speak, but Stedman jumped in. His bald head glistened with nervous perspiration. "Excuse me, Tracey, but it's best that I go first. Until two nights ago, everything was just as Baker said: I had enough evidence to make things difficult for Amicable. It's not fair, probably not even ethical, but insurance companies have to watch out for their own."

"Two nights ago, I was attacked. Yes, I understand the reasoning behind it, but I've never been so scared in my life. It's difficult to tell you where my mind took me, but needless to say, I had a deep reality check."

He stared at his hands as he spoke. "I went into that shower as a self-satisfied, smug, arrogant putz, and I exited it a frightened, despairing, humbled human. When I stepped out of the shower, everything had changed."

Janice blinked. "We apologize for any pain we've caused you."

"Thank you. For me, though, this was a crisis of faith. Do I need to be a pawn in ripping off innocent people? Will another thousand dollars make me feel like a better person?"

The council fidgeted nervously.

"Yesterday, after my confrontation with Mr. Baker, I recognized the error of my ways. Unfortunately, Mr. Baker is planning to finish what I started. Which is why," Stedman spread his hands, "I'd like to be part of the recovery and rebuilding effort."

Janice's smile appeared strained. She was still unconvinced. This man, up until two days ago had been...

"I'm prepared to offer up to one hundred thousand dollars of matching funds for the enactment of Tracey's plan."

243

Jaws dropped.

"Well, Mr. Boswell, you've got our attention." Steve Evans entered the conversation. "You said matching funds…?"

"Yes. I'm willing to match funds from anywhere, not just Amicable. As we continue to market the recovery, I'm certain people will be motivated by the story. I'm willing to put my money where my mouth is." Stedman's eyes wandered around the circle. Even Butcher was taken aback. Amazingly, he had not seen *that* coming. The future is etched in wax, not stone.

"So then, Mr. Boswell, what do we do next?"

Stedman smiled and nodded to Tracey. "Councilors, yesterday we had a discussion with Rhonda, Butcher, Reverend Deakins and Leslie. They encouraged us to start wrapping our heads around what leadership could look like in the next two decades."

"I outlined the short version of the plan this morning at church, but I'd like to add a few more details if I may.

The council waited with bated breath.

"I spoke with Principal Moganan who could, in theory, agree to adapt the curriculum at Amicable High School to support the community recovery program. I spoke with some farmers about volunteering machinery and labor to help speed the restoration process. Even those who were hesitant said that they'd think about it."

"Then, Derek talked with some high school youth. No one in Amicable wants to be left out."

"Great so far," Janice said.

The rest of the council agreed.

"How would you like us to help?" Janice continued.

"Here is where we most need your help. We," Tracey motioned to the younger people, "know very little about event planning and organizing large-scale projects. We need your help in coordination, but also in teaching us how to do it."

"Done." Janice's face beamed.

Tracey took a deep breath and smiled at Summer. "Ms. Teichman can help us in this area."

Chapter 23.

"Good afternoon. My name is Summer Teichman. Over the last few years, I have been involved in marketing Baker Insurance. Now it's time to switch sides."

"During the next months, we'll blitz the media with a spin on the tragedy. Instead of a weak and reeling country town, the state will see a focused and concerted group of people raising the community from the dead. Through social media, press releases, television and radio, we'll let people know that we don't intend to roll over and die."

Janice looked around the circle. "Anything else we should be doing now?"

Summer and Tracey looked at each other and smiled.

Theocrates Baker had somehow fallen asleep on the bed of his motel room. One arm had been thrown over his face, the other lay curled across his belly.

There was a knock at the door. Startled, Baker lifted his arm and looked towards the window. Although he'd threatened to keep the door open, he thought better about the insects. He checked his watch and found that it was dinnertime.

"Who is it?"

"Room service," a woman's voice called out.

"I didn't order any! Go away."

Another knock. "Room service."

"I told you, I didn't order any."

Again, knocking. "Room service," the woman said impatiently.

"For God's sake," Baker said with frustration. Walking to the door, he threw it open. "I told you, I…" He paused. Standing in front of him was a nurse. Definitely not the kind of room service he was expecting.

"Hello," Linda said breathlessly and suggestively, "Room service. I'm here to service you. Oops," she covered her lips, "I mean, I'm here to service your room."

"What the hell?"

"Can I come in?"

"Are you the cleaning lady?"

245

She giggled. "If you're a dirty boy, then I'm the cleaning lady."

He wrinkled up his nose. "Are you a prostitute?"

"No, silly," she placed a hand on his chest and pushed him inside, "we don't have those in Clancy. I'm what you'd call, a call girl, and you can call me anytime, handsome."

"But... but..." he stumbled backing into the room, "I didn't call you."

"No, but your friend did. I can't remember his name. Stickman or something like that."

"Stedman. It's Stedman. Why would he call you?"

"He said you might be lonely and he also said you might want to celebrate your big victory. I don't know what he meant by that, but I love, love, love to celebrate." She clapped her hands with each 'love.'

"Well, that's very kind of you," he said, "but aren't you a little..."

"A little what, Sweetie?"

"A little... old for this kind of work."

She took a playful swipe at him and dropped the range of her voice. "Oh, you say the nicest things. I might be more mature than some of the other girls, but I've got a whole lot of experience." She licked her lips suggestively.

As she closed the door behind her, she pushed him into the room. "Now," she said, "what's your name, big boy?"

"Uh, Baker."

Linda pushed him onto the bed. Trying hard to distract him from her snagged nylons and scuffed shoes, Linda touched her hair and clapped her hands. "Patty cake, patty cake, Baker man. What do you think about warming up the oven?" She reached to the top button of her nurse's outfit and slowly popped it open.

Meanwhile, outside room thirteen, the Angels circled the yellow Lamborghini. Each one had a handful of bumper stickers with an assortment of messages like:

PLEASE DON'T HIT ME. I'M NOT 100% SURE ABOUT MY COVERAGE.

Chapter 23.

DON'T TOUCH ME, I'M NOT THAT KIND OF CAR.

JESUS LOVES YOU. EVERYONE ELSE THINKS YOU'RE A MORON.

The women placed thirty separate bumper stickers all over his car, from the hood, to the doors to the trunk.

When they had finished placing them, they stepped back to admire their work. As per their now normal practice, Angela stepped forward and put chicken poop all over the windshield. Finally, Carley opened up her purse and squeezed Liquid Ass into the radiator. Moving to the vents in front of the windshield wipers, she inserted three or four more drops there also. For good measure, she dripped the last drops on the door handles. Baker would never be able to get rid of the smell.

Around the corner, Leona and Jeannie walked. They had changed their clothes. Now, both of them were dressed in police uniform costumes. Carley was beside herself as she watched Leona and Jeannie strut to the door of room thirteen.

Leona looked at Jeannie. "Don't laugh, okay? No matter what!" Jeannie snorted and then calmed her face. Leona pounded on the door. "Police! Open up!" Jeannie started laughing.

"Stop it, Jeannie!" She pounded on the door again. "Sir, we know you're in there. We have reason to believe that you're not alone

The door opened a crack. It was Baker. His shirt was ripped open. "What seems to be the problem, officer?"

"Sir, we need you to step outside."

"Why, officer?"

Jeannie covered her mouth and pretended to cough, but she was actually biting her hand.

"We have reason to believe that there is a prostitute in this room. Prostitution is illegal in Iowa, sir."

"I don't have a prostitute in here," he squeaked.

"Sir," Leona said as she pulled the walkie-talkie in her hand closer to her mouth as if about to call backup. "Please, step aside."

"But…"

Leona pushed the door, hitting Baker in the face. They were met by the sight of Linda, leaning against the bathroom sink. She smiled. "Hello, officers."

"Ma'am," Leona said attempting to control her laughter, "I'm going to have to ask you to come with us."

"What for? I'm just visiting my Uncle Pete."

Jeannie's eyes bugged. Laughter was near. "Okay. Okay. Uncle Pete. I've heard that one before." Leona looked at Jeannie. "I think we have enough here, Officer Daniels. We'll take both of them downtown for questioning. It's embarrassing, a man your age…"

"But…! I didn't call her to come here! One of my employees called. I was just minding my own business, and she knocks at the door and starts coming on to me. I didn't know what to do."

"Mmhmm." Leona sounded unconvinced

"It's true, officer. She is definitely *not* my niece. I was scared for my life."

"I'm sure…" Leona said slowly. "Okay, Officer Daniels, cuff the woman and take her out to the squad car."

"Yes, Officer Tomkins." Jeannie was hanging on by a thread. Walking over to Linda, she pulled out her plastic children's handcuffs.

"I like cuffs," Linda said with a smile.

A small whimper escaped Jeannie's lips. Her mouth pinched and her eyes began to water. Finally, the cuffs clicked shut and Jeannie pushed Linda towards the front door. Leona wagged a finger at Baker. "Let this be a warning to you, Uncle Pete. Prostitution is no laughing matter." At that moment, Jeannie cleared the door and hurried around the edge of the building where her laughter rang out in the courtyard. Leona and Linda followed quickly after.

When they had finished laughing, Linda looked at Angela. "Did you get it?"

Angela nodded. "They have the whole thing recorded."

Mrs. Baker was going to love it.

Chapter 24.

A light snow was falling.

Unused to white Christmases, Stedman enjoyed the lights glittering in the powder. He marveled at the carols and joyful songs. There was something deeply moving about this time of year that he'd never felt before. It felt natural, like the sun rising in the east, or gravity pulling objects to the ground. He couldn't help it.

Fired from their jobs, both Stedman and Summer had been relieved of their duties by Theocrates Baker who, over the course of three months, had also been asked to leave the company because of actions 'detrimental to the good name of the company.' Things got so bad after the negative publicity regarding Baker's handling of Amicable's insurance claim that the board of directors legally changed the name of the company to United Insurance Company of Kansas City. Baker moved to Colorado with just his reconditioned Lamborghini. The bumper stickers had taken a lot of work to remove. And the smell…

Summer and Stedman stayed in Amicable to help with the rebuilding and restoration efforts. After their firing, the town hired them as consultants during the rebuilding. They were worth their weight in gold, especially as Stedman was donating so much money to the cause. As it was, Amicable was a growing place, especially the high school.

Demetrius Chandler met with Stedman and Summer two weeks before Christmas to give an update. As the students were working towards one goal, educational morale had never been so high.

In Mathematics, a professor from the University of Iowa had taken a sabbatical to teach upper-level physics to six twelfth graders as they prepared the various systems for the new grain elevator.

In Science, BASF loaned a chemical engineer to work with students to develop new fire resistant chemicals to work in the silos to reduce the chances of explosions.

In Drafting, Gensler Corporation, the wealthiest architectural company in the United States, sent their vice president of architectural engineering to teach for an entire year.

In Home Economics, two of the best chefs in the Midwest made weekly trips from Omaha to teach restaurant management and cooking.

In Business, a retired banker from New York, Clayton Meissner, made the trip to hang out with Amicablean youth to teach them about finance.

Principal Moganan strutted like a peacock in front of the cameras. His red face beamed as if the entire process had been his idea.

In one of the most fascinating turn of events, a convoy of trucks showed up to help move debris. When the cab of the first one opened up, a bright-faced trucker smiled from behind his bushy beard. "Where is Azrael?" He cried at the top of his lungs.

Linda Harmsen pushed her way through the crowd, and ran to the trucker. "Hello, Big Tom Tom," she said with a large smile. "I'm Azrael - the other Angels are over there." She pointed behind her to where the others were waving wildly. "Thanks for coming. We really appreciate it."

He pushed his cap back on his head. "Wouldn't have missed it. We couldn't help but want to pay you back for all the laughter on the road."

These memories coursed through Stedman Boswell's mind as his feet trudged through the snow towards Summer's house. They had become steadfast friends. Even though it had taken three months for his hair to grow back, he felt inclined to keep it nice and short. For Amicable's sake.

Stedman and Derek spent many nights together. Eventually, Derek told Stedman that he was going to ask Tracey to marry him.

Derek asked Stedman to be one of his groomsmen.

Summer met him at the end of the sidewalk. Side by side, they strolled the last few blocks to St. Clements church for the Christmas Eve service. Somehow, Amicable had brought out the best in both of them. Even though it had been a difficult start, they were glad to be there. After the elevator was rebuilt, neither one was sure what was going to happen next.

"Did you have a good day?" She asked.

"Exquisite," he said. "I've never been in a winter wonderland before. It's like... well, perfect."

She put a hand through the elbow hole in his arm. "I know what you mean."

"Don't you think it's weird, Summer, that for most of my adult life, I've been working for things that might make me *feel* more important - like that round the world trip, a house in Vale, a new Porsche..."

Summer laughed. "It is pretty funny that you sold the Porsche and bought a used pickup."

He laughed. "Yeah, small towns change a person. And now," he continued, "I understand that what I've always wanted was something I couldn't buy. Community. Respect. Reputation."

"Is that it?"

He smiled and looked up into the floating snowflakes. Around the streetlights, halos of night rainbows were casting rings into the sky. Various townspeople traipsed happily and loudly towards the church. Some of them had paused to make snowballs. A few children had fallen backwards to manufacture snow angels. None of them seemed to have a care in the world, and yet the world was full of cares. Stedman leaned his head down onto hers.

"I suppose there is that one thing more."

Neither one needed to speak the word. They felt it.

As they were welcomed into St. Clements Methodist Church, greeted by the happy sounds of 'Merry Christmas' and the beautiful sound of the organ playing Christmas carols, Stedman and Summer realized that the most expansive part of life was love.

It was good to love.

Epilogue

Dearest Reader,

This feels like I should write, 'And they all lived happily ever after.' But that would not be real life, would it? As much as I would desire to tie up this story, wrap a little bow around it and put it under your Christmas tree, both you and I know that fairy tales are just stories that cause us to think differently. That's what this is, and I hope you can once again think differently about Amicable.

At long last, Nash and Shania were pronounced man and wife. They left the butcher shop and the Greedy Pecker in the care of others and went on a honeymoon to Branson, Missouri, of course.

Mentored to be the next mayor of Amicable, Tracey Thomas continues to lean on others for advice and expertise. She has a quick mind and an endless source of energy and creativity. With Derek, Nash and Shania, they have formed a formidable foursome in leading the town into the future.

The Deakins and Jensen families continue to raise our children knowing that life will never be easy, but it can be entertaining. Almost weekly, we go to the site of the old grain elevator to watch the community work to clear rubble, run machinery and practice trades. J.T. especially likes to watch Demetrius Chandler, who he thinks is the most wonderful person he has ever seen.

The sign standing in front of the elevator construction area reads:

Future site of the Enrique Fernandez Memorial Grain Elevator.

As all good tales must do, this one ends here.

By the way, the Amicable football team won its last two games of the year. They partied like it was 1989.

Sincerely,

Leslie Deakins

"Archangel, come in Archangel, this is Cherub."

"Copy, Archangel, this is Cherub. What's up?"

Leona glanced at her husband who was sleeping in front of the television. It was nine o'clock on New Year's Eve. Leona was not ready to go to sleep.

"I'm bored."

"Yeah, me too."

"Do you want to do something?" Leona released the button and waited for Jeannie to reply. They were surprised when a different voice came through the walkie-talkie.

"Hey Angels. This is Raphael."

"Carley! I mean, Raphael. What are you doing?"

Carley whispered into the walkie-talkie. "I'm about to sneak out."

"What are you going to do?"

Carley giggled and her eyes twinkled. "I got a Christmas present for myself."

"What is it, Raphael?"

Holding the small white bottle up in her hands, she twisted it around to read the label.

"I got Barfume."

www.ingramcontent.com/pod-product-compliance
Lightning Source LLC
Chambersburg PA
CBHW061924130726
47909CB00012B/816